AFTERBURNERS, CONTROLLED CRASHES, CONSTANT DANGER

FIRE

ON THE

FLIGHT DECK

DARREN SAPP

Collins & Halsey Publishers / December 2014

ISBN-13: 978-0692326541
ISBN-10: 0692326545

Cover Art: Sunset Recovery, ©William S. Phillips, licensed by The
Greenwich Workshop, Inc. www.greenwichworkshop.com

Cover Design: www.vividcovers.com

Formatting: www.perfectlypublishable.com

Editing: Lauren I. Ruiz of Pure Text / www.pure-text.net

Dedicated to AN Ronald Krauss and AA William Berry
who gave their lives working on the flight deck
of the USS *Theodore Roosevelt*, CVN-71

"The 'performers' do their act with all the grace of ballet dancers, seemingly oblivious to the danger around them."

Brad Durfee, referring to flight deck workers
in *Stars and Stripes*, August 16, 1975.

PART ONE

"Keep Your Head on a Swivel"

CHAPTER 1

Lloyds of London has ranked working on an aircraft carrier flight deck as one of the most dangerous jobs in the world. The men on the USS William Halsey's flight deck believed it and were paid an extra $100 of hazardous duty pay every month to remind them. Though, most presumed they'd never see a violent death.

Back in 1987, Brian Donley worked as the gear puller—fifty feet from landing planes. He looked up and down the landing area and signaled a clear deck, before stealing a peaceful glance of the ominous Mediterranean Sea.

Thud! A C-2 Greyhound propeller stopped and started in an instant.

Donley's head whipped left toward the sound.

A burst of some substance flew into the landing area as a brown shirt dropped to his knees. His arms hung to his sides, powerless. As his torso fell to the deck, a gush of blood flowed out of his neck where his head should have been.

The pilot lowered his head. The flight deck chief dropped to his knees. A blue shirt stood catatonic and covered in blood. Another guy vomited.

A piece of the victim's helmet landed at Donley's feet—spinning. As it slowed to a stop, he noticed hair, skull, and gray matter clinging to it. For a brief moment, nothing happened. No sound. No movement.

A shimmer of light reflected from the dog tag tied under his shoestrings. The older guys had said to keep one dog tag around your neck and one in your boot. If several men lost their heads in a mass casualty, they could be identified by that dog tag in the boot.

Donley stood still. He didn't know who had died at that point, but he knew how. Something he'd heard could happen but never thought he'd witness. A man had walked into a propeller.

"Ahhh!" A scream broke the silence.

Chaos ensued. Men in blue, yellow, green, and white shirts ran to the scene. An F-14 Tomcat approached, seconds from landing.

Donley realized that pieces of the dead man's skull littered the landing area, jeopardizing the landing. He signaled a foul deck by raising his arms over his head in a cross symbol.

"Foul deck! Foul deck!" blasted over the flight deck 5MC loudspeaker.

The Tomcat engaged full power and roared past him, just feet from the deck. The landing signal officer, who guided the pilots for landing, turned around and stared at Donley with hands in the air.

The officer didn't see a headless torso fall to the deck. Donley did.

"During the day, the propeller appears as a blur," a chief once warned him. "If you stare at it too long, the hypnotic effect draws you toward it. Nighttime is the most dangerous when darkness makes the spinning prop invisible."

Donley heard the handler—the officer in charge of flight

deck control—announce over the 5MC that "We just lost a sailor."

Who was it? he thought. He ran over to the scene and saw red gloves on the fallen man. That's when he knew.

It was Schmidt.

Airman Thomas Schmidt served as a plane captain caring for one or more planes much like a member of a pit crew. Like many squadron personnel, Donley knew little of him. Their past conversations covered mundane flight deck business.

"You ready to move my Hawkeye?" Schmidt would ask.

"Yep, brakes off," he'd say, freeing the wheels so the tow tractor could take over.

Everyone wore brown or black gloves, but Schmidt had odd, bright, red gloves.

Those red gloves.

How did this happen? Donley thought.

Schmidt, an experienced flight deck worker, had safely worked around that type of aircraft a thousand times. His death scared Donley, a nineteen-year-old yellow shirt.

The guys on the "roof" knew many below decks sailors envied their job believing they experienced daily adventure. Some of the roof rats walked around like that line from T. Coraghessan Boyle's *Greasy Lake*, "We were nineteen. We were bad."

Donley loved the flight deck. It excited him. A rush. He had some misgivings about navy life, but he craved the action on deck. Few things compared to the raw power of an F-14 Tomcat in afterburner. The intense heat. The smell of jet fuel. It felt like a monster truck rally with him in the middle of the action.

He had no problem with aircraft landing so close at speeds that would unnerve many. For most of his fellow flight deck workers, it was just another day on the job. The danger lay in complacency.

The veterans often said, "Keep your head on a swivel."

In other words, don't let your mind drift off like Donley once did, causing ABH1 Simon Beckley to stare at him and pull his closed fist from his other open hand—meaning get your head out of your ass. Sure, it was crude, but indelible enough that most men only received the sharp rebuke once in their careers. He deserved it but hated that it came from Beckley—the sorriest SOB on the boat.

Standing next to Schmidt's torso that day, Donley despised the flight deck.

His buddy, Victor "Li'l V" Randolph stood next to him. He earned the nickname Li'l V due to his overuse of the word "little."

"That's a little weird," or "Tell that little dude to get on deck."

"You coming to chow, Li'l V?" someone might ask.

"In a little bit."

Their friendship seemed unorthodox—Donley a white guy from the south, and Li'l V, a black guy from the Bronx. Li'l V called Brian by his first name—a rarity in the Navy. Donley admired Li'l V's skill and resolution. Unlike Donley, Li'l V loved the Navy.

"I'm a lifer," Li'l V would say.

Li'l V edged six feet, with proportionate muscles, and wore the uniform as intended—a regular recruiting poster model.

Li'l V had directed that plane to its parking spot and had given the signal to insert the chocks and chains. He had ordered Schmidt to perform the functions that led to his death. Li'l V, like Schmidt, had done this a thousand times.

Routinely, Schmidt had connected a tiedown chain, turned 180 degrees, and safely walked out perpendicular to the fuselage.

"He walked right into the propeller," Li'l V's voice sounded hollow. "I don't think he even saw it. Just ripped him apart."

"Men, we are in Blue Water Operations," the air boss said over the 5MC.

"Li'l V, what's Blue Water Operations?" Donley asked.

He pointed to several planes in the approach pattern. "Where do you think they're all gonna land? We're too far at sea for them to find another landing field."

It dawned on Donley that the landing area, littered with the debris of Schmidt's body parts, presented unsafe conditions for incoming aircraft that would eventually need to land on the flight deck.

It's why you signaled the foul deck for the Tomcat, you idiot, Donley thought.

The air boss came over the radio headsets: "Launch the two tankers." Those tankers, refueling the birds in mid-air, bought them time to clean up the deck.

Li'l V grabbed guys by their shirts. "Let's go! Let's get this done."

Donley stared once more at the body only a few feet away.

"Let's cover him up," said one medical responder to another.

"C'mon Brian," Li'l V said. "We got birds in the air."

Schmidt's torso lay in a litter on elevator one while hundreds of us walked down the flight deck picking up the rest of him. Hair and gray matter that clung to pieces of skull. Little pieces of his head and helmet scattered all the way to the port catwalk. Someone found a portion of the earpiece in vulture's row—a vantage point on the island sixty feet up.

"Let's use fire hoses to clean up the rest," Petty Officer Beckley said.

A sickening command, but one that had to be carried out.

Within an hour, the final planes landed, and the deck fell silent.

CHAPTER 2

Donley walked into the yellow shirt shack and threw his bloodstained gloves in the trash. Bloodstained, red, like Schmidt's gloves.

"What the hell happened?" he asked.

No one responded. They simply looked at each other.

Donley worried about Li'l V having had a front row seat for the terrible incident. He sat silently wearing a yellow jersey and a life vest—sprinkled with Schmidt's blood. He maintained a tough exterior, but Donley knew him. He knew him on the inside. He knew he hurt.

The captain addressed the entire crew. "Attention, men. We have experienced a tragedy on the flight deck. Stay focused as we recover from this episode and persevere."

That's it, Donley thought. The Navy way—short and to the point.

Beckley walked in. "Hey, let's go cook up some of that meat we picked up."

This became their second shock of the day. Is he making a sick, crude joke out of this? Donley thought. Another reason for him to hate Beckley—another in a long list.

"Fuck you, Beckley," Li'l V said. One of a few who could get away with that.

"What did you say to me?" Beckley said with a fake, puzzled look.

Li'l V hopped up and stared directly at him. "You heard me."

Donley made a feeble attempt to stand between them. Li'l V, for all his attributes, possessed a temper. Not like an angry drunk, or the surly type, but like someone who'd loudly tell you his true feelings without thinking. In other words, he'd jump down someone's throat if needed.

Beckley threw his hands up while walking out. "Listen, if you dwell on the negative, you'll be timid your next time out on deck and make a mistake."

Li'l V had overstepped a boundary speaking to Beckley in that manner, but it was no ordinary day.

Donley stared at Li'l V. "I can't believe he said that."

Li'l V lit a cigarette. "That's his way of telling us to put it behind us and get back to work. Old Beckley is too big a jerk to be sensitive about it. We still got planes to fly. Doesn't matter if it's actual war or training."

Beckley's statements aside, Donley agreed with his philosophy. The aircraft handler sent them out for the next launch.

Chief Fitch stopped Donley and Li'l V on their way back out to the flight deck. "The three of us need to go to sick bay to provide urine and blood samples. Anyone that had control of that aircraft. They want to make sure we are clean of drugs. There will be an inquiry, and the Navy wants to report that we didn't do anything wrong. You know, covering their asses."

They reached sick bay where the chaplain consoled Schmidt's buddies. "We don't always know why God allows things like this to happen."

Some cried. No one thought the lesser of them for this. They were a bunch of scared young men. The average age of flight deck workers was nineteen-years old—Donley's age. He thought he'd acted bravely. Not in a life saving sort of way but by performing his duties under those circumstances. However, he wasn't sure he could do it again.

Me, brave? Maybe not, he thought as doubts entered his mind about working on the flight deck.

Li'l V put a hand on his shoulder. "You OK, man?"

"I don't know. I'm scared." Donley made a feeble attempt to hold back his emotions.

"You're going back on deck if I have to drag you."

Donley looked off to the side. "Man, I don't know. I don't know if I can handle it."

The next day, the flight deck crew assembled near the island structure for a memorial service as Schmidt's pallbearers loaded his casket onto the same plane that killed him. The engines started with their blurred propellers—now seemingly magnified. Everyone stood back from the deadly blades a little further than usual.

Donley overheard two of Schmidt's squadron buddies talking. "He had a couple of weeks left in the Navy and planned to go home and marry his girlfriend. A short-timer."

The other guy shook his head. "Yeah, I know. He had fifteen and a wake-up on his locker."

Li'l V had overheard too. He turned to Donley who said, "He was probably thinking about home instead of his job. Counting down the days 'till he'd head home."

Li'l V raised his voice so a couple of blue shirts could hear. "Fellas, you hear that? That plane captain lost sight of his job for one brief moment, and it cost him his life."

One of the blue shirts chimed in. "Forget those props. What if that arresting gear cable snaps?"

"I heard that happened on the Kennedy—a cable snapped and cut some guys in half," Donley said. "Props, cables, or an intake could suck you in. It's all dangerous. All around us."

Li'l V nodded. "Just hope there's never a fire on the flight deck."

No one spoke after that comment.

That night in his rack, Donley thought about those things, but mainly the worst thing—a massive fire. He'd heard others call the flight deck a ballet of controlled chaos, but it now seemed to him a ticking time bomb. He had joined the Navy looking for adventure and found it on the flight deck of the USS *William Halsey*. He truly had one of the most dangerous jobs on earth.

PART TWO

The Making of a Sailor

CHAPTER 3

A few years before Schmidt walked into that prop, I sat in Mrs. Reddell's English class pondering my future while she read from an Elizabeth Barrett Browning sonnet called *Past and Future*.

"...And write me new my future's epigraph," she read.

I liked that line. At seventeen, I didn't have much of a past and saw few opportunities for my future. I thought the epigraph imagery a bit much but saw my future as a blank slate begging for meaningful words to be written on it. Words like exciting, adventurous, worthy, and honorable.

"What will your future be?" Mrs. Reddell said.

Empty stares surrounded me.

She smiled. "I hope all of you will attend the college fair at lunch."

As a high school junior, I assumed college the next logical step in the process toward adulthood. I could get a business degree and work at some office, get married, and have kids. All that sounded normal and routine. It also sounded boring.

Students started their "waiting for the bell to ring" conversations. The talk centered around the college fair.

"I'm joining the Marines," one guy said.

I cocked my head at that comment. "The Marines? Will

they be at the college fair?"

"Yeah. And the Army will have all that 'Be All You Can Be' crap and the Navy—"

"It's not just a job, it's an adventure." I surprised myself by blurting that out.

What about the military? Did they need me?

I lived a youth of innocence. My parents worried about Vietnam and their parents endured World War II. Sure, there was the Cold War, but I hardly thought about it, much less worried about it.

Should I go into the military instead of college?

As the oldest of four, I knew my parents worked hard to provide for us and I'd overheard their concerns about paying for college.

After the bell rang, I joined those gathered around the cafeteria for the college fair. All the area colleges manned their booths, but a crowd of young men and one young girl congregated around grown men in uniform. The Army and Navy had the largest crowds.

I grabbed my buddy Dale's arm. "Let's check out the Army booth," I said.

"Forget that, man. You'll shoot your eye out. Let's check out the colleges. Think of the frat parties. That's how you pick a college."

"Dale, you don't even know what a fraternity is."

Dale threw his arms up. "That's why I'm going to college. To learn."

I left Dale to his clever plan and paced back and forth in front of the military booths. Stalking really. The Air Force encouraged us to "Aim High," while the Marines suggested we join "The Few. The Proud. The Marines." Apparently, central casting saw fit to send this marine with his high-and-tight haircut and square jaw that obliterated any notions of Gomer Pyle. His uniform impressed me, but something even more striking caught my eye.

The Navy poster showed an F-14 Tomcat on the flight deck of an aircraft carrier. Mesmerized, I imagined myself flying that fighter jet and then walking away after landing in a flight suit; an officer and a gentleman.

I mustered up some courage and approached the Navy recruiter. "How do you become a pilot?"

"You need a college degree and then you go to officer candidate school. You could join the Navy now, work with Tomcats, and earn enough to pay for college. Then you could see if you even like it."

I'd heard of unscrupulous recruiters that would say anything to meet their quota so I kept my guard up. "So I'll work with Tomcats?"

"I cannot guarantee where you will serve, but the college money is a sure thing," he said. "You give your country four years, and your country will help you pay for college."

Ecstatic, I drove home in my beat up '76 Camaro with Van Halen blaring from the Alpine speakers. This seemed like such a great fit. I could serve my country, work with jets, earn money for college, and most importantly, "live the adventure."

At dinner, I announced to my family, "I joined the Navy! I mean, I'm going to join the Navy."

All heads turned toward me followed by three seconds of silence.

My father grinned. "I'm proud of you, son."

My mother offered a different reaction. "You'll be killed on the way to boot camp or fall off a ship. It's too dangerous.

Absolutely not!"

My sister, the family smart-aleck, said, "Helloooo… you're a junior in high school."

"I'm not going tomorrow. I can join now and go to boot camp after graduation."

A few weeks later, my recruiter sent me for a day of written tests at a military processing center. I received an overly personal physical with the whole turn your head and cough thing, gave up fingerprints as if it were a booking, and donated a full beaker of urine.

Next came the good cop, bad cop routine. The bad cop—a pocked-faced marine with eyes that stared through me—spoke first. He worked me over in a room void of décor. Nothing but a table, two chairs, and bright florescent lights.

"Have you ever committed any crimes?" I shook my head left to right. No verbal response.

"You ever stolen anything?"

"Uh, uh, noooo—"

"If I find out you lied to me, I will personally bury you in the deepest, darkest brig."

He scared the crap out of me. After a few minutes of this pressure, I admitted my only crime. "Whe…when… I was ten, I stole one of my little brother's Reese's Peanut Butter Cups from his Halloween basket."

The good cop—a cheerful, smiling sailor— had one simple job: to get me to sign on the dotted line. Actually, about fifteen or twenty dotted lines.

"You've passed all the tests. Sign here and you'll be guaranteed the aviation field after boot camp."

"What am I signing?" The pressure intensified. My sweaty palms gripped the pen.

"Don't worry. This is why you came. You're going to be sailor." The good cop's assumptive close worked on me. I signed every line.

Unsure of what had just occurred, I left thinking I had signed up for thirty years and agreed to hand over my first-born. My recruiter, who instructed me to call him Tom, assured me otherwise.

"Tom, I'm not ready to be in the Navy." That's what I said but what I was thinking was: What have I done? I made a mistake. I need to get out of this. I need a lawyer or something.

"Memorize the chain of command, learn your general orders, workout, and you'll be ready."

Tom worked with me over the next year calming my fears.

Graduation arrived and I spent my last few days of freedom saying goodbye to friends and continuing my regimen of pushups, sit-ups, and running in preparation for boot camp.

Fear crept in again. What if I fail? What if they yell? What if I can't take it? I tried my rationalization exercises. It's only eight weeks. The Marines had the most arduous boot camp, and it lasted thirteen weeks. All the yelling in that Richard Gere movie, *An Officer and a Gentlemen*, involved wannabe pilots. Navy boot camp is more of a mind game. A process that you take day by day. Yeah, I can do this, I told myself.

"Don't take it personal," Tom said, during a training session before I left. "Do as you're told, don't screw up, and be a team player. Don't do anything to stand out. Oh, and if you fail, don't you dare walk back into this place because I won't want anything to do with you."

No pressure, I thought.

CHAPTER 4

My first day in the Navy began with my digital alarm clock flashing 4:30 AM. An ungodly hour, but one that seemed fitting for a military man. My mother sobbed and embraced me in our driveway as my father rolled down the window of his '74 Impala.

"Let the boy go, Momma. He's in the Navy now."

We met Tom at his office at 0530—I learned that 0530 translated to 5:30 A.M.—for delivery to the local MEPS (Military Entrance Processing Station). Military time owned me now.

My father put his hands on my shoulders, said he was proud, and offered one suggestion. "Do as you're told."

That sounded reasonable to me. My grandfather survived the Battle of the Bulge and instilled a military ethic in his two sons. My dad certainly passed that on to us in a Ward Cleaver sort of way.

Dad looked at me in a way he hadn't in years. A look of deep concern. His head tilted and I noticed his eyes beginning to water. "Seems like just yesterday I was teaching you how to swing a bat. Good luck, son." He shook my hand and made a quick exit.

Tom parked the car in the MEPS parking lot. Getting out

of that car comprised my last free act for quite some time. Sure, the Navy owned me from the day I signed those enlistment papers, but this was the real deal. Minutes would measure my free time for the next eight weeks. At MEPS, I traveled from one processing point to another with several persons barking orders.

"Fill this form out."

"I need your urine."

"Go get in that line."

And then came the most thorough physical I'd ever endured.

This one represented the more realistic Navy way. My prior physicals had involved one doctor in an examining room, but this was a group physical. The details defy decency. A line of men bent over, underwear around their ankles, with cheeks spread, as a doctor walked by inspecting. I made the mistake of looking to my left as the guy next to me looked back with terror in his eyes. Then, because I failed to learn from my mistake, I looked at the guy on the right. His horrified expression mirrored my own.

We pitied one poor soul when the doctor stopped behind him for what seemed like an eternity and called over another doctor for consultation. "Doctor Smith, what do you think of this man's anus?"

He didn't really say that, but he might as well have. Ugh!

By noon, we finished processing, had lunch, and entered a large wood-paneled room with a flag. In that regal room, I took the oath of allegiance:

"I, Brian Donley, do solemnly swear that I will support and defend the Constitution of the United States against all enemies, foreign and domestic; that I will bear true faith and allegiance to the same; and that I will obey the orders of the President of the United States and the orders of the officers appointed over me, according to regulations and the Uniform Code of Military Justice. So help me God."

I beamed with pride. One of the proudest moments of my life. Despite my trepidations, I felt as if I had arrived, ready to contribute to the betterment of society, and defend my country.

A librarian-looking woman, a civilian, handed me a huge packet. "Get on the bus for the airport to report for your next duty station, Great Lakes. Good luck!"

In those days, the Navy had three locations for boot camp; beautiful San Diego, sunny Orlando, and dreary Great Lakes near Chicago. Naturally, the Navy ordered me to Chicago with seven other guys from the area. After a four-hour wait at the airport, we boarded our flight for Chicago's O'Hare Airport.

On arrival, members of the USO—a volunteer group that serves those in the military—offered us a refreshing beverage while we waited for the bus that would take us to Great Lakes Boot Camp. The USO lady gave me a Coke and then a smile. The last smile I'd see for some time.

So far, this Navy stuff had been simple. As the bus entered the gate, my seatmate's watch read 10:16 PM, which I translated in my head to 2216. Exhausted, I imagined a good night's sleep in some barracks. Oh, how naive I was.

The yelling seemed to begin before the bus wheels came to a complete stop.

"Get off my bus!" I moved quickly tripping over my own feet.

"Get on that line!"

"Get off that line!"

I saw one thick yellow line but had no idea if my toes

should touch it or not.

"Get in line!"

Multiple people yelled and I lost track of who ordered whom to do what.

In mass confusion, we looked at one another hoping somebody would know what to do.

"Don't look at him."

I froze in fear, unsure if the guy yelling meant me.

I realized one thing; lines are important. Afterwards, they corralled us into a building to fill out forms, and tell us what to do. And what not to do, most important of which was, "Keep your mouths shut."

I mastered keeping my mouth shut. Much of the time, I simply waited. I had no clue why we waited. We just sat, stood, or pondered. Those yelling out orders completely controlled our lives. They seemed to have a firm grasp on what they wanted, but we remained clueless.

I arrived at boot camp in decent shape after running daily for several weeks. From the looks of several guys around me, they hadn't seen a pushup in years. Several bellies hung over belts. I wasn't exactly Jack LaLanne, but some of these guys were in serious trouble. My recruiter had told me that men who needed to lose weight would and men who needed to gain weight would. I didn't need to do either, but I'd hoped to gain some muscle to accentuate my fair-haired, boy-next-door look.

Sitting in a classroom of sorts at one of those school desks with the chair attached, I looked at the clock, and it said 0018—eighteen minutes after midnight. They issued us black, ballpoint, retractable pens with the words "U S GOVERNMENT" stamped on the side. I assumed that I would have "U S GOVERNMENT" stamped somewhere on my person before this night ended.

Click, click, click, click. A full room of bored men clicked those retractable pens over and over.

The fellow that directed us in that room seemed nice enough up to this point, and I assumed he and I might enjoy a friendly conversation any other day. Busily writing at his desk in the front of the room, he suddenly looked up and said, "Quit clicking your fucking pens."

Every pen click ceased at that moment. Most guys put their pens down and did not give it another thought. I, however, pondered the profanity directed my way. I had certainly heard the "F" word before. It's possible that it had left my lips on one or two occasions in the past. But he directed this foul language at us, haphazardly. Specifically, at me, perhaps.

How dare he use such a filthy word in such a public way?

Many dared to use—and successfully delivered—that filthy word over the next few hours in a variety of forms. They used it as an adjective, a noun, and an interjection in the most colorful ways.

"Shut your fucking hole."

"What the fuck did he say?"

"Fuck!"

I quickly shunned my civilian sensibilities. The abbreviations, acronyms, terms, and profanity all combined to form the naval language.

They directed us to empty our pockets and then confiscated any contraband we had, such as knives, over-the-counter medicine, magazines, etc.

"You keep that," the sailor said. "Put that in the box. Move."

We clumsily marched into a large barracks and they told us

to use the head (bathroom) and hit the rack (bed) in our civilian clothes. Other than the loan of a raincoat, no other military clothing had been issued.

One poor guy made the mistake of asking what time they would wake us.

He received a curt response from the mysterious man in charge. "Shut the fuck up, and go to sleep."

The time read 0345 according to the clock that hung at the end of the barracks. I realized near twenty-four hours had passed since I woke up in my bed the previous morning. Surely, they knew this and planned for us to sleep late.

Naivete clung to me.

CHAPTER 5

Clang! Clang! Clang!

The metal trashcan lid that banged against its receptacle provided an excellent alarm clock. My body seemed to fly from my rack in some sort of involuntary convulsion.

A man I'd never met bellowed, "Reveille, reveille, reveille, get up, get up, get up!"

The man pulled blankets from several racks.

"Go to the head if you need to," he said.

I existed in some middle state between sleep and consciousness.

My last trip to the head had been a mere forty-five minutes earlier. That's right. The clock read 0430. We'd slept less than an hour.

Could this really be happening?

I had learned my first valuable lesson in boot camp. Our personal comforts counted for nothing.

The CC—company commanders—paced up and down the barracks. "Don't worry about making your racks. You don't know how to make them anyway. Put your raincoats on."

Make my rack? I could hardly stand. I stood upright while the rack exerted some gravitational pull on me. I desperately needed more sleep. I realized that not only did my sleep last a mere forty-five minutes, but that I likely faced seventeen to eighteen hours until the next opportunity to sleep. It literally hurt. At that moment, I understood why sleep deprivation had been an effective torture technique. How would I ever survive this day?

My second valuable lesson came shortly thereafter. Never say or do anything stupid. Sounds simple, but in every group there's always one ignoramus. He's the one that mumbled, "This is B.S., man."

"What the fuck did you say?" the CC said in an obviously rhetorical tone.

Seaman Recruit Ignoramus deserved the fifty pushups for his mumbled comment. "Everybody drop."

But in the eyes of the CCs, we all deserved fifty pushups for SR Ignoramus's comment.

A string of fifty pushups challenged many. Counting out each pushup with, "one, sir—two, sir—three, sir," at 0433 in the morning, wearing a raincoat, on forty-five minutes sleep, while pissed at SR Ignoramus for the dumb comment challenged everyone.

When the CC consistently stopped us, made us start over, and otherwise interfered with the process, the difficulty morphed into an impossibility. Thank you, SR Ignoramus.

"Fall out for chow."

What does fall out even mean? I quickly learned that boot camp is a team sport and I followed the crowd.

The Great Lakes weather in early June at 0445 ran about fifty-five to sixty degrees. For me, a southern boy, it may as well have been twenty degrees. Despite my fight to regain muscle control, my teeth refused to stop chattering until I was inside the chow hall.

"No talking."

I had no appetite that early in the morning, but like many things, chow was not optional. I held out my tray as one guy tossed on a piece of toast and another slung a pile of slop on the toast. For breakfast, they served SOS (shit on a shingle) or as the menu stated—ground beef in gravy on toast.

Hundreds of men moved through the lines or sat devouring their food. I sat and managed to swallow three bites when the CC stood up.

"On your feet!"

Next came the proverbial haircut rite of passage. Like students forced to watch another student paddled before their turn with the principal, we watched our fellow recruits lose the little dignity they had left. Most had the same look as when we received our group proctologic exam.

The barber pointed at me. "Next."

That simple haircut seemingly transformed us from boys to men. Sailors, no less. Those thoughts quickly faded as a group of "real" sailors marched by mocking us. They wore the white Dixie Cup sailor hat and marched confidently. Technically speaking, they were not true sailors yet, but they seemed far ahead of us in training.

Standing in line became my nemesis. Staring at the ugly, bald head of the guy in front of me. Many times, I was right up against the guy in front of me.

"C'mon. Tighten up. Nuts to butts," the CC said.

For several hours, tailors measured us, issued us uniforms, and pushed us along the assembly line. After packing my civilian clothes in a bag for storage, I clumsily put on my dungarees and attempted to balance a green seabag on my back. I covered my bald head with a navy-blue watch cap. 100%

wool. A sailor's friend in the winter. A recruit's enemy when the heat came. Wearing a uniform for the first time, I should have felt pride, but I only thought of sleep.

Afternoon chow offered us our first chance to talk to one another. "I'm Brian Donley," I said, extending my hand to the guy in front of me.

"Victor Randolph. Good to meet you, Brian. I'd say call me Victor but that might be a little against the rules," he said.

I noticed Randolph earlier. He seemed confident, so I mirrored him.

"Where you from, Rand—"

"On your feet!" some voice said, and we obeyed.

We lined up in ranks for a march of what seemed like miles. The full seabags on our backs accentuated the forced march. Nothing seemed beautiful about this place. All business. One similar looking building after another with strange names such as NSTC or TPU. I had no idea what those letters meant. No ships. Nothing like the recruiting posters. Just buildings and the guy's head in front of me.

We arrived at our new home—the barracks at the extreme end of the base. As I walked in, cleanliness and order glared back at me. The only thing that seemed out of place was me.

Twenty-two bunk beds lined each side with lockers in-between. We unpacked our seabags on our racks and began the meticulous process of stenciling everything we owned. Each of us held a card with our first and middle initial, last name, and Social Security number.

The CC scribbled "I.M. Dickhead" on the chalkboard, the name he chose for demonstration rather than John Doe or something like that. "Like SR I.M. Dickhead, you take your stencil card and pen in hand and put your name on everything you've been issued." The CC proceeded to show us how to stencil each item in a particular spot in a particular way.

My less offensive stencil simply read B D Donley. I stenciled my name as instructed on every item including my newly issued tighty-whitey skivvies—the underwear of the Navy.

"Now take off the pair of dungarees and skivvies you're wearing and stencil them."

With bare butts in the air, we laid our skivvies on the floor and stenciled them. This act stripped away the pride I felt from the previous day's swearing-in ceremony.

The greatest stress occurred when we stenciled our last names on our dungaree shirts.

The CC yelled a sentence in one breath that would mortify any grammarian. "Place your dungaree shirt flat on the deck with your stencil in your left hand and your stencil pen in your right hand and proceed to stencil your last name above the left breast pocket to the right from left to right, begin."

Bewildered, my right hand shook as I placed ink to cloth.

The CC stood over me. "If you screw this up, you have to put one straight line through the mistake, and then re-stencil in the correct location. Don't screw this up."

There are no do-overs. Screw this up and the mistake would follow me, seemingly, for my entire naval career.

I managed to survive that task, but a couple of guys failed and faced the prospect of wearing that scarlet letter for all of boot camp.

The indecipherable screams of the CC amplified their mistakes. Without taking a breath, the CC walked away from them. "Pick up all your clothes and stand in front of your racks!"

For some pointless reason, and there seemed to be many of those, the CCs ordered us to hold all of our folded clothes in our hands and run around the barracks in an oval pattern. For most of us, the clothes extended above our eyesight. Running blind, I continually bumped into the guy in front of me as the one behind me kept bumping me. This caused my first, flagrant offense in boot camp. I stepped on my CC's shiny, corfam, right shoe.

I stopped as several guys behind me bumped together. I looked down and saw his reflection in the non-smudged corfam of the left shoe. I peeked up and around my stacked clothes as he glared directly at me. I imagined this the same look he'd give someone that ran over his dog or crossed a boundary with his daughter. With all the breath he could muster, he yelled, "You stepped on my fucking shoe, you fucking dickhead!"

The teeth chattering I'd experienced at morning chow returned.

"Move!"

"Yes, sir!" I said with a shaking voice and resumed my running.

"Stow your gear and prepare for chow."

Our barracks seemed to reside miles from the chow hall. Specifically, one-and-one-quarter miles away.

Our marching looked ridiculous and I had to think through each step. Left, right, left, right, right, no that's not it. I noticed another company marching by and every one of them had the scarlet letter on their dungaree shirts. They had their names stenciled on the right side with a line struck through them and their name also listed on the left—the correct location. The CC leading them held a look of disgust at the recruits under his charge.

Although twelve hours had passed since reveille, it seemed

like a second day had begun. I remembered waking up in my own bed the previous day, but that day ended at 0345. I'd never felt so exhausted physically or mentally in my eighteen years.

I knew better than to think they would give us the evening off after chow. I knew better than to think they'd let us go to sleep early.

Naivete left me on this, the longest day of my life.

CHAPTER 6

My second day in the Navy beckoned a realistic glimpse into my future. My overworked body welcomed the evening chow slung on my plate. Eating, like marching, became a robotic exercise as my mind and muscles screamed for rest. Yet, a whole evening remained.

More stenciling, running around the barracks, yelling, and confusion. After unpacking and learning to brush our teeth the right way—that is, the Navy way—CC Brown instructed us on proper sleeping, as if we needed any guidance.

"You will lie on your rack, on your sheet, head on pillow, body under blanket. Is that clear?"

"Yes, sir!" we said in unison.

"You will not leave your rack except for an emergency head call. Is that clear?"

"Yes, sir!"

I did the math. I'd slept forty-five minutes in the last forty-two hours.

"Taps, taps, lights out. All hands turn into your bunks. Maintain silence about the decks. The smoking lamp is out in all berthing spaces." My body thanked the mysterious voice that came over the intercom at 2130 (9:30 PM).

A mere seven hours later, I cursed him for calling "Reveille,

reveille" and other instructions I failed to comprehend at 0430.

I popped up and made a feeble attempt to make my rack. I occupied the top one and realized I never introduced myself to the man occupying the rack under me. "Hey, I'm Donley."

"Julio Lopez Guillermo from Boise, Idaho," he said.

I thought this odd on two levels. He introduced himself by his full name, and he came from Boise. Perhaps my bias intervened, thinking Boise void of Hispanics. Rather than utter an artless comment toward him, I focused on my rack.

"You work on that end of both racks, and I'll do the same on this end," Guillermo said.

He understood the essential element of teamwork, and I considered myself fortunate to be rackmates with him. A friend maybe.

"Guillermo, we need to do this every day."

He replied with a thumbs up.

Brown walked down the line of racks noting every error in our rackmaking skills. "That looks like crap. Do it again," Brown said.

Not "Good morning" or "Did you sleep well?"

His next quip startled us. "Any of you girls afraid of needles?"

CC Joseph E. Brown fit the quintessential stereotype of a boot camp instructor. His biceps stretched his tight uniform sleeves. Merit ribbons piled high on his chest. One eye seemed to always rise slightly higher than the other, offering a stern demeanor. But his greatest asset lay in his ability to rattle off a profanity-laced tirade in a moment's notice. Every recruit feared him.

Guillermo whispered, "I heard he's been in the Navy twelve years."

I thought this curious since his rank fell below that of a sailor with that much time in service. Had he committed some infraction in the past? Mystery surrounded him like the crazy recluse that lived in the old house at the end of the lane. I wanted to investigate Brown but feared the potential findings. I sure wasn't going to ask him.

Brown's powers bordered on telekinetic. Without saying a word, his mere stare forced recruits to drop and do twenty pushups. I'm not sure he took pleasure in our abuse. Maybe he thought it a necessary rite of passage. He had no toleration for failure.

"Listen up," Brown said. "The true meaning of discipline is not punishment, but that development of self-control and team work which enables men to strive for perfection and accomplish greatness."

I'd already heard this boot camp mantra three times from him. I'd been yelled at before—I played high school football in the South. But Brown operated on a different level. He was a professional tormentor. And this was the man whose shoe I'd stepped on, putting me on par with SR Ignoramus.

After an incompetent march and morning chow, we entered the medical building for a day's worth of probing and prodding. The Navy pursued efficiency with a passion. This included inoculations via an air-powered jet injector, or as we called it—the shotgun. As we moved single file down a hallway, men stood on each side, guns in hand, shooting the fluid into our arms.

Kachunk. Kachunk. The shotgun unleashed on me and reloaded.

The corpsman made no attempt at bedside manner. "Next!"

I moved up for another. After four of these, I turned the

corner only to see two more corpsmen at the ready like those creepy Santa's elves in the movie *A Christmas Story*. Six shots total and my arms hung near incapacitation, blood streaking down the left one. No needles, as Brown had implied, but still a penetrating affront to my body.

Thank God that's over, I thought.

"Go in there and drop your pants," the next corpsman said.

One more in the backside. That one stung like the others, but it was even worse; it hurt every time I sat, pulled my notebook from my pocket, or simply thought about my right buttock. A little later, I noticed everyone sitting on the floor, leaning slightly to the left.

Processing days like that one were long, boring, uncertain, and worst of all, they delayed day 1-1 (week one, day one), the real first day of boot camp counting toward graduation.

Evening chow provided our first opportunity in two days to rest, think, and recover. Thirty minutes of peace.

"What is this on my plate?" I said to the guy across from me. I had yet to learn his name or the names of many of the eighty or so others experiencing this crucible with me.

"Beef and noodles," he said.

"Yeah, but what kind of beef?"

"No wait, I think it's pork, and this may not be noodles. Mystery meat, I guess. It's dead, cooked, and not moving. Just eat it."

Brown stood. "Company 165, on your feet!"

With a full belly, I entered the barracks hoping the evening involved some rest and reflection. Perhaps some time to sit around and chat. The CCs planned something much different—a mashing.

The verb "mash," in the context of boot camp, translated

to punish or discipline. MASH stood for "make a sailor hurt," according to boot camp gossip.

"Get those racks back," Brown yelled.

We moved the racks against the wall to facilitate more room for our punishment. The infraction we committed remained a mystery.

Did I do something, I thought. Did Guillermo? SR Ignoramus. Yes, must be him.

Brown pulled a card from his breast pocket. "This is a mash card indicating the type, number, and severity of exercises authorized by higher command that I may use on you. I can take you through this card twice with no rest. Any questions?"

"No, sir!"

After hundreds of sit-ups, pushups, and jumping jacks, we ran around inside the barracks for several minutes, before Brown introduced us to two brutal exercises.

The flutter kick required me to lie on my belly and kick my arms and legs as if I were swimming.

This is easy, I thought. Then pain entered the equation. Searing pain all through my legs, arms, and torso. Then the second minute started. I'll never make it, I thought. Why isn't he reading from that mash card?

I quickly deduced that Brown didn't use the card. He probably showed it to us as a perfunctory requirement. He operated on feeling. Or maybe sadism.

"On your feet! This is a body builder." Brown dropped into a squat, then did a leg kickout, a pushup, and a jumping jack.

That's easy, I thought, forgetting the flutter kick scenario. Thirty bodybuilders later, death seemed imminent.

"Rest!" Brown said.

His idea of rest was twenty seconds.

"Pushup position!"

A diabolical exercise called the three-inch puddle caused me the greatest pain. Brown smiled. "This exercise ends when you have a three-inch diameter puddle of sweat on the deck."

I pressed up and released down at varying speeds upon Brown's command. I discovered that my chin, appropriately placed and moved about in my sweat, altered the size of the puddle. In other words, I cheated—as did many. The mashing ended after forty-five minutes.

"You men remember this and don't let it happen again," Brown said.

Let what happen? I thought. He never told us what we did wrong.

The next morning after chow, we returned to the barracks and found CC Phelps in a perturbed state. He ordered us to push back the racks and held up a pen that some recruit had supposedly left on his rack.

"Get in pushup position," he said.

CC Brown partnered with Chief Raymond Phelps, a rookie CC. I thought Phelps an amiable man, almost uncomfortable with the mashing. His yells included the occasional squeak causing Brown to shake his head in disgust. With thick glasses and paunch, Phelps seemed a bit of a nerd. He lacked Brown's swagger, but Phelps did his due diligence.

"I will make you sailors," he'd say.

Chief Phelps considered a "missile" the most egregious of errors. He found it unacceptable to leave any item out on a rack, a table, or the deck.

Holding up the pen, Chief Phelps yelled, "This is a missile. This or a loose piece of clothing on a ship might stop up the drain of a flooding compartment."

The lecture proceeded as my arms began to ache from simply holding myself in pushup position.

"Down!" Chief Phelps said. "A loose tool could fall on someone's head."

The pauses made these pushups excruciating.

"Up!" Another pause. "A loose CO_2 cylinder might tip over, have the head break off, and shoot through a bulkhead."

My arms labored through the mounting pressure. Shifting my weight back and forth to each side gave moments of relief.

"Down!" Phelps continued pacing back and forth between our ranks. "If I ever find a missile left out, you will pay."

The burning made me deaf to Brown's lecture.

"Up!"

My arms began convulsing. This scared me. I knew that dropping to my knees meant more punishment, but I began to panic.

"Down!"

As much as I tried, I couldn't go down, or move my arms left or right, or drop to my knees. I remained in a paralyzed state, other than my shaking arms.

"Up!"

Will this ever end?

"Recover!"

Finally, Phelps gave the command to stand at attention. My arms gave way and I collapsed on my belly.

I don't think Phelps even understood the length of time we held the pushup position. His mind focused on his lecture whereas Brown would have focused on the torture. Phelps taught, Brown disciplined. Both methods worked. Both sucked.

CHAPTER 7

As the first week transitioned to a second and third week, company 165 learned to work as a team. We sang a cadence as we marched to chow in unison.

Randolph called the cadence and we repeated.

"Get out of the way. *Get out of the way.*

We're coming through. *We're coming through.*

Company 165. *Company 165.*

Is marching through. *Is marching through.*

So make a hole. *So make a hole.*

And make it wide. *And make it wide.*

'Cause 165. *'Cause 165.*

Is marching by. *Is marching by.*"

The CCs appointed Randolph as our RCPO (recruit chief petty officer), our leader in the absence of the CCs. No one questioned that. He epitomized self-assurance and leadership.

All types surrounded me. Jocks, brainiacs, hillbillies, smart alecks, the shy, and the gullible. Overachievers and underachievers marched with pride. Jerks to my left, and loners to my right.

I'm not sure which classification I fell under, but I got along with most of the others.

Overweight guys shed pounds. Underweight guys gained

muscle. The shy learned to use their voices with authority, and the loudmouth learned to keep his mouth shut. Not everyone adapted to the Navy way. Certainly not SR Ebert.

One day after chow, we entered the schoolhouse for classroom instruction, which offered a nice break from the marching and mashing. These classes typically covered topics such as US Naval history, ship safety, and personal hygiene.

A hospital corpsman lectured us on sex education. He showed several slides of genitalia in various states of decline from venereal disease.

SR Ebert raised his hand and the instructor pointed to him. "What?"

"I'm a black belt in karate," Ebert said.

"So what? You gonna break a board with your dick? Who gives a shit?"

Ebert sank in his chair. The room erupted in laughter.

The statement, so bizarre and out of place, baffled us. SR Ebert was our odd duck. The only thing I could deduce was that Ebert wanted to tell us how physically fit he was. Perhaps his karate kept him so fit, he deemed himself immune to venereal disease. We didn't understand why he did and said some of these crazy things. Maybe he had a screw loose. It was impossible to have a normal conversation with the guy. His rackmate talked to him out of necessity, but nothing more.

We continued laughing about this throughout the day. That's a bad thing while you're marching, and Brown—not privy to the classroom lecture—mashed us for laughing in ranks.

Ebert lined up for a routine inspection one day with an enormous bulge in his breast pocket. Regulations required nothing in our breast pockets other than our identification card in the left, with the picture side facing out and up. There was no latitude or augmentation allowed. Eighty guys stood at attention expecting no infractions. The CCs always found infractions.

CC Brown walked by each of us pointing out the slightest mistake. "Poor shave."

He stopped in front of Guillermo. "Crooked cover."

I prayed, Please, God, don't let him find anything wrong.

Brown turned and looked at me. A bead of sweat rolled down my cheek. His eyes rolled, and he looked to the side in disgust. "Dirty—" Brown froze. No movement of foot or lips. He stared at something or someone down the line from me.

Then he moved at a quickened pace. Had this been a cartoon, Brown's ears would have blown steam. I was supposed to look straight ahead, but I had to know the cause of this fury.

"What the fuck is in your pocket, Ebert?" Brown said this through clinched lips as if conserving strength for the inevitable screaming.

"Money, sir," Ebert said.

Our first payday occurred the day prior. Nearly all of us had sent the majority of our money home as instructed. We kept only a few bucks to buy a Coke or cigarettes. The rest stayed in our lockers.

"Ebert, why the fuck do you have money in your pocket?" Brown said, his voice rising.

"I don't trust banks and don't want anyone to steal money from my locker," Ebert said.

"Get those racks back," Brown yelled.

His individual mistake meant group punishment. We allowed everyone a screw-up on occasion, and they might receive a bit of disgust from us, but Ebert committed deliberate infractions. He willfully disobeyed orders and refused to work with us. Ebert's real punishment was the shunning that occurred over the next several days. No one talked to him other than in obscenities. No one helped him. His rackmate abandoned him. He began to break under the pressure.

Ebert did one thing really well: the sixteen-count manual of arms—a multiple point exercise with an old M-1 Garand rifle, minus the firing pin. We called them our pieces—not rifles or guns, but pieces—and we carried them most places.

Four days into the shunning, our company entered the drill hall after noon chow. The heat, combined with a lack of any breeze, made our sixteen-count manual drilling unbearable. My dungaree shirt had two tones: a dry light blue and a sweat-filled dark blue.

As the CC commanded, "Right shoulder, arms," or "Present, arms," we attempted to place the rifles in their appropriate positions. Ebert usually did this without error. I rarely did the count twice in a row without messing up as happened with many. How Ebert managed this exercise with perfection, and more importantly, with team unity, mystified me.

On this hot day of drilling, though, Ebert did the count but began shouting the commands at the same time as the CC.

I think the first time, Phelps and Brown thought they had just heard something like an echo. The second time they looked around.

"Who the fuck said that?" Brown screamed.

No one responded.

"Port, arms," CC Phelps said, with Ebert simultaneously chiming in.

This time, they looked directly at Ebert who continued the count while shouting the commands.

I froze and stared at Ebert.

When Ebert finished, Brown walked up curling his index finger. "Follow me."

"Sir, yes, sir! I will follow you sir!" Ebert said.

We returned from the drilling session to find Ebert and his possessions gone. I don't know what happened to him. I suppose he had a mental breakdown and was sent home. I was glad to see him go. He had no business operating million-dollar equipment on a ship.

Ebert failed boot camp because he lacked the mental toughness needed to follow orders—even those that seemed meaningless, such as the sixteen-count manual.

Some guys had no problem following orders, but struggled with simple little tests required in boot camp. Like Purcell.

SR Purcell never learned to swim. He stood six-foot-six and carried a healthy amount of weight. His pleasant demeanor curtailed his imposing appearance. Everybody liked him.

Swim test day terrified him. He only needed to jump in the deep end from a six-foot board, swim to a point, tread water for five minutes, and swim to the end of the pool

Purcell stood on the diving board shaking while his fellow recruits of color mocked him without mercy.

"What's the matter, Purcell, black man afraid of the water?"

While nearly everything we did required the strictest discipline, the company commanders allowed a relaxed atmosphere around the water. The intent was encouragement, though, not mocking.

Purcell could crush any of us with his bare hands. His rackmaking perfection thrilled CC Brown. He never failed to bark his eleven general orders of the sentry word-for-word.

I stood in line behind Purcell. He looked at the water, looked behind him, and looked to each side as if hoping for some escape. "Oh, Jesus," he said.

The mockers clapped and began to encourage him. "C'mon dawg. Let's do this thing."

"Purcell, hit the water," Brown barked.

Purcell stepped off the board, hit the water, and sank to the bottom. Unlike the others, who came right back up, Purcell stayed at the bottom. A lifeguard quickly rescued him. Purcell broke the surface of the water, gasping for air, to see Brown staring back at him.

"Looks like you'll be spending your evenings in the pool until you pass."

I felt bad for Purcell. Everyone had difficulty with something in boot camp. I struggled with boredom. The CCs certainly kept us busy, but the inevitable waiting in line, standing guard, or standing at attention for no particular reason tried my inactive imagination.

I hated standing watch. Recruits had to guard the barracks, twenty-four hours per day, with a useless rifle that had the firing pins removed for safety. Technically, we watched for fire or theft, but nothing ever happened. One night, I had the 2400 to 0400 watch, also known as balls-to-four.

Guillermo had the 2000 to 2400 watch that night. "Donley, get up. It's your watch."

I rubbed my eyes. "What time is it?"

"2340. You have to relieve me in five minutes."

"What?"

Guillermo shook me. "Donley, get up."

I finally accepted the reality of the situation. I slept so little already in boot camp and now I had to be awake for the next four hours.

Every fifteen minutes, I walked the length of the barracks and logged in my report, "ALL SECURE." Sheer boredom! I woke up my relief at 0340 and hit my rack for a mere forty-five minutes. It hurt. It hurt all day.

I enjoyed few things in boot camp but we all liked Coke and Smoke—ten minutes to drink soft drinks and smoke cigarettes. Guys that never smoked in the past began smoking, if for no other reason, than a break from the normal routine. It gave us a few minutes at the end of the day to relax. To rest our minds from the constant stress.

As bad as balls-to-four watch was, little things like Coke and Smoke made boot camp bearable.

CHAPTER 8

"Who do you think'll get Deep Sink?" I asked Guillermo as we made our racks.

Guillermo shook his head. "I don't know. Ebert would've gotten it. I'm hoping for something simple. Cleaning tables in the mess or something like that. All I know is we're halfway through boot camp. Service Week is easy duty."

"You don't think I'll get it, do you?" I said.

"Get what?" Guillermo said.

"You know. Deep Sink. Scrubbing pots and pans all day. That's gotta suck."

Guillermo smoothed out the bottom sheet. "Nah. That's for screw-ups like Ebert. I don't think the CCs even know your name."

I shook my head. The stress gnawing at me. "I hope so. I'll take laundry or some paint crew any day over Deep Sink."

I'd heard stories of Deep Sink as some abyss in the mess hall where CCs punished recruits for Service Week—seven days of support work for the base. I'd envisioned recruits chained to the deep sinks, scrubbing pots and pans all day, the men suffering from the intolerable heat of steam, sixteen hours per day, with no breaks. A stern Simon Legree stood by ready to pounce on any recruit that complained. Torture. No less than slave labor.

That afternoon, the CCs posted the list for our Service Week assignments, which would start the next morning. I scrolled to the D's and found my name. "Donley...Deep Sink." As I read those words, my shoulders and chin dropped. What the heck did I do to deserve this?

I approached CC Brown in a sheepish but respectful manner. "Sir, permission to speak."

"Speak." Brown looked at me with no emotion.

"Why...why was I assigned deep sink? I thought I was doing pretty good. My name is Do..."

"You're on Deep Sink nights, Donley. Report there at 1600 today. " With no further explanation or chance for rebuttal, Brown turned and walked away.

So he did know my name. I assumed that to be a bad thing. I looked back at the sheets and noticed the "Deep Sink" and scrolled to the right with my finger to find the words "night shift." All the other guys we expected to get Deep Sink had the day shift. They had to report at 0400 the next day.

Guillermo walked up smiling. "Hey, Donley, I got Processing. I'll be the one saying, 'You keep that. Put that in the box. You keep that.' What did you get?"

"Deep Sink." I hung my head, shaking it left to right.

"Huh? You're kidding me."

"Nope. It's nights, though, but I guess that means this will suck all night instead of all day."

Guillermo laid a hand on my shoulder. "Sorry, man. I don't know what you did to piss off the CCs"

Bewildered, I reported at 1600 as ordered. Deep Sink looked a little less dungeon-like than I'd envisioned. The heat seemed unbearable, but no chains. No Simon Legree. Those hard at work did have a look of desperation. Hopelessness. Exhaustion.

"You Deep Sink nights?" said another recruit who appeared to be supervising.

"Uh...yes," I said in a slow and methodical voice.

"I'm Caughey, in charge of Deep Sink nights. Grab an apron and gloves and start over there."

Training took about one minute. I dove into the hot mess of pans and water and scrubbed, unsure why this hell had been unleashed on me. The guys that started work the same time as me laughed as they scrubbed, sprayed, and stacked.

Two hours later, Caughey yelled, "Coke and Smoke, ten minutes."

Everyone dropped their pan. So, we do get breaks, I thought.

I decided to confide in Caughey. "I don't understand why my CC gave me Deep Sink. I haven't done anything wrong."

Caughey laughed. "Listen, we have another break at 2000 when the day shift leaves. I'll explain everything then. Trust me."

Slightly encouraged, I joined the others for Coke and Smoke. The guys that started work with me—the night shift—laughed and inhaled their Marlboro Reds. The day shift guys sat, dejected. Some smoked as well, but had no smile, no cheer. Several questions raced through my mind. Why the difference? Were the day guys just beat? Why did Caughey say, "trust me"? What the hell is going on? Is this a dream?

At 2000, the day shift slowly walked out in pure exhaustion as we headed for another Coke and Smoke.

As guys lit their cigarettes, Caughey said, "Hey, everyone this is Donley. He wants to know why he's being punished with

Deep Sink."

They all laughed. Caughey continued. "This is easy duty. We do a lot more Smoke and Coke than scrubbing pots and pans. The day shift guys work from 0400 to 2000. Sixteen straight ball-busting hours. We come in at 1600 and help. By 2200 we're done. They may need us to help crack some eggs or unpack some boxes, but most of the time we sit around, smoke, and sleep. Yeah, we work hard for six hours or so, but then we lie around for the next six."

They all laughed because they'd thought the same thing as I did. They all thought that Deep Sink meant punishment for something. The relief overwhelmed me. Caughey pushed out a cigarette from his pack. "You want a smoke?"

"Sure. Guess I need to buy my own pack."

My fellow Deep Sink night workers tore into the work with laughter. With much of the mess hall staff gone, the noise lowered enough that we could talk. A rare commodity in boot camp. We rarely had time to just talk.

"Caughey, how long you been in Deep Sink?" I asked.

"Four days. Tonight, two more, and I'm done."

We talked about sports, music, girlfriends. All kinds of topics.

Caughey seemed a lifetime ahead of me in boot camp. That's the way it was. Like a junior in high school seems so far ahead of a sophomore. He wasn't really, but that's the way it felt. I envied guys ahead of me in boot camp. You always wanted to reach that next milestone. Caughey was only four days ahead of me, but seemed so much more experienced.

"Who'll be in charge then?" I asked.

Caughey shrugged. "I dunno. Maybe you."

Around 2215, we finished and headed to the break room

for a Coke and Smoke. I noticed guys using old coats and various items for pillows. I followed suit and slept on a bench for five glorious hours. Caughey woke me in time to greet the day workers who looked like the walking dead. I couldn't imagine how bad they felt. Working sixteen long hours, marching perhaps one mile to their racks, sleeping six hours or so, marching back the mile, and working sixteen more hours.

Back at the barracks, I showered and slept nine more hours. The longest I'd slept since the weekend before I left for boot camp. And it felt great.

On my second night, they had us crack eggs, four to a bowl—making it easier for the cooks to make eggs to order. At first, I got shells in the bowl and made a big mess. By morning, I could take one egg in each hand, crack it, and leave no shell in the bowl. Easy duty. That's the way Service Week went for me. I realized the CCs gave me an easy gig.

Two days later, Caughey finished his Service Week, and a guy that started the day before me became the supervisor. That was fine with me. A whole week with little responsibility, free from stress, and no yelling.

I double-timed to the barracks after my final shift; recruits not in formation could not walk, we had to jog. Guillermo caught up with me, having finished his final shift.

Out of breath, he said, "Tomorrow's the day we don leggings, the guard belt, and the Dixie Cup hat."

I shook my head. "It also means they're gonna kick our asses with drills, and mashing, and yelling."

"Hey man, that's why they call it Hell Week. We get to sleep 'till 0530 now. No more 0430 reveille. A whole extra hour of sleep."

I scoffed. "We'll see."

CHAPTER 9

"C'mon, Donley. Let's get these racks made," Guillermo said.

"I'm trying to lace up these stupid things."

Panic! Sheer panic consumed me. Reveille had sounded at 0530 with no extra time to orchestrate the complicated task of putting on leggings—ridiculous pieces of cloth that served no purpose. The World War I soldier likely found them quite useful, but they only represented an extra task for us, along with making bunks, brushing our teeth, and if we could find the extra minute, using the head. Like we had time to run laces through several eyelets and buckle them around our boondocker boots. No shortcuts with these things.

"Let's go, let's go," Brown said. "Fall out with your pieces."

Oh, great, I thought. More drilling with useless rifles. They could've at least let us have some fun firing those things. But we were going to be sailors. No real weapons training for us.

I ran to the head to relieve myself. I glanced in the mirror. Rather than the boy from day one that wore the watch cap over a bald head, there stood a man with the famed white sailor hat. Since the day they had issued us the hats, we hadn't worn them because we hadn't earned it. We only wore a wool watchcap in the first several weeks. For one brief second, I was proud of the boy who was becoming a sailor.

Brown burst into the head. "Fall out, now! You can piss when you get to the fleet."

Unlike in our first few days, our ranks showed the sharp skill of an organized unit as we assembled on the parade grounds. Despite the useless leggings and rifles—a change began in our step. We'd reached a milestone and wore the white hat.

RCPO Randolph looked up and down the ranks. "Forward, march."

We marched with confidence and a sense of accomplishment. It lasted about five yards.

"Halt!" Brown said and just stared.

It was 0542. In the last twelve minutes, we'd wakened, dressed, brushed our teeth, used the head, made our racks, and ran down three flights of stairs to fall in. We had only marched ten steps toward morning chow. Welcome to Hell Week, I thought.

Brown, hands on hips, slowly approached my direction.

Oh crap, what have I done?

He walked inches past me. "Sidwell! What the fuck is wrong with you?"

Everybody liked SR Sidwell, other than one little thing. The guy possessed no military bearing. It's a difficult concept to describe but essentially entails the ability to comprehend and follow orders. It's more than discipline or simple obedience. Sidwell joined the Navy to work as a paper pusher, so none of us feared him operating million-dollar equipment like Ebert.

Brown walked back a few steps and surveyed the ranks. "Since Sidwell doesn't know his right from his left, we're gonna help him learn. Order, arms!"

Sidwell didn't have a bad attitude. He wasn't disobedient. But he had a knack for screwing up. He's the kind of guy that might have snot running down his lip and not even know it. There we stood with our rifles on our right shoulders and Sidwell had his rifle on his left.

At 0542 on the parade ground, sleepy and hungry, we were made to perform the sixteen-count manual of arms. A more experienced company marched by, grinning at our misfortune. They had finished their Hell Week.

Brown launched obscenities like we'd never heard before. "You ladies will do sixteen-count manual until Sidwell is perfect. Maybe you need a visit from the Watash."

Several puzzled faces looked at Brown. "Yeah, that's right. You girls don't know about the Watash. Chief Jean-Pierre to you. He's the baddest fucking CC to ever run a company. He will mash your ass for hours. You better hope you don't meet him."

I internally debated whether Chief Watash really existed or Brown was just trying to scare us. I'm sure others wondered the same thing as we continued the sixteen-count manual arms, praying for Sidwell to get it right.

Sidwell never performed anything perfectly, but after forty-five minutes Brown relented, and we eventually made it to chow.

That first day of Hell Week passed quickly. Lots of yelling. Lots of pushups. Lots of confusion. By evening chow, I thought, this is Hell Week? I can do this. My old nemesis, naivete, crept back in. I should have remembered that boot camp constantly makes you think one thing, when in reality, another happens. The specter of Watash kept popping up in my head. At that point, I wanted nothing but peace and quiet. I certainly didn't want any more stress.

SR Ruffalo walked by my table and whispered to Sidwell who sat across from me. "Your ass is mine." Sidwell pretended to ignore him but I could tell he heard the threat.

I imagined Sidwell as the type that suffered insults from bullies on a regular basis in high school.

And Ruffalo fit the bullying profile. He didn't have a big, imposing physical nature, but rather a short, hardened look. Tattoos covered his body. No matter how closely he shaved, his face remained darkened in the beard area. Most of us, at eighteen or nineteen found it difficult to relate to the twenty-nine-year-old Ruffalo.

Guillermo and I talked about Ruffalo that night while shining our shoes. "What does a guy do for ten years after high school and then decide to join the Navy?" I said.

"Maybe he's one of those guys that the judge told jail or the Navy, so he chose the Navy," Guillermo said.

I pondered that. "That makes sense. I bet he's an ex-con. What do you think he did?"

"Probably shot his mother," Guillermo said. We both laughed at that.

"What's so damn funny?" We looked up to find Ruffalo staring at us. "Well, what the fuck are you two faggots laughing at?"

"Uh…nothing," I said, hoping it would satisfy him. "Just a dumb joke."

"Faggots," he said as he walked off.

He loved that word "Faggot." Sometimes when we stood in lines, they packed us in like sardines. Nuts to butts they called it. When we strapped our rolled up raincoats to our lower backs in case of rain, it gave us a little bit of a buffer. Ruffalo called them "fag bumpers." He possessed no political correctness or decency.

Typical bully. I'm sure if he had heard Guillermo me and talking about him, the results would have been explosive.

I remembered Ruffalo's threat to Sidwell. He made all of us angry for the extra sixteen- count manual, but we had all screwed up at one time or another, causing punishment for the entire company. I felt sorry for Sidwell. It was almost as if he couldn't help it.

A few minutes before Taps, a crowd gathered around Ruffalo, nodding and whispering. The CCs had left an hour before. I walked up.

"As soon as Sidwell's asleep, we're gonna give him a blanket party," Ruffalo said. "We're gonna make that little faggot pay for his screw-ups."

"Blanket party?" one recruit asked.

Ruffalo let out a big smile, pointing guys out. "About thirty minutes after Taps, you two will hold a blanket over Sidwell so he can't move. The rest of you wrap your soap in your towel and whale away at him."

I stood there, shocked. I'd heard of blanket parties but assumed them to be a myth. Something that never really happened.

Ruffalo received enough nods from the crowd to maintain his smile, but a couple of guys failed to acknowledge the plan and he pointed them out. "Every one of you will take your licks on that faggot. You. And you. You too, Donley." Ruffalo stared directly at me.

"I...I...don't know if I can do that," I said.

"You'll do it or get the same. Any of you chicken out and

you'll get the same."

I offered no agreeing gesture, but didn't object either. This presented quite the dilemma. I walked to my rack and pulled Guillermo behind our lockers. "Guess what?"

"Why are you whispering?" Guillermo said loud enough for anyone nearby to hear.

"Shhh. Listen." I looked left and right to make sure no one heard. "Ruffalo and those guys are going to give Sidwell a blanket party. You know, hit him with soap in their towels."

Guillermo's eyes got big. "I knew it. I knew Ruffalo would try something."

"It's worse," I said. "He told me I have to hit him."

"What are you going to do?"

"That's why I'm telling you. Help me think of something. I'd have told him 'no,' but he had all those guys around him."

"You could warn Sidwell," Guillermo said.

"Yeah, but what if Ruffalo finds out? Then he'll be after me."

Guillermo rubbed the stubble on his head. "You can't tell the CCs. They left." Then he held up his index finger. "I got it. Randolph. Tell him. He's the RCPO. He's in charge when the CCs are away."

I slapped him on the back. "Oh yeah. Good idea. Thanks, man."

Guillermo's idea made sense. A recruit could screw up in a lot of ways, but disobey the RCPO when the CCs were away and that recruit might find himself back on 1-1 day— repeating boot camp.

I had spoken to Randolph a few times since that first day we met at morning chow. He grew up in the Bronx. My stereotypical thinking, based on movies, pegged him as a tough guy. Weren't all black guys from the Bronx tough? I never questioned his toughness, and he exuded confidence. He grew up in a house where his parents demanded hard work and excellence. They never allowed any grade below an "A." Randolph's mother worked as a nanny for a rich family in Manhattan and his dad operated a construction crane. They told him and his two younger sisters the same three things every day before they left for school. I love you, Jesus loves you, and find someone to help today. He shocked his parents by joining the Navy. They intended for him to become the first in the family to graduate from college. He told them he could help someone every day by serving his country and go to college after. Some would call him a born leader. I reasoned that his parents deserved much of the credit.

I found him sitting on his rack reading a letter.

"What's up, Randolph?"

"Got a little letter from my girl back home." He sniffed the letter with closed eyes. His head rolled back in appreciation of the perfume his girlfriend had apparently sprayed on the letter.

"You got a girl back home, Donley?"

"Uh, no. Hey, you got a minute? There may be a problem." Randolph's brow furrowed. His professionalism always took precedence. He always kept us in line on the march. He always got onto guys that screwed up.

"What's the problem?"

"Maybe I shouldn't say anything. I don't wanna be a nark."

Randolph stood up. "Little too late for that. Tell me."

"I'm afraid for Sidwell."

Randolph chuckled. "Hell, we're all afraid for Sidwell. That little dude screws up everything he touches. We ought to be afraid. Can you imagine his finger on the button for a missile launch?"

"No. I mean afraid for him tonight." I looked over each shoulder to make sure no one could hear me. "Like he's gonna get hurt."

Randolph inched closer. "Tell me what you mean."

I looked around again. "It's Ruffalo. He and some other guys are gonna give Sidwell a blanket party because he screws up all the time."

"A what?" Randolph said, cocking his head.

"You know. A blanket party. Where they hold a sheet down over him and beat him."

"Ah, hell no." Randolph surveyed the barracks.

I put my hands up. "Wait, I don't want anyone to know I told you."

"Sometimes you got to stand up and be a man, Donley. "

A terrifying thought. Then Ruffalo would target me.

Rubbing his chin, Randolph said, "Chill out. Just hit your rack at Taps. I'll handle it."

After Taps, I watched Sidwell and Ruffalo's rack for movement. Both lay across the barracks from mine, and enough light from the street lamps allowed me to see any event that might unfold. Randolph didn't share his plan with me. He didn't say how he planned to handle this or whether my name would come up. I'd have to trust him. I could think of no scenario where both Sidwell and I could escape Ruffalo's wrath.

Sidwell went right to sleep in his top rack after Taps. The barracks remained still and quiet except for the occasional footfalls of the guy on watch. I wondered how Randolph would handle the blanket party.

On cue, at thirty minutes after Taps, Ruffalo got out of his rack. A couple of other guys tiptoed over to him. They fumbled around with what I presumed to be a sheet and some towels.

Oh, crap, I thought. This is really happening. Where's Randolph?

A couple of other guys started walking toward the group. Sidwell tossed and turned a little, oblivious to the imminent attack. The group inched closer to Sidwell, two guys ready with the sheet. Ruffalo and two others stood by with towels in hand, ready to swing.

I sat up, not sure what to do. Should I scream out? Should I yell for the watch? Should I run over and throw myself over Sidwell in sacrifice? I froze. Sidwell was seconds away from the blanket party.

"What the hell are you dudes doing out of your racks?" It was Randolph. He didn't whisper. I could hear him clearly.

Ruffalo turned in shock at the sight of Randolph. "None of your damn business." He quickly gained his composure and tried to whisper a better response, but I heard him. "We're gonna teach Sidwell a lesson. We're gonna get him in line."

Sidwell, only a few feet away, stayed asleep. Other guys began to rustle and wake up.

"Who's talking?" and "Shut up" type comments rang out from all over the barracks.

Randolph placed his hands on his hips. "Here I get up to take a piss and find you guys stalking around the barracks like fools." Pointing guys out, Randolph kept talking loud enough for everyone to hear. "I don't know what you think you're gonna do with sheets, and soap, and towels, but you ain't gonna teach nobody no lesson tonight. Get your butts back in your racks. Anybody I catch out of their racks will stand balls-to-four watch."

Purcell jumped out of his rack. "Anything you want to do

to Sidwell, you might as well do to me. He's my rackmate." The imposing Purcell stared down a few of the would-be assailants. Several guys had awoken by this time.

I'd forgotten about Purcell. He may have had trouble with a simple swim test, but he excelled at everything else. He always helped his rackmate, Sidwell.

Randolph pointed to the towering Purcell. "You are on permanent watch over Sidwell. You report to me anybody that tries to lay a hand on him. Got it?"

Ruffalo's bandits looked up at Purcell.

Purcell stared down at them. He crossed his arms and said, "You got it, Randolph."

By now, Ruffalo's followers began deserting. One by one, they drifted back to their racks. Ruffalo, ever the tough guy, looked around in disbelief. "You faggots, get back here." He pointed to Randolph and Purcell. "This isn't over."

"Yeah it is," a voice from far away in the barracks blurted out.

Other voices rang out with similar comments.

"It's over."

"You're done, Ruffalo."

"You ain't doing shit to nobody."

Finally relenting, Ruffalo dropped his head and walked toward his rack. Totally defeated.

Sidwell turned over. All that commotion, and the guy never woke up. He never knew how close he'd been to serious pain.

It felt great to see Ruffalo thwarted. It felt great to know I'd avoided him knowing about my betrayal. Randolph came up with the perfect solution. He likely prepared Purcell for the whole act of catching Ruffalo by surprise.

Then it hit me. I felt terrible. I realized what a weakling I'd been. I should've stood up to Ruffalo from the beginning.

Earlier that morning, I'd stood before the mirror in my white Dixie Cup hat, so proud. I felt like a man. In one day, I lost all that pride because I failed to stand up to Ruffalo. To protect Sidwell. I'm glad I told Randolph. But what if I had no Randolph? What would I have done? Day one of Hell Week left me more emotionally drained than physically. I finally fell asleep sometime after midnight.

The trashcan banged as loudly as that first morning we met our CC's. Brown's screams replaced the professional voice that typically announced reveille.

"Get out of those racks! You've got seven minutes to fall in outside."

Brown and Chief Smith paced up and down the barracks. I glanced at the clock. It had only reached 0400.

Chief Smith stood on a chair in the middle of the barracks. "Since you people want to stay up late playing grab ass, we'll begin our day early. We're gonna have a full locker inspection after morning chow."

I whispered to Guillermo. "How did they know about last night? I figured we had a nark, but how did they tell the CCs last night?"

He shrugged. "I don't know. Maybe they're making it up."

Our march to chow and back took two hours longer than normal with Brown and Smith continually stopping us to point out some infraction or offer a lecture. Sometimes, Brown would shout, "Halt!" and then stare. That was the worst. You'd almost rather know what you did or what someone else did. The not knowing sucked. The final "Halt!" that morning occurred in front of our barracks.

Chief Smith, hands on hips, cleared his throat. "On my

command, you will fall out and prepare for locker inspection in fifteen minutes. Is that understood?"

"Yes, sir!"

"Fall out!"

We ran into the barracks, tripping over one another up the stairwell to the third floor. Upon arrival, something terrible met us. A white tornado. We'd heard this might happen. Our T-shirts, underwear, towels, and other effects lay strewn across the floor. Most of the items were white, hence the white in "white" tornado.

Purcell threw his hands up. "What the hell are we gonna do?" I'm sure all of us felt extreme stress over this situation, but none more than the neat freak Purcell.

The items not only lay on the floor, but several blankets, sheets, and pillows covered them. The complaints and grumbling became very loud.

"Everybody shut up!" Randolph stood on a chair as Chief Smith had done that morning. "Listen up. Get the racks made first, then everyone start sorting the clothes and put them on everyone's racks. They all got names on them. We got fourteen minutes."

No one argued. We scrambled to resolve this terrible mess. Guillermo and I worked our partnership in rack making. Guys started calling out random names and throwing clothes at anyone claiming ownership. We managed to get everything off the floor and began folding.

I noticed a pair of underwear on my rack that read "Farmer." "Hey, this isn't mine," I shouted.

"Just fold it and put it up. We can sort it later," said Guillermo.

Fifteen minutes after Chief Smith told us to fall out, the

racks looked horrible, and all of us still had clothes to put away.

"Attention on deck!" Randolph said. We immediately dropped everything standing at attention at the foot of our racks.

Footsteps broke the silence. Not two sets of footsteps, such as Brown's and Smith's. One set. I turned my head enough to the right to see which one entered. I'd hoped for Smith. He might mash us, but he'd lecture more than anything else. The person that entered was one I'd never seen before. He wore the uniform of a chief and stood at least six and a half feet tall. Tall as Purcell. He walked in slow, careful steps. He had deep, ebony skin. I don't think he carried an ounce of fat on him. All muscle. This was a hard man.

He reached the end of the barracks and slowly turned.

No one talked. No one moved. No one breathed.

He folded his arms. "I am Chief Jean-Pierre."

"Oh shit," I mouthed. "The Watash."

"You motherfucking guys will learn to properly prepare for a locker inspection. This motherfucking place is unacceptable."

He spoke with an accent. Caribbean I thought.

His opening comments reached a crescendo. "Get those motherfucking racks back!"

And so it began. The worst mashing we'd experienced. The Watash greatly surpassed Brown in both intensity and profanity. The Watash managed to yell in each of my ears multiple times as well as in those of several others. Our clothes became drenched in sweat. One poor guy had a puddle of urine from between his boots. I don't know how the man managed to yell that much and not get hoarse.

Nearly ninety minutes later, he walked to the door at the front of the barracks. "You motherfuckers remember this." And, as mysteriously as he arrived, the Watash walked out.

Only one thought entered my mind; this is definitely Hell Week.

CHAPTER 10

I survived Hell Week, despite the Watash. We never heard from him again or knew where he'd come from. No one dared ask the CCs. We talked about it. For several days, when the CCs were gone, heads turned whenever the door swung open. We feared those footsteps—those of the Watash.

Graduation approached as boot camp wound down. A relaxed atmosphere subtly entered our company. The eight-week tension slowly released. Our boots held their shine and our racks kept their tightly-snugged sheets. CC Brown actually joked with us in those last couple of days.

"Hey, Donley. You enjoy Deep Sink?" Brown said, slapping me on the back.

"Uh, yes sir. Wish I could do it again."

A funny thought between us, but not to the guy a few racks down who had Deep Sink day shift as punishment.

We still woke at 0530. Still cleaned the barracks every day. Still cleaned pissers (urinals) and shitters (commodes) everyday. Words like "pissers" and "shitters" became part of my daily vocabulary. A blunt code between recruits morphing into sailors.

One final test remained—firefighting. It seemed that half the guys looked forward to it and half feared it. I couldn't wait.

From morning chow, we marched toward the tunnel that led to the other side of the base which housed the firefighting facility. I'd noticed the facility many times, with smoke clouds billowing toward the sky. Deep, black clouds that turned to gray several times a day, as recruits feverishly extinguished pits of fuel.

The tunnel ran under a busy roadway, and tradition demanded the company sing "Anchors Aweigh" while marching through it. We'd been through the tunnel dozens of times. As new recruits, we abused the song with our lack of harmony and fumbled lyrics; as seasoned recruits, we sounded almost choir-esque. Not quite, but close.

We arrived at the firefighting facility with full bellies from morning chow. We stood in ranks as CCs Brown and Smith turned us over to our instructors.

"I'm Petty Officer Teal, and I will be your instructor for the day." He paced up and down our ranks, occasionally stopping for effect. A short stub of a man with a bushy mustache—barely within regulation. "You ladies will find it wise to listen to everything I say. It may save your life one day." He turned and looked directly at me. "It may save your life today."

Up to this point, I had not realized my life was in jeopardy.

"If you think burns on over seventy percent of your body will not kill you, you're mistaken," Teal said.

I switched over to the side that feared firefighting training. I'm sure many joined me.

Teal held up a fire hose. "This is your salvation. If a fire breaks out on a ship, there's no fire department to call. You're the fire department. You must put out the fire. Every sailor is a fireman."

The Marines had a saying that every marine is a rifleman.

Whether infantry or a desk jockey, every marine could shoot. Likewise, every sailor needed to know how to fight a fire.

Teal continued, "But first, you need to know what a smoke-filled compartment feels like."

He led us to a long building that seemed to have only one door at each end. Oval doors with large bars to open and close them. Hatches, as they're called on a ship. No windows, though. Sort of like a Jehovah's Witnesses church. The entrance had a sign over the threshold that simply said, ENTRANCE ONLY (NO EXIT).

Teal pointed toward the building. "Ladies, meet George. If you follow our orders, you'll enter George as ladies, and come out as men."

I had no idea why this building owned such a proper name—a human name. What would George do to us? What terrible rite of passage lay hidden within George's walls?

"I need a volunteer." Teal reached out and grabbed Sidwell from our ranks, before anyone raised a hand. Volunteering always presented a dicey proposition in boot camp. You gained nothing and had everything to lose. N-A-V-Y stood for Never Again Volunteer Yourself.

Teal's fellow instructors placed an OBA (oxygen breathing apparatus) on Sidwell and demonstrated its usage. The device, also called a rebreather, loosely resembled scuba gear, with a mask connected to a contraption that hung over the torso, and a green canister the wearer inserted into the unit. They broke us up into groups and showed us how we'd wear these in the event of a fire. The clunky contraptions enabled us to breathe in a smoke-filled compartment.

I managed to put mine on quickly, but the contraption's operation confused me. In other words, I didn't care how it worked and was ready for the fun stuff—putting out fires. Teal interrupted my desire to move on.

"Now that you ladies know how to don your OBAs, you will enter George ten at a time. When instructed, you will remove your OBA mask and continue along the handrail toward the exit. There will be no pushing, running, or panicking. If you push, run, panic, or otherwise fuck up, you'll start George all over. Understood?"

"Yes, sir!" we shouted in unison.

Guillermo and I stood halfway back as they lined us up at one end of the building. The first few groups of ten walked in, but I couldn't see the other end of the building.

Did they even come out?

We only saw the instructors carrying back the OBAs for the next group. It seemed that men wearing OBAs went in one end of the building and only the OBAs came out.

As we inched closer, and my nerves heightened, I regretted the extra glass of orange juice I'd drunk, which now produced a full bladder.

I did some quick math and realized that I'd be in the next group—middle of the pack. I put on my OBA, lit off the green canister that magically produced oxygen, and breathed in the sweet smelling air.

Teal, wearing a much nicer and newer OBA, opened the door and waved us in, as a puff of smoke billowed out. His sarcastic, one-sided grin hinted that some medieval torture awaited.

We waddled along, grasping a metal bar that stood waist high, guiding us through a couple of rooms. I reached for the bar with caution, assuming flames had heated it, but I saw no flames. They ordered us to stop, and the entity known as

George, suddenly awakened. Dank, gray smoke filled the room. Our visibility reduced to a few feet in front of us.

"Now, remove your mask, and follow the bar out of the building. Do not run!" Teal said, his voice muffled by his own mask.

I loosened the straps and slid it off. Instantly, coarse smoke invaded my nose, and I involuntarily gasped, forcing smoke down my throat. My eyes watered, and I saw nothing but the back of Guillermo's head one foot in front of me. He moved, so I moved, still grasping the bar. Every inch of my body screamed for me to push, run, and panic.

You're almost there. You're almost there, I reasoned.

"Ahhh! My eyes!" one guy screamed.

"Move! Move!" the poor guy in the back yelled.

Seconds seemed like hours.

Plunk!

I heard the sound of the hatch opening, and a ray of sunlight pierced through the smoke.

Freedom!

I stepped through the doorway, liberating myself from George. My fellow pod of ten recruits joined me in a fit of coughing and hacking. Tears flowing from eyes met snot blowing out of noses. Our faces blackened from our bout with George.

"Go over there and wait," one of the instructors said.

The guys that had gone before us sat in various stages of recovery.

For the remainder of the day, I don't think a single soul daydreamed in our firefighting lectures. I don't think anyone failed to comprehend the gravity of fire on a ship or of a smoke-filled compartment. I don't think anyone doubted the effectiveness of a properly functioning OBA.

The actual firefighting was more work than anything. The instructors lit burning pits, and we hosed them down. The heat of ten-foot flames backed us up a step. We learned the value of teamwork when handling the high-pressure water flowing from two-and-one-half-inch hoses as we stepped back toward the fire.

As evening approached, our dirty and exhausted bodies marched back through the tunnel singing "Anchors Aweigh." We stepped with a little extra pride after defeating the danger of numerous fires. I assumed my days of meeting huge fires face-to-face were over.

Purcell stumbled over the finishing line and Sidwell managed to pump out the requisite pushups for the company's final physical fitness test—the last hurdle each recruit had to complete for graduation.

We had only worn our dress whites to make sure they fit, so the day of graduation sent everyone to the mirrors in the head. No stripes on sleeves or ribbons on chest, but enough uniform to show accomplishment—to see a real live sailor staring back.

After the graduation ceremony, called Pass-In-Review, CCs Brown and Smith shook a few hands.

"Congrats, Donley," Brown said, extending me his hand. "Keep up the good work when you get to the fleet."

"Yes, sir."

I appreciated the gesture, but then heard him offer the same line to several other guys.

Guillermo, a few others, and I walked out the front gate to hail a cab. For eight weeks, the base held us captive, but now a yellow cab offered our liberation.

We squeezed in as Boston played on the radio. I realized I had not heard my favorite band in eight weeks.

"Where we going?" Guillermo asked.

We all looked at each other, not knowing what do with our newfound freedom.

Finally, I stated the obvious. "Fast food."

All agreed as we enjoyed an evening of simple pleasures. We repeated this the next day, took in a movie, and walked around the mall. Not exciting. Not adventurous. Just different than the constant marching and yelling that had been our life for the past two months.

Our next week involved processing out of boot camp. Several guys left immediately for their "A" school—the initial step for earning their ratings such as aviation electrician, mess cook, or gunner's mate. Guillermo planned to go nuke—that is, nuclear reactors. A tough school to get into, so I assumed Guillermo had some math skills.

"I'm outta here, Donley. It's been real," he said.

"Thanks for all the help making this stupid rack. See you out in the fleet," I said.

As an undesignated airman, I sewed two green stripes on my sleeve and planned to attend a four-week aircraft training school. While others excitedly packed their seabags for their trips, I'd have to wait a few days before packing mine for the march across base. My school, unfortunately, resided at Great Lakes.

Brown walked in, carrying several large brown envelopes. "Orders!"

He called out several names and guys carefully unbraided the metal clasps, learning of their permanent duty stations. I had no guarantee as to where I'd serve, only that I'd work with aircraft. That might mean any number of ships that carry aircraft or it might mean an air station. I had no desire to go to sea, so I hoped for an air station, such as North Island in San Diego.

"Donley!" Brown barked, and threw my orders at my chest.

I carefully slid out the papers and navigated my eyes through the military jargon. UPON COMPLETION OF AIRMAN APPRENTICE TRAINING, REPORT TO V-1 DIVISION, AIR DEPARTMENT, USS *WILLIAM HALSEY.*

"*William Halsey?* V-1?" I whispered, unsure what either of those meant.

Brown walked up to me, grabbed the orders from my hand, and began reading. I noticed it to be the exact spot, where eight weeks prior, I had stepped on his shiny corfam shoes.

He scoffed. "You lucky bastard. You got a carrier. The flight deck. That's where all the action is."

Randolph hit me in the arm with his orders. "You said V-1 on the Halsey, right?"

"Yeah."

"Me too," Randolph said, grinning. "We gonna be those guys in yellow shirts that tell the planes where to go."

"Not so fast, Randolph," Brown chimed in. "You're gonna wear a blue shirt and chock and chain for a long time first. It's hard work. You have to earn that yellow shirt."

I sank a little at the hard work comment. Not that I feared work, but rather the uncertainty of the kind of work. PBS had run a documentary about the flight deck of an aircraft carrier, which I recorded and watched over and over. So, I knew a little about where I'd be going.

"Where's the Halsey, Petty Officer Brown?" Randolph asked.

"Norfolk. It's an older carrier. Been in the shipyard for awhile getting retrofitted. It's named for Admiral William "Bull" Halsey. They call it 'the Bull.' This one's a *Kitty Hawk* class."

"*Kitty Hawk*?" I said.

"Built like the *Kitty Hawk*," Brown replied.

"Hey!" Randolph yelled. "How many of you guys got the Bull?"

A few others raised their hands, but none were with V-1 Division, or even the Air Department.

"Looks like it's just you and me, Donley." Randolph kept his grin, excited to get to the fleet. The guy was all military, ready to serve, ready to fight for his country. No stress.

The final event of boot camp for the thirty-five of us waiting to leave, presented itself out of sheer boredom. Ruffalo never carried out any physical assault on Sidwell, or anyone else. His assaults remained verbal. Several of us vowed to shut him up once and for all.

We'd spent many Coke and Smoke's fantasizing about how we'd get him. Some ideas were funny, like sewing him to his rack with his underwear and T-shirt. Some were gross, like dunking his head in a toilet after Purcell had used it. The most vicious involved things that would leave him without the ability to father children. All of them harmless though, since they were mere fantasy.

On the final day, Sidwell came up with an idea that required a little planning, but it was one we felt Ruffalo deserved, in particular due to his favorite pejorative, "faggot." It required bribing the yeoman in the division office with a pack of cigarettes and a Coke.

An hour later, the yeoman walked in with the same brown envelope we'd all received with our orders.

"Ruffalo!" he yelled.

"Yeah, that's me," Ruffalo said walking over. He had already received orders for a base near Seattle.

The rest of us tried not to stare. We milled about acting busy, while casually glancing over.

Ruffalo pulled the papers out. "Change of duty station?"

A guy near me snickered and received a sharp elbow from Randolph.

Ruffalo kept reading silently, moving his lips. His mouth dropped. He looked left and right and quickly tucked the papers into the envelope.

Randolph approached him. "You get your orders changed, Ruffalo?"

Ruffalo fidgeted with his locker, acting busy. "Uh…yeah. They're sending me someplace else."

"Where?"

"Uh…Florida. Some base down there."

Randolph turned his head to smile and tried to compose himself. "What base in Florida?"

"It doesn't say."

"Doesn't say? Sure it does. Let me see them." Randolph reached for the envelope.

Ruffalo grabbed it quickly, and stuffed it in his seabag. "Leave me alone, Randolph. You aren't the RCPO anymore."

"C'mon, Ruffalo. Let's see your orders," I said.

"Yeah, c'mon, Ruffalo," another said.

Several of us bull rushed Ruffalo and held him down. I grabbed his right leg, after receiving a swift kick in the side.

Randolph grabbed the orders and handed them to Sidwell. "Read 'em, Sid."

Sidwell cleared his throat. "Due to your failure to comprehend teamwork and common practice of addressing your mates as 'faggot,' it's been determined you need to repeat recruit training." He began to snicker. "You will report to the processing station for 1-1 day."

We lost it and broke out laughing, letting Ruffalo go, one by one.

Ruffalo, face reddened, tore up the orders. "I'll get everyone of you fuckers."

I lay in my rack, smiling at the realization that boot camp had ended just as it began, with profanity.

CHAPTER 11

"They say the third floor is haunted," the cab driver said, as he dropped me off at Nimitz Hall, one of several barracks on Naval Station Norfolk.

I leaned forward and handed him a five-dollar bill. "Haunted?"

"Yeah, back in World War II they used the third floor for a brig. See the bars on the windows? A bunch of prisoners committed suicide, and they say it's haunted."

I looked up at the third floor. Dark windows with what looked like bars stared back. I awaited the proverbial clap of thunder, but none came. My mind said to run away, but my uniform commanded me to report for duty.

"Hey. Want your change?"

"Uh…no thanks," I said, continuing to inventory every window.

The previous four weeks of airman apprentice training in Great Lakes and a week home on leave had passed by quickly. My arrival to the USS *William Halsey*—or the Bull as we called it—would have to wait while the aircraft carrier sat in Newport News Shipbuilding for the next three months for repairs. Meanwhile, new arrivals and some of the ship's company berthed in barracks.

The huge, brown-brick building would have to settle for my entrance into the fleet. I strapped my seabag over my crisp white dress uniform and squarely secured my cover. I performed the check I learned in boot camp using two fingers to measure the distance from the top of my eyebrow to the rim of the hat.

A sailor walked by me, laughing and shaking his head at my boot camp freshness.

"Idiot," I whispered to myself.

After checking in and receiving my rack assignment, I unpacked, thankful they put me on the second floor as opposed to the third. I stowed items that were issued to me in boot camp but wouldn't wear until winter. A heavy peacoat—a symbol of the old navy. Dress blues with thirteen buttons for the pants; the strangest garment accoutrement ever invented. And to add to my discomfort, a thick, wool sweater.

"Attention on deck!" a voice barked behind me.

I dropped my bag and popped tall.

"Ha, ha."

I turned to find Randolph laughing. "Gotcha."

I extended my hand. "How long you been here?"

"Couple of days. Don't unpack too much. They're sending us out to sea in two days."

"What? I thought the ship was under repair."

He sat on my rack. "It is. We're going on a little ten-day cruise on the Kennedy."

"To do what?" I asked.

"To work. Learn. I guess we'll be blue shirts. Chocking and chaining."

"Oh, cool...wait...what do we take? What do we do? Where—"

Randolph stood up. "You worry too much. Put your dungarees on, and I'll show you where the chow hall is."

Morning muster occurred in the parking lot between two extensions of Nimitz Hall. Cars pulled in and out of spaces. Sailors strolled down the sidewalk near us. Steam rose from a large metal unit attached to the building. Nothing about this felt naval.

ABH1 Simon Beckley walked out—clipboard in hand. He twirled his mustache, but his whiskers were too short to produce the desired point. I imagined him with a stovepipe hat and rope on railroad tracks, about to tie down the damsel in distress.

"Atten-huah!" Beckley shouted, with his own version of the attention command.

We popped tall and looked straight ahead.

Randolph leaned over to me, whispering out of the side of his mouth. "This guy is old-school navy. Calls everybody 'shipmate.' He—"

"Shipmate!" Beckley stared Randolph down. "You have something to share with the rest of us?"

"Uh...no...uh," Randolph stammered.

"Then shut your hole."

The remainder of our ranks stiffened as Beckley paced back and forth. The usually calm and collected Randolph had always been on the other side of those confrontations. I snuck a glance and noticed Randolph standing at perfect attention— eyes widened.

"At ease," Beckley ordered. "Most of you newbies will be going to sea with me on the Kennedy in two days. That means we will get this barracks inspection ready. Fall out for work assignments when I call your name."

Our ranks dwindled as Beckley sent sailors to various duties, such as cleaning heads, sweeping, swabbing, and painting. He looked up from his list to see only Randolph and me left.

"I have a special assignment for you two. Go up to the third floor of this wing and move every box to the storeroom. We need to make room for more shipmates coming next week. And I want the boxes lined up. Stacked to perfection. Understood?"

"Yes, sir!" we said simultaneously.

"Sir?" Beckley's brow furrowed. "This ain't boot camp. You mean, 'yes, Petty Officer Beckley.' Now get moving."

The third floor? The same third floor the cab driver had pointed to? Did Randolph know what evil entities might lurk up there?

I grabbed Randolph's shoulder on the way up the stairs. "Maybe we need more guys."

"What are you talking about? Beckley said just you and me. There may not even be that much. C'mon."

Randolph probably hadn't heard about the ghosts of Nimitz Hall, or he didn't care.

I trailed a few feet behind him as we opened the door to the third-floor barracks. We stepped into a pitch-black space.

"Feel around for the light switch," Randolph said. He stepped further into the space.

I held the door frame tightly and ran my hand up and down the wall.

Click!

Down the long barracks, lights powered on in sequence, producing a buzzing sound.

"Why you standing over by the door?"

"Uh…yeah…let's find the storeroom," I said, avoiding his question.

We found the storeroom empty and smelling even danker than the rest of the barracks. The boxes we were to move sat in stacks the length of the barracks.

Randolph poked through a few of the boxes. "Look at this. They're like old training manuals from the '60s. Here, let's get to moving 'em." Dust flew in the air.

I carried the first of many boxes toward the storeroom, hoping our stacks would please Beckley. The light didn't work in the storeroom, so I made my trips in and out of the room as fast as possible. Thoughts of prisoners, brigs, and suicides filled my mind.

"I gotta use the head," Randolph said, as I retrieved another box.

I curiously fumbled through the contents, giving my muscles a rest.

Thump. Thump.

Footsteps behind me. Couldn't be Randolph. He'd walked into the head at the other end of the barracks. I turned slowly. A tall, lanky sailor stood there wearing a white Dixie Cup hat slanted the way they wore it in World War II. No expression.

The spirit of a former prisoner?

I opened my mouth to speak but no words came.

Then he spoke. "Hey, is there a Randolph up here? They want him downstairs."

"Oh," I chuckled. "Yeah. He's in the head."

"Thanks," the real, live sailor said.

I carried several more boxes toward the storeroom, laughing at myself.

How stupid! I'm eighteen years old. I'm in the Navy. I

shouldn't fear ghosts. I strained to heap the box to the top of the stack in the storeroom.

Slam!

The storeroom door shut. Total darkness. I felt around for the door. Full panic ensued. I found the knob, but my hands slipped as I struggled to free myself. What if someone or something had trapped me in here? What if it is in here? The slick knob wouldn't turn. I used my shoulder to push it open but an opposing force fought against me. That scary opera music they play in horror movies rang out in my head. I pounded on the door. I started to scream for help when the door opened. My weight carried me a few feet past the threshold.

Randolph stood there laughing. "Get locked in?"

I stared back, bathed in perspiration. "Did you lock me in?"

"What? No, man. I just came back. You alright?"

"Uh...yeah."

We finished our task in time for noon chow. With all the boxes removed, I remembered the supposed bars on the windows that the taxi driver had pointed out. These windows had no bars attached to them. However, they did have the bars of several bunk bed parts pushed against them.

No bars on the windows. No ghosts. Only an overactive imagination, a naive sailor, and a seasoned taxi driver.

The bus dropped us off at Pier 12 with our partially packed seabags—enough uniforms and gear for the ten-day trip. Two carriers rested at the pier, facing in opposite directions. Ships of all shapes and sizes lined the shore as far as I could see. Destroyers, battleships, frigates, and one black-painted submarine.

Randolph smiled. "Now, this is the Navy."

The salty air smelled good. It smelled naval.

We walked down the pier as the aircraft carrier towered over us, its length longer than three football fields. I looked up as if viewing skyscrapers in a downtown area. Huge mooring lines ran from the ship to the pier. Each line had a rat guard—a cone that prevented rats from climbing the line and infesting the ship. A few men walked along the edge of the flight deck. Above that, the island structure reached several more stories with all kinds of antennas pointing in every direction.

The carrier was painted haze gray except for the black at the waterline. A few streaks of rust appeared in various places. Aside from many voices, a steady humming emanated from the ship. Several sailors loaded boxes on a long metal track that ran up to the hangar deck. Hundreds and hundreds of boxes of food and supplies.

The aircraft carrier had become the most formidable force on the ocean—striking fear in America's enemies. Its arsenal of ninety-five aircraft, with the ability to launch from seas throughout the world, offered a timely response to most national defense crises. The picture of naval power.

For most sailors, this was just another day on the job. For me, it was the most exciting day of my life.

Halfway down the pier, we reached the L-shaped gangplank—steps leading toward an opening into the hangar bay.

We took turns performing the boarding ritual that entailed standing at attention before one of the ship's crew on watch. The procedure required showing our ID cards, and saying, "Permission to come aboard?"

I watched several guys perform the task perfectly, and

receive the response, "Permission granted."

I took my turn, stood at attention, held up my ID, and said, "Can I come aboard?"

The watchman didn't blink, "Permission granted."

Beckley shook his head at me in disgust.

We made our way through the enormous hangar bay that ran two-thirds the length of the ship and then through a hatch. I stayed close to the man in front of me as we snaked down passageways and up ladders.

We entered a large compartment with racks lining the walls.

"Find a rack and stow your gear," Beckley said.

I noticed all the middle racks had already been taken. I chose a top one while Randolph threw his bag on a bottom rack. The clothes-folding skills we had learned in boot camp came in handy as we squeezed our gear in the tiny compartments of our coffin lockers, the space below the racks.

"Hey, we're pulling out. Let's go see," Randolph said.

We walked onto the catwalk while tugboats pushed the carrier away from its berth. Several women and children waved goodbye from the pier. We waved back as if they were saying goodbye to us.

The people on the pier shrunk as the tugs pushed us further through the bay. In a fluid motion, the tiny boats pulled away and the carrier powered out to sea on its own. The blue water turned dark green as waves bashed the side of the ship. In one direction lay the shore and all I'd ever known. In the other direction, the endless ocean and uncertainty.

After losing our way no less than three times, Randolph and I found the chow hall. The mess cook called today's entrée, beef yakisoba. Complementing my meal, I chose rice, a brown 'n' serve roll, an unidentifiable cake, and bug juice—also known as Kool-Aid.

Plop!

ABH2 Eddie Eppers's tray spewed bits of Jell-O as it landed on our table. "You boys ready to ch...ch...chock and chain?"

Eppers sometimes stuttered, but I got used to it. His sleeve displayed two chevrons, but his years in the Navy should have earned him three. We'd heard stories about his antics in the last couple of days, and he lived up to the billing. Everybody liked him.

He shoved half a roll in his mouth and looked back and forth at us.

"I guess we're ready," Randolph said. "You gonna teach us a little?"

"Yep. I can chock and chain faster than anybo...bo... body." A piece of food fell out of his mouth and onto his tray. "Just don't get killed on your first day. It might make me look bad."

"Killed?" I said. "I hope not. We're only watching and learning, right?"

"Nope." Burp! "You gotta get your hands dirty. Just stick by me. And if the cable snaps, jump or hit the deck. But don't just stand there."

My mouth dropped.

"Excuse me," Randolph said. "What cable?"

Eppers set his fork down. "The arresting gear cable that catches the plane. One snapped on this boat about ten years ago. Cut a bunch of guys in half. There was this photographer taking a picture when it happened. Took the photo right before the cable cut his head off. So, if the cable snaps, don't just stand there. Jump or hit the deck. Got it?"

We both nodded, slowly. I assumed Randolph shared my shock and fear.

Eppers shoveled more food in his mouth. "Probably won't happen, though."

Slightly rattled by Eppers's pep talk, I settled into my rack that evening for my first night of sleep aboard a ship. Water flowed through pipes, two feet over my head. The ship grumbled and growled like any working machine. Guys talked incessantly. Some argued over their card game while others complained about their girlfriends or the Navy, or whatever. AC/DC drowned out Run DMC.

The rack measured three feet wide and about six and a half feet long. If I sat up too fast, I'd hit my head on the lamp. I tucked myself in and closed the blue curtain for a small amount of privacy. Lights began turning off at 2200 for taps.

I noticed a subtle motion. A rise from my right to left that lasted for several seconds. Then the movement went left to right. The massive aircraft carrier was nothing to the sea. The carrier obeyed the waves like any other ship. My focus on this fact sent a message to my stomach and the queasiness began. Seasickness loomed. I could think of nothing else but the ebb and flow until I forced myself to think of other things—saving a trip to the head.

I lay there, eyes open, a little excited, a little scared. We had walked around the flight deck and received some safety training earlier that day. We watched helos land, but all matter of aircraft would arrive the next day.

I'd been issued a blue shirt worn by those of us tasked with inserting chocks and chains on parked aircraft or breaking them down for launch. Coolies, they called us—the lowest rung of the flight deck food chain.

The blue flight deck safety vest had a pull string for quick inflation should one fall in the water. The guy handing it to me called it a float coat. The helmet had blue plating, and may very well have been the most uncomfortable thing I had ever put on my head.

I assumed I'd feel cool and adventurous in all this gear, but I felt like a little league football player on his first day of practice. I fell asleep a fresh recruit, barely enough whiskers to shave. The next day I'd be on the flight deck with live aircraft. I'd be a fleet sailor.

CHAPTER 12

Petty Officer Beckley paired us with an experienced blue shirt—most of them from the Kennedy's flight deck crew. Kellen Garfield worked with me. He came to the Kennedy two months before but had recently been assigned to the Bull. I'd met him on my first night in Nimitz Hall. A short, scrappy type, he was all muscle from his daily regimen of pushups and sit-ups. He'd spend several minutes brushing his closely cropped afro. I noticed that it never seemed to change, but he insisted that all that work was necessary.

He walked on to the flight deck with me in tow.

"You stay close by me, OK?" he said, nodding. "Everything will be fine."

I nodded back. "But what do I do if—"

He pointed to the sky, "Here they come."

Two airplanes, side-by-side, flew past the starboard side of the boat. The one on the left broke off into a hard turn over the bow. The roar of their engines trailed off.

Garfield said, "You see that? That's how they get into the landing pattern. That A-6 Intruder that broke off will come in and land. In regular flight ops, we'll park 'em and shut 'em down, but this is gonna be what they call CQ. Stands for carrier qualification. They land and go to the CAT to take off again."

"We don't do anything?" I asked.

"Not until they need fuel. Then they'll park 'em here." Garfield pointed out the middle part of the flight deck to the right of the foul line—a red and white line running the length of the landing area. During training, Beckley warned us never to cross it while a plane was landing.

I watched as one plane after another landed violently. The steel deck vibrated under my boots. I noticed each pilot thrust forward in the cockpit, and then settle back, looking at a yellow shirt for instructions. A "bird" would roll back to free itself from the arresting gear cable, and taxi up to the bow CATs for another launch. They called it a CAT shot—an action as noisy and thrilling as the landing. The aircraft powered up and were "shot" down the bow. Most of them slightly dipped as they freed themselves from the bow before gaining altitude.

Every bird impressed me, but then there was the F-14 Tomcat. A sleek design of 62,000 pounds of machine. Pilots with interesting nicknames. Afterburner on some take-offs. Wings that slid back, rather than folded over. Ominous missiles hanging from the sides. It oozed coolness.

And then we got busy. Yellow shirts moved into various positions in the middle part of the flight deck, known as Fly 2.

"C'mon, let's grab some chocks," Garfield said as he took off running.

I followed him to the island structure, a huge building in itself, at the middle, starboard part of the flight deck. The chocks—yellow rectangular boxes attached to a galvanized steel bar—lined the island. We used these to secure an aircraft's wheels.

"Gr…" Garfield said.

"What?" The aircraft noise intensified and I couldn't hear

him.

"Grab two and follow me," he repeated.

We stood near Eppers in his yellow shirt as a thundering beast of an aircraft headed toward us. Obeying Eppers's signals, the pilot turned the nose wheel as needed. Eppers brought his hands in front of his chest with closed fists, as that aircraft, an F-14 Tomcat, stopped. Eppers pointed his thumbs in and rolled his hands, signaling us coolies to insert chocks and chains.

Garfield yelled, "Throw it on like this!" He inserted the chock and closed the boxed ends on the wheel in one seamless motion. "Set your chocks down and grab some chains!"

A guy with brown flight deck gear handed me two tiedown chains. I'd practiced with these in apprenticeship training, but not enough to attach them with any speed, or correctly, or at all.

I hooked one end on the ring attached to the wheel strut, and one end to a padeye—one of many tie down points on the flight deck. I fumbled with the operation of inserting the chain into the locking mechanism with proper length and spinning the tightening wheel to an appropriate tautness. I either had it too loose or got my glove caught in the apparatus.

"Like this," Garfield yelled. He popped in the chain, and spun the wheel tight. "C'mon."

I followed underneath the two large exhaust nozzles of the bird. Another Tomcat rolled into its parking spot and another brown shirt handed me tiedown chains.

Garfield pointed to the parked aircraft. "You chock this one."

I threw in the chock and managed a secure fit after a couple of adjustments. Another aircraft parked, and we repeated the process over and over. I even managed to secure a few tiedown chains, but lacked Garfield's speed.

Garfield grabbed my ear protector and pulled it an inch away from my ear. "Go get more chocks."

I ran to the island. Randolph approached at the same time, out of breath like me. "How's it going?" he said.

I shrugged. "Just trying to keep up."

I noticed his watering eyes. He cradled four chocks under his arms and ran up the deck. Fumes from the parked aircraft caused my eyes to water, too. The parked planes hot fueled, meaning the engines kept running while they took on fuel. The exhaust filled the air. Jet fuel offered a distinctive smell, tolerable to the nose, but the exhaust burned my eyes.

I grabbed four chocks but after a few steps realized my vision had blurred. The aircraft looked like a hunk of mass, and I could barely make out the figures moving in front of me. I turned away but found no relief. I set the chocks down and wiped my eyes, worsening my condition.

Someone grabbed my arm and pulled me behind the island. Through my blurred vision, I noticed it was Eppers. "Stand here for a minute and clear your eyes. Then get back out there."

Ten minutes into real action on the flight deck, and I stood there, eyes watering. I slapped myself in the head and started for more chocks.

Eppers walked up with Randolph who was suffering from the same affliction. "Listen, you're gonna get hurt or screw up if you can't see. Cl…cl…clear your eyes and suck it up. You'll get used to it."

I delivered more chocks, but the fumes still assaulted me. I quickly learned that with consistent blinking, turning my head at the right time, and moving around, I didn't need any more trips behind the island.

Fresh "non-skid" offered my next rude awakening. Similar

to asphalt, non-skid covered the flight deck with a coarse and sometimes sharp coating that provided better traction for aircraft and mobile equipment. The Kennedy had recently applied a new layer.

An A-6 Intruder did a quick turn with its exhaust pointed directly at me. Garfield crouched to brace himself. I looked at him—standing upright—when the exhaust blew me six feet backward and onto my backside. The gloves I wore spared my hands, but my elbow and butt incurred a nice dose of road rash.

Aircraft 2. Donley 0, I thought.

The unrelenting pace forced me to constantly move and improve. I attached the chains faster, and I managed to do the job without Garfield standing over my shoulder. After what might have been three or four hours, Garfield got my attention by putting his fists side-by-side and making a breaking motion—the flight deck signal for "take a break."

"I'll show you flight deck control," he said, walking away and waving for me to follow him.

We entered from the rear of the island structure. Several men in colored shirts surrounded the Ouija board, a glass-plated replica of the flight deck with pieces representing every aircraft on board.

Garfield whispered, "That guy in the big chair is the handler. You don't need to talk to him and he sure as hell don't need to talk to you. If he does talk to you, you probably screwed up."

I noticed a room off to the side. Eppers and Beckley sat there smoking with five other yellow shirts. I took a step toward the room out of curiosity, my foot breaking the threshold.

Garfield grabbed me. "What are you doing? You can't go in there. That's the yellow shirt shack. They'll kick your ass if you go in there."

Indeed several yellow shirts stared at me, as if I'd insulted their mother. "Get the fuck out of here," Beckley said, flicking his arm at me.

Eppers sat calmly and took a drag of his cigarette.

We entered the blue shirt shack, one level down and tantamount to a hole in the side of the ship. We sat on lockers that had been turned on their sides to provide seating. The smoke-filled room seemed as uninviting as the yellow shirt shack, but no one told me to "get the fuck out."

A casual smoker, I hadn't developed the dependency most guys had. After all that exhaust, a normal person would likely avoid the inhalation of more noxious gas. But sailors smoke on break. I had a pack in my locker but didn't think I could bring it to the flight deck.

Garfield reached into his locker and pulled out a pack of KOOLs—the preferred menthol smoke.

"How you like the flight deck?" Garfield asked. Several other blue shirts looked for my reply.

"OK, I guess. Busy."

"CQs are harder because it's non-stop. Most of the time we have regular flight ops and we get more breaks." Garfield took a long drag off his KOOL. "And the birds shut down after they land, so you and Randolph don't have to run behind the island, crying like little girls."

Several blue shirts laughed.

Garfield elbowed me. "I'm just kidding. Happens to everybody. You get used to it."

I'd heard "get used to it" twice that day. It seemed as though there were hundreds of things to get used to, and I'd never worked so hard in my life.

I showered off the day's work and climbed into my rack—mentally and physically drained.

Could I do this every day?

The question seemed irrelevant, because I had no choice. I was a sailor. And now a flight deck worker. A Fly Two blue shirt.

The routine of flight deck operations had its interruptions. The ship held numerous drills such as man overboard and general quarters. One drill that required speed was the rigging of the barricade—a huge net that would catch an aircraft on landing should the plane's tailhook fail or have some other malfunction with the ship too far from an alternate airfield.

We also ran mock fire drills on the flight deck. An F-14, purposely parked in the landing area, served as our fire. Yellow shirts directed hose crews to move in. I manned a hose, working with others to sweep the base of the imaginary fire with imaginary water. A white miniature fire truck, called a P-16, drove up with guys in red flight deck gear. Two of them wore silver proximity suits that would protect them from flames. A large forklift raised them up in a cage to rescue a theoretically injured or unconscious pilot.

I'd noticed these guys in red going to and from the aft of the island. I assumed they had their own shack for breaks and to store their gear.

After the drill, I caught up to Eppers. "Who are those guys in the red shirts?"

"That's the crash crew."

"How do I get to do that?" I asked.

"You gotta serve your time as a coolie. If you work hard

and show some skills, you might get moved up to a tractor driver, elevator operator, or crash crew. After that, you get to be a yellow shirt, like...like me."

"Yeah." I smiled. "I want to be in the crash crew."

"You got a lotta chocking and chaining to do."

We returned to Norfolk ten days later. Randolph and I stood in the catwalk, much the same as when we had departed. A few loved ones stood on the pier, anxiously awaiting their husbands and fathers.

"I'm so ready to get off of this boat," I said.

"It's not a boat. It's a ship." We turned to find Petty Officer Beckley standing behind us. His graying hair and wrinkled brow suggested he was a little too old for his first class petty officer rank. Guys his age had at least made chief by now. I wondered what had held him back. Did he commit some grave offense in the past? He sometimes wore a jacket with a "Tonkin Gulf Yacht Club" patch, referencing his service in Vietnam. While he occasionally offered a few pearls of wisdom, he seemed more like the cranky old man on a porch saying, "get off my lawn you young whippersnappers!"

"Yeah. I mean the ship," I said.

"You boys be careful when you hit the beach."

"The beach?" Randolph said.

"The beach. Liberty. There's plenty of people that will take advantage of young sailors on liberty with money burning a hole in their pockets. They'll sell you a car with no down payment but big monthly payments and then have the Navy take it out of your pay until you retire. If you see a sign that says 'We finance E-1 and up,' run." Beckley twirled his mustache. "Or there's some pretty girl that will act like she's interested, and the next thing you know you're signing up for some magazine subscription. She'll take all your money and you'll never see her again."

"Did that happen to you?" I said, putting my hand over the pocket holding my wallet.

"Hell, no. You think I'm an idiot?"

"And another thing. You'll be sitting in some bar drinking a beer and some guy that looks like a sailor will start a conversation. He'll say he's on this boat or that boat and he'll start asking you about details. Like what ship you're on, when you're going out to sea, how many aircraft you got. Stuff like that. Well, he's probably a Russian spy. You men will know things we don't want the Russkies to know, so keep your traps shut. That man don't have a need to know. Hell, you hardly have a need to know."

I "hit the beach" with Randolph and Willie McGee, my Nimitz Hall rackmate. Like me, McGee was fresh out of boot camp. It only took a few sentences to reveal his northern accent. He towered over most of us and carried enough weight that no one doubted his claim that he played offensive line in high school. A few guys called him "The Bear," but never to his face. As McGee didn't care for his body type, he preferred to be addressed as "McGee" or "Willie." When you're built like a bear, you get what you want.

After a long bus ride on a dreary day, we arrived at Military Circle Mall. We heard it was a great place to get a slice of pizza and catch a movie. After a few moments, I realized that dozens of other sailors had the same idea.

McGee swallowed half a slice of pizza and burped. "Look at that squid."

"Squid" referred to any sailor that exhibited sailor characteristics when they weren't necessary. Sort of like a sailor nerd. Our haircuts, and traveling in groups of two's and three's, made us stick out as sailors, but we tried to avoid any outward display of our naval conformity whenever possible.

The squid McGee had pointed out had two strikes against him. He wore his birth control glasses—the kind issued in boot camp. The BCDs (birth-control devices) as we called them, earned that name because no one of the opposite sex would come near you if you wore them. His other strike was the white mesh laundry bag slung over his shoulder.

"You gotta wash your civilian clothes, but carrying that through the mall?" I said.

Randolph sat silently—shaking his head.

McGee also shook his head while sipping his drink. "A serious coolness infraction. You'll never catch me doing that."

McGee became my regular running buddy. We "hit the beach," specifically, Virginia Beach, and found every bar that had a live band over the next several weeks. McGee's parents lived four hours away and he planned to take me to his house for the weekend once he bought a car.

While we made the most of liberty, we wanted to get to the Bull and out to sea again. We tired of all the mindless cleaning and painting. We scraped paint off stair railings and then re-painted them. We stripped wax off the floors and then re-waxed them. Most of this was obvious busy work—killing time until we got to the ship.

"Petty Officer Eppers, I need to go to the personnel office about my paycheck," one guy would ask.

"Go," he said, without even looking at who asked.

"I need to make a dental appointment," another would say.
"Go."

Eppers believed that sailors worked their butts off at sea, and should take it easy in port. We didn't argue.

Beckley, on the other hand, wanted us busy all the time. He especially wanted us new guys to always be training. He had us set up a classroom on the third floor of Nimitz Hall, with or without ghosts. We covered a wide range of SOP (standard operating procedures), flight deck basics, aircraft basics, and maintenance programs. Staying awake during these sessions proved challenging.

He also arranged for us to have more firefighting training at a facility in Norfolk. We began by watching a film that had become infamous amongst carrier sailors, *Trial by Fire*. The film showed sailors on the USS *Forrestal* fighting a huge fire that killed over a hundred men. I watched in shock at the real danger of a fire at sea. The film showed a brave chief that ran to the fire with a CO_2 bottle and became engulfed in flames. Like the "crispy critter" videos many of us watched as sixteen year olds for driver training, the *Forrestal* fire video was a wake-up call. I never needed anyone to remind me of the seriousness of firefighting training.

"I didn't sleep through *that*," McGee said.

I shook my head. "Me, either."

Our instructors repeated the training we had in boot camp. All the basics. They also introduced us to PKP and AFFF— chemical agents designed to extinguish fires.

The facility had a mock building, and they walked us through the scenario we'd face that day. After extinguishing several small pit fires and donning OBAs, they moved us to the building.

The hatch opened and flames licked the walls. Smoke billowed out, and a wave of heat penetrated my OBA mask. I manned the front of our water hose and pulled the lever back on the nozzle, remembering a cardinal rule—every good firefighter checks their agent before approaching the fire. Meaning, make sure your water hose or extinguisher works before you get close to the fire.

Water gushed out. The pressure pushed my hose team of five a step in the opposite direction.

"Move in," Randolph, our scene leader for this drill, yelled.

The heat and flames indicated anything but a drill. We stepped in, slowly, and I directed the hose at the base of the fire, left to right. The flames subsided on one side and grew on the other. Our entire team forged ahead into the building as we poured water onto the flames. We made some progress but the fire seemed intent on winning.

A gush of water lightly sprayed me as I noticed another firefighting team working from another hatch. Within a minute, we beat the fire.

Unlike during our boot camp experience, we fought much larger fires while enclosed in buildings. More heat. Taller flames. Fewer places to run away. On a burning aircraft carrier at sea, there's no place to run. There's no place to hide. There's the fire, your shipmates, and your duty to fight the fire.

CHAPTER 13

I walked the Nimitz Hall barracks at 0330 with a red flashlight while working the balls-to-four coop watch. Any place we slept, we called the coop, as in chicken coop. Nothing glorious about this duty. My job, from midnight to 4:00 AM, entailed watching the front door with a partner, and one of us walking the entire barracks every fifteen minutes. Theft watch. Fire watch. Any way one looks at it, the tedious duty in the middle of the night, when I'd still be required to muster at 0700, sucked.

I walked the barracks listening to guys snoring, thinking about *The Charge of the Light Brigade,* a poem by Alfred, Lord Tennyson I had to memorize in high school. "Theirs not to reason why, / Theirs but to do and die." That said it all. It seemed a more dignified way of saying, "Don't question orders, just follow them."

We stood six-section duty. Every six days, we had to stay on base and stand duty. That balls-to-four watch was my last on shore. We moved onto Bull the next day, readying for sea. Beckley told us that we would have several work-up cruises for the next year in the Caribbean and North Atlantic. Then we would depart on a six-month Mediterranean cruise.

Our shipboard coop lay under catapult one at the bow of

the ship. All the petty officers took the middle racks and I drew a bottom rack under Eppers. After unpacking, I looked around at my new home for the next few years.

"Hey, Petty Officer Eppers."

"Hey?" he said. "Hey is for horses. You must be a jackass."

I looked at him, brows furrowed.

"Just joking, what?"

"How long do you think I'll be a coolie? I mean, when can I get in the crash crew?"

Eppers slammed his coffin locker closed and inserted the combination lock. "If you work your ass off, and a spot opens up, they'll promote you. But you have to start with wo… working your ass off. Don't go sucking up to nobody. Maybe the bos'n or crash chief will see you."

"The bos'n?"

"The officer in charge of the crash crew."

"Got it. Work my ass off."

Eppers started to walk away, but turned back. "And don't be farting in the bottom rack. Heat rises and I don't want to smell it."

I nodded. "You got it."

After two weeks at sea, I settled into a regular routine. Chocking and chaining seemed anything but adventurous. Neither did the pier watch I stood on Christmas morning a few days before we left. They don't show that in the brochures. I did my best to follow Eppers's advice to work hard. Like most, I jumped when ordered and attached tiedown chains with relative speed.

Still, I admired the moving complexity and orchestration

of the flight deck. Nearly sixty-five planes in close proximity, some moving within feet of one another. Ground crew equipment and ordnance carts scattered throughout the deck. And hundreds of men hustling between. I loved it. The work was hard, but I loved it. The F-14 Tomcat launching with afterburners, especially at night, beat anything I could imagine. Like a tractor pull on steroids. Pure excitement.

The noise never ceased. From the explosive sound of an A-6 on the catapult to the whining of an F-14 taxiing. Even between launches, a piece of ground equipment hummed, chains crackled on top of a tractor, or the wind whipped past my head.

As I did on the Kennedy, I worked the Fly 2 in the middle of the flight deck. Randolph worked Fly 3, the aft part of the deck.

"Man, I'm a little beat. You got a smoke, Brian?" Li'l V said, walking into the blue shirt shack.

Guys caught on to Victor Randolph's habit of overusing the word "little" and dubbed him Li'l V. He had continued to call me Brian, ever since boot camp.

I extended a Marlboro Red from my pack.

Li'l V shook his head. "Damn, Donley, I don't know how you can smoke these cowboy killers."

I pulled the pack back. "Fine. You don't want one?"

"Nah, give it here."

Li'l V looked across the room as a heated, but harmless discussion elevated.

"I don't give a flying wombat's ass what you say. They suck!" McGee said.

Garfield fought back. "Man, you're full of shit; my boys will whoop yours any day."

I wasn't sure of the exact details of their argument. Something about football. The subject mattered little. The way in which they argued and the colorful use of language entertained us. McGee's "flying wombat's ass" showed originality and aggressiveness. Garfield's comeback lacked flair and hinted that it had no substance. We sat back, smoked, and enjoyed the show during a short break before the next launch.

"Your quarterback is a little bitch," McGee said.

Garfield stood up to deliver his closing argument. "Look, they beat your wimpy ass team last year in—"

"Rig the barricade! Rig the barricade!" we heard over the 5MC.

Beckley burst through the door. "Get your asses out there and rig the barricade! This is not a drill."

I jumped up and stubbed out my cigarette. I buckled my helmet while bumping into others exiting through the door.

We ran from behind the island to Fly 3 where Eppers was hooking up the barricade to a tractor that would drag it across the deck. My fellow blue shirts and I grabbed the metal plates that fit into the deck and served as the foundation for the barricade. We had drilled on this many times.

Unlike the dirty, gray barricade we had drilled with, this one had no marks. It was a bright white weave of four-inch fabric that attached to base plates and was raised by two stanchions. The last hope for a troubled aircraft facing a ditching into the sea.

After inserting my base plate, I looked up and noticed an S-3 Viking flying aft off our port side. A small explosion occurred over the cockpit. Unlike many of the jets that required one or two pilots, this aircraft carried a crew of four. Over the explosion, only one parachute opened.

"Let's go! Let's go!" Beckley yelled. "C'mon, get those plates down."

Eppers and a few other yellow shirts pulled on the plates and made sure the bottom of the barricade net was properly tucked.

I looked up again to the S-3 approaching.

"Clear the deck! Clear the deck!" a voice said over the 5MC. I assumed it to be the voice of the air boss in pri fly—primary flight control.

Beckley waved his arms. "Get behind the island. Move! Move!"

We scrambled to safety. I caught the S-3 out of the corner of my eye, seconds from the deck.

Who was flying? Somebody ejected. But who?

Every other machine on the deck stood silent. The calm before the storm.

Slam! We heard the bird land out of view with its familiar vacuuming sound.

Eppers ran in front of the island, and we followed. The S-3 rested in the same spot it would on a normal landing—the white barricade net cocooning the aircraft. The crash crew moved its P-16 firefighting truck into position. Men grabbed firefighting hoses, and I latched on to the third position of one of those hoses.

There was no fire.

The pilot sat there, still but alert. The canopy had one hole over the copilot's seat.

The bos'n held up his hands. "Everybody stay back!"

I immediately recognized him as the man in charge of this situation. We later learned that the pilot had attempted to eject all four crew after realizing a safe landing, even in the barricade, seemed improbable. However, all but the copilot's seats failed. The rest of them sat on a hot seat, meaning their ejection seats could light off at any minute sending them through the cockpit, now wrapped in the netting of the barricade, and killing them instantly.

A squadron chief, wearing white flight deck gear, cautiously entered the S-3 to secure the ejection seats should they attempt to light off. After less than a minute, he and the three remaining crew safely exited.

A helo landed, and a wet, but smiling copilot emerged, shaking hands with the other S-3 aircrew.

Within thirty minutes, we cleared the deck of fire hoses, the used barricade, and the downed Viking. Flight deck operations resumed immediately. No hesitation. Back to work. Back to the business of launching and recovering aircraft.

I'd experienced my first flight deck mishap. A strong lesson that anything could happen at any time. We trained for a reason. Experienced guys told us to keep our head on a swivel, always looking for danger. This was the adventure.

Chief Fitch walked up to Randolph, McGee, and me as the final bird of the night parked and shut down. "You men like that excitement today?"

ABHC Howard Fitch looked like the Watash, but acted nothing like him. A man of impeccable character and knowledge, he epitomized the leader we'd gladly follow into battle. He instinctively knew when a sailor needed a pat on the back or a just admonishment. He perfectly fit the saying that "Chiefs run the Navy." He stood at an imposing six feet six inches tall. He wore his hair well within regulations and likely manicured his mustache daily. I never saw him without military creases in his uniforms. While everyone else had dirt and grime on their flight deck gear, his stayed a brilliant yellow. Not that he didn't work. He worked as much as anyone. He merely kept order about himself at all times. He never walked. He marched.

We each offered a partial smile and chuckle at his question.

Fitch folded his arms. "Well, thankfully that S-3 didn't catch on fire."

"You ever see a fire on the flight deck, Chief?" Li'l V asked.

"Yeah. A big one. Ever hear of the *Nimitz* fire?"

We all shook our heads.

"About five years ago, a sky pig clipped a helo and slammed into a bunch of parked birds."

"Sky pig?" I said.

"One of those big ugly bastards. If pigs could fly, they'd look like that." Fitch pointed to an EA-6B Prowler.

Some also called this bird "a stretch," because it looked like an A-6 Intruder, but with an elongated cockpit housing four crewman. Most aircraft had various nicknames. An F-14 Tomcat was called a Turkey. Some called the F/A-18 Hornet a cockroach due to its bug-like appearance at certain angles. The S-3 Viking sounded like a vacuum cleaner on take-off, so it earned the nickname Hoover.

"Were you on deck when it happened?" McGee asked.

"Yep. Standing right where I'm standing now." Fitch pointed to the ground as we stood in the six-pack, an area in Fly Two along the foul line where six planes were typically parked. "I watched that sucker miss all the wires and skid right past me and hit birds on the bow. Barely missed me. Just lucky, I guess. A huge fireball went up. Real bright since it was nighttime."

McGee and I stood there, mouths agape. Li'l V put his hand on his chin, as if studying this event.

Fitch continued, "I ran toward the fire, dodging birds and tractors. Jumping over guys on the deck, unconscious. We had a well-trained crew, and hose teams came from everywhere. We got that fire contained pretty quickly, but some hot ordnance exploded. Like a chain reaction. More fire. The hose crews kept at it. The corpsmen responded quickly. We finally beat it. Took over an hour."

"Hot ordnance?" Li'l V asked.

"You see that?" Fitch pointed to a Sparrow missile hanging from an F-14. "We thought all the weapons were cooled off but one of those exploded. Killed two guys instantly. That's why we don't rest when the fire is out. We keep pouring on the water. Keep cooling the ordnance."

"Some guys died?" McGee asked.

"Oh yeah. It was hell. Fourteen. Fourteen guys that never made it home. And about thirty-nine injured. When you see body parts lying around and burnt skin coming off, you never forget it. One guy's foot was missing and he was screaming nonsense. Another guy walked around carrying his left thumb in his right hand. He didn't make any noise. He just strolled toward the island like he was headed for a smoke break."

I'd reached a comfort level on the flight deck in my short career, and the S-3 barricade rig excited me. But Chief Fitch's *Nimitz* fire story left me rattled.

"So, Chief, that wouldn't happen again, right?" I said.

"Hell. Of course it can. Anything can happen. This whole flight deck is an accident waiting to happen. We're in a dangerous business. That's why we train. That's why you keep your head on a swivel." Chief Fitch walked a few steps away and turned back. "You need to ask yourself what kind of sailor you are. What kind of man you are. Because there's two kinds: Those that run to the fire to fight it and those that run away from it."

No more flight deck mishaps that day. The rest of that short cruise progressed with the normal routine of launches and recoveries. Eppers poked his head into the blue shirt shack on our final day before entering port.

"Donley. Randolph. Petty Officer Beckley wants you in the yellow shirt shack."

We entered that shack, cautiously, careful not to breach any etiquette. A few yellow shirts looked at us but no one said to "get the fuck out."

Beckley waved us over and stubbed out his smoke. "You two are getting promoted. Randolph, you're gonna learn to drive tow tractors. Donley, you're going to crash."

We looked at each other with slight grins. I had definitely made it known that I wanted to join the crash crew. Randolph wanted to be a yellow shirt, but working in crash, driving a tow tractor, or working as an elevator operator were typical jobs one had to do before moving up to aircraft director.

"But first, you gotta do your TAD," Beckley said, sipping his coffee.

Our grins subsided. TAD (temporary assigned duty) meant three months of serving on the ship, much like Service Week in boot camp. Most guys did their time working for the mess cooks. Basically, TAD meant mess cranking like scrubbing pots and pans. But other jobs included laundry or cleaning officer's staterooms.

"You two need to pack your gear and report to supply. But go see the master chief in flight deck control first."

No one ever wanted to see the master chief. Nothing good ever came from that.

The yellow shirt locker connected to flight deck control. Entering, from a logistical standpoint, was easy. From the standpoint of hierarchy, it presented another matter altogether. We stepped toward the door, each waiting for the other to go first. Blue shirts have no business in flight deck control.

"C'mon, man," Li'l V said, without moving.

"I'm going," I said, standing as still as him.

I spotted Master Chief Gerald Platt talking to the handler. We'd seen Master Chief Platt many times but had never spoken to him. He stood at about five-foot four with a belly that hinted at a healthy appetite for both food and beer. He worked a toothpick between his teeth as he pointed toward spots on the Ouija board.

A week before, a yellow shirt had us hook up a tow bar to a bird while we were waiting on a tow tractor driver. Master Chief Platt walked up, and the yellow shirt explained the predicament. Platt hopped on a nearby idle tractor and pulled up to the bird.

"You can drive that tractor, Master Chief?" the yellow shirt said.

"Hell, I got more time in this seat than you got in the fucking Navy."

The master chief is a mythical creature. Part man and part god. Junior officers fear them. Senior officers respect them. When asked how long they've been in the Navy, they always answer "longer than you've been alive." They'd seen every liberty port in existence, sailed every ocean, and most of them had the supernatural ability to peel paint with their stare. Master Chief Platt possessed all these qualities.

Platt turned around to find us having inched up on him. "What the fuck do you two want?"

"Uhhh," I said.

Randolph elbowed me. "Master Chief...uh...Petty Officer Beckley told us to see you. We're supposed to report for mess cranking."

Platt folded his arms. "Is that so? Well, everybody's got to do that duty. But remember, you represent V-1 Division. That means you represent me. Don't fuck up. Work hard for three months and get your ass back on the flight deck. And don't let those fuckers in supply mess with your heads. You're gonna do a lot of shitty work, but it's work that needs to be done. Understand?"

"Yes, Master Chief," we said, in unison.

"Alright then, get the fuck outta here," he said, and turned back toward the Ouija board.

CHAPTER 14

"You fucking guys. You're not cleaning the deck. You're making it dirty." The Filipino chief began his lecture with lots of head shaking. "You see this swab? It's dirty. You see this water in the swab bucket? It's dirty. How are you going to clean the deck with a dirty swab and dirty water? You fucking guys. Clean it again."

We looked over our work and noticed several dirty streaks from our dirty swab and dirty water. As ordered, we started over. Six weeks into my time mess cranking had left me less than motivated.

The Supply Department had ordered Randolph to three months of cleaning staterooms, and I had hardly seen him since. They relegated me to three months of serving on the mess decks. It was easy duty, but long days. Twelve-hour shifts with the occasional day off while in port.

The sailor at sea has few drink options. There was always water and coffee. Fresh milk was available until the supply ran low and then one had the option of dumping powdered milk on their frosted flakes. Most chose bug juice.

Several times a day, I'd fill a five-gallon metal cream can with water, add two packets of Kool-Aid, a pound of sugar, and stir. I'd then pour that concoction into the drink dispenser for all sailors to enjoy. My hands developed a stain from all the bug juice colors, some of it lasting in my fingerprints for months.

For ninety days, I made bug juice. And I cleaned. Scrubbed. Swept. Swabbed. Waxed.

Before departing on our North Atlantic cruise, the crash crew sent me for several weeks of training away from the ship. Kellen Garfield, the guy who trained me on the Kennedy, recently earned a promotion to crash, and traveled with me.

The US Marines trained their aircraft firefighters at Naval Air Station Millington. The idea of training and learning from Marines seemed odd to me, but I was too excited to care. I hoped they would spare us of all the "ooh-rah" stuff.

Garfield and I faced the outside of the training facility across the street from the main base with several marines. Four old metal buildings stood with no markings. We saw no men in charge, nor anyone to welcome us. Other than the guys milling about me, the place looked like a ghost town. Our orders required us to report for muster at 0700.

"Fall in!" a mysterious marine said, appearing in a doorway.

The marines jostled and formed ranks within seconds.

Garfield stubbed out his cigarette. "We better join them."

Our pace ran a bit slower than the marine's. The sergeant that had ordered "fall out," noticed us.

"You fucking squids want to join us?" he said.

The rolled up sleeves on his shirt struggled to contain his biceps. Tattoos ran down both arms but there were too many for me to make them out. He paced back and forth while opening and closing his fists. I thought he might knock someone out to appease his wrath. The only thing missing from this package was smoke blowing from his nostrils. He looked at us as if we were the bane of his existence.

"My name is Sergeant Vasquez. I will be your instructor for the next three weeks. We'll spend every morning in the classroom and fight fires every afternoon." He paused and slowly turned. "You will learn to love fire."

Vasquez spoke in a robotic tone, loud enough that someone one hundred yards away could likely have heard, though only fourteen men stood before him in two ranks.

"Right face!" Vasquez said.

The marines turned right in perfect unison. I clumsily turned to join them. Garfield made his turn with a scoff. Sailors never marched after boot camp. We simply walked from one destination to another. Strolled, if you will.

Vasquez ran quick paces toward him. "You have a fucking problem with my command, squid?"

Garfield popped tall. "No, sir!"

"Don't you ever call me sir. I ain't no fucking officer. Do I look like I sit on my ass behind a desk all day?"

"No, sir…uh, no, Sergeant."

Vasquez turned toward me.

A bead of sweat ran down my face. I pictured him as a soldier in Iron Maiden's song "The Trooper." A warrior riding a horse with reckless abandon into certain death—into the mouth of Hell.

I wondered if we'd reported to the right place. To the right base. This was worse than boot camp. This was like Marine boot camp.

"You two fucking squids will fall in line in my school. I don't need no fucking Gomer Pyle. You will learn to fight aircraft fires. You will learn to rescue pilots. Drive the P-4 firefighting truck. Handle hoses. First aid. Every one of you swinging dicks in my school will pass this course. Is that understood?"

"Yes, Sergeant!" we said, in unison with the marines.

Sergeant Vasquez lightened the rhetoric as we transitioned to a classroom. He talked at a feverish pace, and I struggled to write sufficient notes. Aside from his tough demeanor, the man possessed a strong academic ability. This school, and Vasquez, meant business. Unlike at a conventional school, if we answered his question incorrectly, he'd throw an eraser or piece of chalk at us. No Socratic method for us.

By afternoon, they lit the large round pit on fire and we extinguished it. The pit measured about fifty feet in diameter with an old F-4 Phantom in the middle. The carcass of the old aircraft maintained a permanent blackened state. A nozzle fed the pit with fuel. The instructor would light it, and a wall of fire would shoot up several feet in the air. The heat always knocked us back a step.

Unlike previous firefighting training, there were only fourteen of us. As soon as one fire was extinguished, an instructor lit another. By 1700, all the energy had drained from my body.

I'd seen fire constantly for the last two weeks. We rotated through every job within a crash crew, within numerous scenarios. Lead rescue made for the most exciting and most difficult. On this particular drill, I would climb up to the cockpit on the mock aircraft to rescue the pilot.

Wearing a silver proximity suit, I stepped toward the

enflamed aircraft. Climbing to the cockpit, my body struggled to overcome the bulkiness of the protective suit. Sweat poured down my body. Everything got quiet. I tried to focus on my training. On everything that Vasquez had drilled into our heads.

I reached down to grab the pilot, represented by an empty, five-gallon bucket, and pulled him out. A burst of flames came out from under the bucket.

I looked back and couldn't understand why the hose team trained their nozzle straight at me. The blast nearly knocked me down. I wore a silver proximity suit designed to withstand extremely high temperatures. The lens on the hood provided little visibility.

With bucket in hand and fire out, I stepped from the fire pit and pulled off my hood, slightly peeved. "What the hell? Why did you point the hose directly at me?"

Vasquez chuckled. "Because you were on fire, dumbass."

"Huh?" I said.

"Yep. This whole side of your body was on fire," Garfield said, pointing up and down at my right side.

I held my hands up. "I didn't feel a thing."

"And that, men, is why we wear the proximity suit," Vasquez said.

I realized that I'd been too careless with my protective equipment. The suit saved me, but I'd become too accustomed to fire. Reckless. I spent my final week focused on safety.

Vasquez lightened up on the "ooh-rah" stuff. Our classroom time involved more testing, and we participated in several contests, like trying to don a proximity suit the fastest or trying to most accurately diagnose a mass casualty. I won an unorthodox contest. Hose teams are teams for a reason. A fully pressurized hose takes a lot of strength to handle. If loose, it whips around in a frenzy. One man can hold a one-and-a-half-inch hose, but the two-and-a-half-inch exerts a tremendous amount of pressure. Vasquez had us hold the hose, alone, and open the nozzle. The contest involved seeing who could hold it the longest without turning off the nozzle. It kicked my butt, but I held mine over a minute and won.

Garfield high-fived me.

"I can't believe you grunts let a fucking squid beat you," said Vasquez.

The marines lowered their heads.

"We kicked their asses," Garfield said.

Vasquez whipped his head toward Garfield. With no warning, he tackled him and put his left knee on his chest.

"You don't think these marines could kick your ass if I let them?" Vasquez said, and then looked at the marines. "Any of you guys want to kick his ass?"

They looked at each other but none made a move, unsure if Vasquez was serious or joking. He'd been prone to these outbursts and we never knew if he was kidding.

Vasquez lowered his head toward Garfield, who had a look of terror on his face. "You think you kicked their asses?" Vasquez said.

Garfield shook his head.

Vasquez quickly got up and pulled Garfield up by his arm. "Well, you squids held your own."

That was our life with Vasquez's bipolarity. His unpredictability. But I suppose that's firefighting. A certain amount of unpredictability. Just when you think the fire is out, a burst of flame explodes in your face.

Garfield and I had held our own with the few and the proud.

Sergeant Vasquez offered some parting words as we prepared to leave Millington. "I told you on your first day that you'd learn to love fire. I lied. You need to fear it. Not be afraid of it. But have a respectful fear."

I agreed. I kind of felt that way toward Vasquez. A respectful fear. But he scared the crap out of me.

Garfield and I went straight to NALF Fentress, a naval auxiliary landing field. Navy birds practiced their touch-and-go's there, simulating a carrier flight deck. The old World War II base now housed twenty aircraft firefighters. The crash chief ordered us to serve with them for two weeks and get some "real world" experience.

What we got, was a lot of time in a P-4 firefighting truck, watching A-6s and F-14s touch and go. I heard the same sea stories repeatedly. We drilled some. Put out a few pit fires. We cleaned the gear. The master chief sent us on a four-mile run through the woods which left me fighting for air. For a shore-based firefighter, that was the real world.

While in the woods, one of the Fentress regulars pointed out some old World War II bunkers that had housed a machine gun defense against the Germans, or Japanese, or whoever attempted an attack on American shores.

With lots of downtime one Sunday, Garfield jumped out of his chair. "Let's go check out those bunkers. See what we can find."

I lay in my rack reading a Stephen King novel and looked up. "What do you think we'll find?"

"I don't know. Bullets or something. I'm so bored with this place. C'mon, let's go explore."

I put my bookmark in the novel and hopped up. "Why not?"

We found no bullets or other hidden treasure. Only empty bunkers. Concrete structures of a different time. I suppose some kid my age manned that bunker forty years ago during World War II—his machine gun armed. He likely sat there bored. Maybe he read a novel. A Zane Gray western. Maybe he longed for excitement.

Garfield picked up a few rocks and threw them into the woods as we walked along the runway. "I'm so ready to get off this base."

"Why?" I asked. "This is easy duty."

"I want some action. All we do is work and train. We've been in the Navy almost a year and havn't seen anything. We put out all these fires, but it's just practice. I want some real action."

I shook my head. "Be careful what you wish for. You should have heard what Chief Fitch said about the *Nimitz* fire. All those guys killed. He said that—"

Bing! Bing! Bing!

The fire alarm sounded. We ran full speed toward the parked fire trucks. My heart raced. Maybe an F-14 needed an emergency landing. I looked up but saw no aircraft circling the landing field. We ran into the garage but saw no one.

The chief walked out drinking coffee. "What are you two doing?"

"We heard...huh, huh...the alarm," Garfield said, out of breath.

The chief sipped his coffee. "That was a test. We test it every Sunday at 1400. Where've you two numb nuts been?"

I pointed toward the woods. "Walking around. Looking at

the bunkers."

The chief smiled. "I see. Well, you better check your balls for ticks. They're thick as hell out there."

"Oh man," Garfield said, running toward the head.

A typical Sunday in the military. No real excitement. Just boredom. False alarms. And ticks on private parts.

Unlike the dingy blue shirt I'd worn as a coolie, my new red shirt, with "CRASH" stenciled across the chest, fit my body and mind. Ever since that day on the Kennedy, I wanted to belong to the flight deck fire and rescue crew. While I lacked the confidence to pull a pilot from a burning aircraft, I was eager to learn.

I tempered those thoughts as I cleaned a fire hose nozzle with a wire brush, careful to remove every speck of verdigris, a green substance that grew on the brass. The crash LPO, ABH1 Climer, assigned me a firefighting station. As ordered, I checked it every day, making sure the station was working, unobstructed, and clean. Fighting the green scum became a daily battle. No glory for me yet. No stepping through fire. No pilots flung over my shoulder. Nothing but me and my archenemy—verdigris.

"Donley," Petty Officer Climer said, leaning over the catwalk. "You got those nozzles clean?"

Sniff.

Climer seemed to end every sentence with a sniff. As if he always had a cold—like Lupus from *Bad News Bears*. He walked and talked with no certainty, meandering around the deck. Always pushing his glasses up his nose. Not so much a nerd, but one of those people that didn't seem to care how others viewed him. Like the kid that got picked last for teams. Totally out of shape. That was only in appearance, though. Climer knew his job and taught us well. During drills, we all knew who led the charge. He seemed like two different people. One minute, he'd waddle along, mild-mannered, then, he'd turn into John Wayne, the hellfighter.

I looked up at Climer, one eye closed due to the sun. "They're almost clean. It seems like this green crap grows faster than I can brush it off."

"Rust never sleeps," he said.

"Rust?"

"Yep. That green crap is like rust. It never sleeps. Just keeps coming back."

Sniff.

Climer turned to walk away and stepped back. "Oh! Go to supply and get issued your foul weather gear. You're gonna need it next week."

"What kinda gear?" I said.

"Foul weather. You'll see."

We planned to leave port the next day and head for the North Atlantic Ocean for six weeks. I heard it would be cold. But foul?

CHAPTER 15

"Welcome to the North Atlantic, gentlemen," the air boss said over the 5MC.

The North Atlantic was anything but welcoming. The massive carrier cruised through four-foot swells topped with white caps. The gray sky blocked out the powerful heat and light of the sun, offering an eternal gloominess. But that wasn't the worse part. A constant drizzle of freezing rain pelted us. Soaked us.

I wore long underwear, my normal dungaree pants and red shirt, a foul weather jacket, and yellow rain gear. The work gloves protected from the rigors of flight deck work, but offered no real protection from the brutal cold and wet weather. Supply also issued me a foul weather mask, suitable for scaring small children on Halloween. After thirty minutes on deck, the water seeped down my neck, into my gloves, and between my toes.

The extra gear helped, but we remained miserable in the intolerable weather that remained below freezing, coupled with a turn into the wind at every launch. The occasional warm blast of a launching aircraft's exhaust or tow tractor huffer unit (used to start planes) offered a brief reprieve.

Petty Officer Climer posted a daily schedule for our flight deck rotations. We manned a firefighting vehicle on deck for one-and-a-half hour shifts. A crash crewman served as the driver for the P-16 firefighting vehicle, and two crewmen wore the silver proximity suit pants—with hood, jacket, and gloves readily available. Climer and the crash chief took turns roaming the deck. They had assigned other equipment to various crash crew in the event of an accident.

"Petty Officer Climer, how come I'm never assigned driver?" I asked. "I can drive."

"Do you know how to light off the system? Do you know how to approach an aircraft fire?" Climer pushed his glasses up his nose.

I veered my eyes to the side. "Uh…kinda."

"That's why. Be patient. You'll get there. And you'll probably learn to drive the 20K and Tilly."

The carrier housed a 20K forklift and an NS-60 crash crane, called a Tilly, in the event an aircraft lay damaged and immovable in the landing area—crucial elements for the salvage part of the crash and salvage crew. We used those pieces of equipment to quickly move damaged birds out of the way so other planes could land. Much of the time, birds in the air have no alternate airfield; they must land on the carrier.

Our P-16 crew typically parked in a location where we could see most of the deck and respond quickly to any incident. This gave me many hours to observe deck operations. Purple shirts dragged hoses toward aircraft to load them with fuel. Brown shirts inspected their birds in preparation for launch, and the pilots did the same. Red shirts, like the ones we wore but from a different division, lifted ordnance to the underside of A-6s and F-14s. Green shirts carefully checked that an aircraft's launch bar rested securely in the shuttle, and white shirts did a final check before launch. Yellow shirts waved their hands, guiding pilots through tight spots. So many colors. So many jobs. A well-oiled machine.

I contributed little but knew my job would kick in should an accident occur.

I walked off the deck toward the crash shack.

Li'l V sat on a tow tractor. "Hey, Donley. Let's go to chow. I get relieved in a little bit."

"Yep. I'm starving."

We worked our way through several passageways and three levels of decks toward the massive mess deck area. A line extended into the hangar bay, meaning we'd have about a twenty- minute wait for chow.

"You ready for sixteen on, eight off?" Li'l V said.

"What?"

"Sixteen hours on and eight hours off. They said we're gonna fly around the clock and we have to work in sixteen hour shifts. It's gonna suck." Li'l V shook his head. "I start tomorrow. Mine is 2100 to 1300 every day. Like ten days in a row."

I cocked my head. "Wait. What?"

"You know, like nine o'clock at night to 1:00 PM the next day."

We inched forward in line. "Dang. That's about what we do in crash now. Sometimes a few of us will go to the coop early and be the first ones back up. About fourteen-hour days."

Sailors complained a lot. It was part of our job description. I excelled at it, but Li'l V needed some work in that area. He rarely complained. The eternal optimist.

"But hey, it'll be a good experience for a real wartime situation," Li'l V said, as we made our way to the front of the line.

I watched as several first class petty officers cut in front of us. A special head-of-line privilege they held.

I noticed today's offering. "Spaghetti and meatballs!"

"Ah, hell yeah," Li'l V said, sniffing the air.

We received the impersonal servings on our trays, including a piece of chocolate cake each, and made our way to the drink stations. I chose milk, ever critical of the mess crankers inability to make bug juice as perfectly as I had made it.

We joined two coolies from our division. I paused a moment. Others may have thought that I engaged in a moment of silence. A word of grace perhaps. I actually took a moment to consider that after several days of miserable weather, little sleep, and what had become a mundane job on the flight deck, I was about to enjoy my favorite meal in the warmth of the mess decks.

I looked around and saw several sailors, with dry clothes and dry hair, whose jobs spared them from the elements. They laughed and scooped food in their mouths and would soon return to their warm, cozy environment.

"Ain't you gonna eat?" Li'l V said to me, and then slurped a piece of spaghetti.

I smiled and dug my fork in. "Yep, I just—"

"This is a drill, this is a drill. Fire, fire, fire. Fire on the flight deck," blasted over the 1MC shipboard public address system.

My mouth dropped.

That announcement meant nothing to most guys. A real fire, yes, but a drill, no. For me, and every flight deck worker, it meant drop everything and get to the flight deck.

Li'l V immediately dropped his fork and jumped up. Some

yellow shirts at the next table did the same.

I looked at my pile of spaghetti, giant meatball, glistening chocolate cake, and creamy milk. "Son of a bitch!"

I jumped up and stayed on Li'l V's heels up to the deck.

An F-14 Tomcat rested in the landing area, simulating a crashed bird. The crew that had relieved me parked the P-16 at an angle to the nose. Hose crews trained their nozzles on the aircraft.

A yellow shirt cupped his hands over his mouth and yelled at the crew to his right. "Move in!"

Typically, the first yellow shirt to arrive at a crash acted as on-scene leader, directing firefighting crews. The hose crews of four to five men swerved their hoses at the base of the imaginary fire, slowly inching toward the blaze in half steps. Those in khaki pants—chiefs and officers—watched and judged our performance.

The two rescue men had donned their proximity suit hoods and jackets. A rescue cage attached to the 20K forklift raised them to the cockpit for pilot rescue. After twenty minutes, hose crews had extinguished the fire, the rescue men carried the pilot to the hospital corpsmen, and we cleared the landing area of debris.

At least in theory. This was a drill. One of many.

Drills never occurred at a convenient time. But accidents didn't either. We performed fire drills on the flight deck and below decks. Man overboard and general quarters drills. They had annoyed me until we rigged the barricade for real, and I saw firsthand why we drilled.

By the end of this fire drill, my stomach growled.

Garfield pulled off his hood, having served as one of the rescue crew, and handed it to me. "You're up."

"Up?"

"Yeah, it's your turn on deck."

I glanced at my watch. "Crap."

My chow time had passed. That was shipboard life. Flight deck life.

I finally got back to chow two hours later, ready to load my tray with spaghetti and chocolate cake. But lunch had turned to dinner and a new menu. Fish sticks. Hard-as-wood fish sticks with rice.

For several mornings, we anchored near the fjords of Norway—an endless chain of green islands with snowcapped peaks. On many nights, the Northern Lights filled the sky. In those brutal conditions of the North Atlantic, a quiet beauty shone through.

For a few days, we made our way into the Arctic Circle and earned ourselves a place in the Order of the Blue Nose. The Navy holds many traditions, some geographical. The most famous one occurs while crossing the equator where pollywogs (those who haven't crossed) are turned into shellbacks (those who have crossed). The Blue Nose represents a simpler initiation where a sailor or officer goes on the bow wearing only skivvies and boots. An experienced Blue Nose applies blue paint to their nose lasting a few days and they earn their Blue Nose status.

I didn't need the paint. The cold weather kept my nose blue most of the time. Our routine entailed waking, working, freezing, and overnight thawing. The weather never relented. As cold as the deck seemed, I imagined the sea's temperature. It only added to one of my greatest fears—an aircraft's exhaust blowing me over the side.

The flight deck towered seventy-five feet above the sea. We had no safety rails. Only a wire net that extended four feet from the edge. One would hope to catch that net, but expect painful injuries in what we called "halfway to hell." I don't think anyone ever feared merely falling off the flight deck. But aircraft exhaust blasted us across the deck repeatedly. The downward exhaust of an A-6 Intruder blew at our feet. We hated the F/A-18 Hornet exhaust the most because it blew at the small of your back. It pushed you. Guys would look as if they floated across the deck—their legs scurrying along, trying to keep up.

I imagined myself walking near the arresting gear while an F/A-18 spun in my direction. The exhaust zeroing in on my body before I could outrun it. I'd look like a lunatic running and hurling myself off the fantail—never to be seen again.

Should I survive the seventy-five foot fall, hypothermia would kill me in minutes. The four-foot waves would swallow me or hide me from the rescue helo. If I inflated my life vest, turned on my strobe light, and activated the dye to mark my path in the water, I might get rescued. But only in calm waters with reasonable temperature. It all seemed implausible. I wanted nothing to do with the sea. Halfway to hell I could survive, but not the hell of the North Atlantic.

The activity in the coop died down as taps approached. The racks rattled as a bird launched, mere feet over our heads. We lived on the 03 level, just under the flight deck. The CAT 1 shuttle completed its catapult run right over my rack. After a fourteen or fifteen hour day, my body's desire for sleep overcame the constant disturbance of the shuttle ending its track run.

McGee had the bottom rack across from me in a pod of six racks—stacked three high. We always hoped our group of six had a different schedule so we could get ready for work or bed without climbing over each other. McGee, now a tractor driver, shared my shift. Unfortunately, he took up the space of two men.

He invited me to his home near Baltimore the weekend before we left for the North Atlantic. I quickly learned where McGee got his size. His parents towered over me, as did his three brothers.

What do they feed this family to make them so big? I thought.

I found out at dinnertime as his mom served meatloaf, mashed potatoes, peas, cornbread, milk, and apple pie. Every meal included hearty fare.

I also found out where McGee's propensity to argue and tell stories came from. One after another, McGee's dad and brothers told stories and argued about the accuracy of each.

"I caught fourteen fish that morning, and you pipsqueaks caught like three altogether," McGee's dad said.

One of the brothers rolled his eyes. "What? You gotta be kidding me. We showed you that fishing hole. We caught more than you."

"Horse hockey," the dad said.

In the middle of the chaos, McGee's mother, who had told me to call her "Miss Carol," asked me about my home, family, and interests. She seemed oblivious to the fighting going on around the table which included lots of laughter and backslapping. It was all in good fun. This was one of those families that worked hard, fought hard, and played hard. The football game in the backyard included bone-breaking tackles. I feigned an injury and sat out as they finished their game, ending up with bruises and torn shirts. They walked back into the house, arms around each other. I lacked the skills to be a part of that family, but I greatly admired them. I was fortunate to make the trip to McGee's house two more times before the Mediterranean cruise.

I returned from the shower to find McGee in only a towel, blocking my rack. "Why do you do this every night?"

"Do what?" he asked, applying some sort of lotion to his face.

I rolled my eyes. "You stand here and apply all kinds of crap to your body. Then you go look in the mirror for five minutes and inspect your face. You primp like a girl."

He smiled and rubbed his hands across his face. "Gotta look good for the ladies."

"What ladies? We're in the Arctic Circle. There ain't no ladies here. Probably none within a hundred miles."

"Donley, it's a process. A routine. I have to maintain myself under these primitive conditions so I hit the beach looking good."

"Well, I need to get to my rack and sleep, so go primp somewhere else."

"You ain't gonna watch the movie?"

I leaned around the racks to see the TV. "*Beverly Hills Cop*? They've shown it fifty times this cruise. No. I'm going to sleep."

Thud!

McGee lowered the bar and dropped his locker top. "Fine. Get your beauty sleep. I don't need it."

I settled in my rack which lay one foot off the deck. I

no longer had any soreness from the work, as my body had accustomed to the daily grind. With my rack curtains closed and my body cocooned in a wool blanket, I noticed the lights going out and voices moving toward a whisper. The four guys that slapped their dominos on the table with excitement transitioned to a quiet placement of each move. The night shift kept the deck going while I looked forward to six hours of rest.

"Overboard, starboard side!"

The 1MC speaker woke me. Lights flickered on and I heard rustling and clanking. I realized I missed part of the announcement.

McGee threw open my curtains. "Donley. Get up. Man overboard."

I'd only slept a short time. "You've got to be kidding me. Another drill." I slowly rolled out of my rack.

"No drill," he said, putting on his flight deck boots.

"Man overboard! Man overboard, starboard side!" came over the speaker again.

Normally, "This is a drill, this is a drill," precedes these announcements. I assumed that I had missed that part while sleeping. Someone actually fell into the water. I immediately envisioned an F/A-18 blowing some poor guy off the fantail.

I threw on my pants, foul weather jacket, and boots, all undone, and followed McGee toward our muster station behind the island. During flight operations, we could not run across the flight deck. We had to work our way through the 03 level passageways, down to the hangar bay, and then up to the flight deck.

The cold air assaulted me. I wore a fraction of my normal protective clothing, and the arousal from deep sleep ill prepared me. We lined up in alphabetical order and walked toward

Petty Officer Beckley as he checked off our names. The same procedure occurred throughout the ship as a designated leader identified every man to determine exactly who and how many hit the water. In addition, man overboard crews readied small boats for rescue.

Night shift guys lined up with us and the scuttlebutt began.

"They're delaying the final recovery," a yellow shirt a few steps ahead of me said.

"What happened?" I asked.

A couple of guys shrugged.

"Maybe some dumbass fell off the fantail in the hangar bay," one guy said.

"No. Somebody probably got blown off," said another.

I could see a lot of commotion near elevator two. Several squadron guys shone their lights over the side of the ship toward the water.

Chief Fitch walked past me.

"Chief, what's going on? What happened?" I asked.

The three guys in front of me turned around and looked at Fitch.

The chief pointed toward elevator two. "Some green shirt got blown off the deck. A squadron guy."

I looked off the starboard side. Three helos flew low to the water with searchlights.

"Cagler!" Beckley said, and checked off a name. "Crowley! Dawson!" Each man stepped up, showed his face, and Beckley acknowledged him.

I inched further up in line.

"Listen up, guys," Chief Fitch said, looking up and down the line. "We're gonna finish the final recovery and then we will probably suspend flight ops until we find this guy. The ship will do figure-eights for twenty-four hours while we look for him."

Eppers walked past me wearing underwear, boots, and his foul weather jacket. Everybody else put on pants, but not Eppers. The weather seemed to have no effect on him. He avoided anything normal. He was created abnormal. Curly, jet-black hair topped his body of pasty white skin and an almost reddish-looking mustache covered his upper lip. He walked like a cowboy, as if he'd been in the saddle a long time. He brought his wife on board one day and she stood a foot taller than him. He listened to rap music, exclusively. The oddest duck in V-1 Division but one of the best yellow shirts on the deck.

"Hey, Eppers," I said. "Did you hear? Some squadron guy got blown over the side."

"Yep. He's a go…go…goner."

"You don't think they'll find him?"

"I hope so. But falling in the water is bad enough. In these cold waters it's worse. But at ni…night? Like I said, I hope they find him, but I doubt it."

I stepped up to Beckley and his clipboard. "Donley!"

I moved out of line quickly and looked over the side. Searchlights darting out from the side of the ship exposed flashes of sea. But mostly, it looked like a black mass. My body shivered and teeth rattled, but I thought I could at least look. The poor guy had surely drifted a mile away by that point.

McGee walked up next to me. "Can you imagine?"

I shook my head. No words seemed sufficient.

"Listen up!" Beckley said. "You men that are off, go back to your racks. Be back on deck at your normal time because we may be on regular flight operations."

I returned to the coop but only slept a couple of hours, wondering what had happened to that guy. I hoped they'd announce his rescue and that everything would return to normal.

The next morning, McGee and I walked through the hangar bay toward chow and saw Li'l V.

"Hey, Brian. You boys get plenty of sleep last night?"

"Nah. Maybe an hour or two. They find that guy?"

"Nope," Li'l V said, shaking his head.

"Do they know what happened?" McGee asked.

"Oh yeah," Li'l V motioned for us to get in the chow line. "A couple of guys saw it happen. An A-6 had pulled out a little for a maintenance turn on EL 2. This green shirt was walking from EL 1 toward the island with a cable wrapped around him. You know, that big yellow cable the squadron guys hook up to the birds. The A-6 turned up the power right when he walked behind him. Guys yelled at him but he didn't even see them. They said the plane's exhaust blew him right off the deck."

"Damn!" McGee said.

A few men in front of and behind us eavesdropped.

Li'l V continued, "I heard a squadron chief say that with that cable wrapped around him, he probably broke every bone in his body when he hit the water. Probably sank like a rock."

"Keep your head on a swivel," I mumbled.

"What?" McGee said.

"Keep your head on a swivel," I said, a little louder. "That's what they always tell us. He must've been looking down or not paying attention."

"That chief said they'll find out if guys were flashing their wands during the maintenance turn. But it sounds like the guy thought it was a low turn," Li'l V said.

McGee grabbed a tray and held it out for scrambled eggs. "We flying today?"

"Don't think so," Li'l V said. "I think they'll look the rest of the day, but they ain't gonna find him."

"Then why keep looking?" McGee said.

"Because they might find him. At least they can tell his parents they tried." I pulled the lever to pour milk in my glass. "What was his name?"

"Smith." Li'l V said.

Smith. We probably had a hundred Smiths on the boat. I didn't know him. But he was one of us. And now he'd vanished into the sea. Just like that. Working on the flight deck one minute and blown over the side the next.

CHAPTER 16

We arrived back in Norfolk, down one man. A man named Smith. I'm sure he left Norfolk thinking he'd hit the beach and have a beer. Or maybe that his girlfriend would stand waiting at the pier. Maybe he'd start his car and tune into his favorite radio station.

None of that would happen, though.

A Navy chaplain probably visited their home to tell the family the terrible news.

I imagined what they'd say: "The Navy regrets to inform you that your son was lost at sea during flight operations in the North Atlantic."

The mother would scream, "Nooooooo!"

The father would hold her and ask, "What? How?"

"It was an unfortunate incident," the chaplain would say. "Your son was well-liked and a hard worker. He died an honorable servant to his country."

What else could he say? The difficult job of a chaplain. I didn't envy them.

McGee and I settled on our post-cruise requirement. Wendy's. Nothing like fast food to readjust to society after six weeks at sea.

"Let's go to Little Creek Tavern and have a beer," McGee

said, his mouth full of meat, cheese, and bread.

We both liked the Little Creek Tavern. It was a great place to relax, have a beer, and watch a live band. A few Norfolk regulars manned their seats at the bar, but mostly sailors frequented the place.

"Maybe for a bit. I've got the duty tomorrow."

"Don't be a wuss. We've been out to sea for six weeks. You don't need no beauty sleep."

Despite McGee's pleas, I knew I didn't want to drag myself in at 0300 for a 0700 muster.

"You don't have the duty. You can sleep in tomorrow, but, fine," I said, and immediately regretted it.

"I'll probably have several ladies buying me drinks and have to send you home anyway," McGee said.

Unfortunately for me, McGee's peer pressure kept me from my rack until 0230. I dragged myself to morning muster for my day of duty. They divided us into six sections for our duty requirement every six days. In port, we had to stay on the ship for twenty-four hours doing menial tasks, standing watch, etc. Since we'd returned from sea the prior day, none of the section leaders felt like accomplishing much, so they had us doing minor cleaning. I'd lucked into the 1200 to 1600 coop watch, meaning I could sit and play cards, listen to guys snore as they slept off the previous night's drunkenness, and walk around the coop every once in awhile, making sure things were secure. Easy duty.

Before the North Atlantic cruise, I had taken the test for petty officer third class. Beckley told us they'd post the results in the mess decks in the next few days. I headed for chow before my watch and noticed the lists posted.

Garfield walked toward me smiling and pumping his fist.

"I guess you made third, huh?" I said.

Garfield raised his arms, "Whoop, whoop! Yeah, buddy. How 'bout you?"

"I haven't looked."

I walked over to the list. Several guys crowded around papers taped to the bulkhead. A few of them ran their fingers down the lists searching for their names.

"Son of a bitch! That's the second time I didn't make it," one guy said.

To earn advancement, we took a test based on our ratings. I took the exam for aviation boatswain mate (handling). If I made third class petty officer, I'd be referred to as ABH3 Brian Donley. Within each rating, only a certain percentage of the top scores advanced.

I worked my way toward the D names and ran my finger down. "Donavan. Donis. Donlan," I whispered. "Donley!" I scrolled over and found my first name and social security number. "I made it!"

I turned to high-five Garfield, but he wasn't there.

I fist pumped and saw him emerge from the crowd.

"I made it!"

He high-fived me. "I was looking at other names. Congrats!"

A week later, we attended a brief ceremony, each with the new rank on our left sleeve. The insignia had an eagle, one chevron, and our rating symbol. We called it the crow. I soon learned of a ritual that awaited us. One that wiped the smile from our faces. The tacking on of the crow.

Although I had my crow carefully and securely sewn on,

experienced petty officers saw fit to "tack on the crow" with a punch to my arm. While some participated with a light jab, many reared back and delivered punishing blows. For days, my arm hung at my side, practically useless. Below the shoulder, a grotesque mixture of blue and black bruising covered the width of my arm. I didn't understand this rite of passage, but I endured it—ever the team player.

Some sailors endured another painful ritual known as the pink belly. Reserved for newbies to the boat, three or four guys would hold down the young airman, while another would pull up his shirt and repeatedly slap his belly until it turned pink.

One evening, I noticed a commotion near my rack, and saw that a newbie kicked and jerked his legs during the initiation.

"Alright, let him up," said Eppers, a participant in this evolution.

The young sailor jumped up smiling, either in defiance of any pain or out of enjoyment for joining as a newly elected member of V-1 Division, Air Department, USS *William Halsey*.

The deliverers of the punishment walked away laughing.

He tucked his shirt back in. "Is that it? That's all you got?"

"Dude. I wouldn't be asking for more," I said.

"Ahhh. I'm kidding."

I extended my hand. "Donley."

"Worthington," he replied, grasping my hand.

We didn't need to say our names. In port, we wore dungarees that had our last names stenciled above the pocket. But that was the etiquette.

Airman Apprentice Worthington had arrived at our last port, fresh out of boot camp. I later learned his full name. Frederick Carlton Worthington. Someone that worked in the division office shared the information in an effort to make fun of him and produce a nickname.

Many times, last names turned into nicknames. Smiths were Smitty. A Polish surname like Wakowski was shortened to Ski. Mauser became Mouse. So Worthington could have been Worthy or Worth. Certain behaviors produced the best nicknames. Like Victor Randolph being called Li'l V for saying "little" so much. We called Kellen Garfield "Cash" because he always counted his money. If a guy tried to create his own nickname, we ignored it.

Frederick Carlton Worthington struck us as a country club name. Country Club sounded OK, but Spalding worked so much better. At first Worthington hated the nickname Spalding and assured us he had no country club upbringing and that his parents raised him on a farm in Nebraska. He stood several inches shorter than me with the sturdy build of a farm kid. His stocky frame didn't match his baby face and high-pitched voice. He failed to fight off the moniker, so Spalding it was.

With some slight turnover in personnel, and my new crow, I moved up to a middle rack, as did McGee with his new crow. Spalding had the bottom rack below me. We both liked him immediately.

Every night when the lights went out, he said, "Night, John Boy." He was the one that woke up as reveille sounded and said, "Rise and shine, boys. It's a fine day to be in the Navy." He was the joker that said, "C'mon, boys, let's move these boxes," during a working party. So annoying yet so funny.

We needed guys like Spalding to break the monotony, especially in port. We worked hard at sea, and the excitement of the flight deck carried us through those long days. We felt as though we really contributed to a necessary and worthy goal— the defense of our country. In port, the work seemed only moderately necessary and far from worthy.

We each did our time on working parties, such as those that would offload materials and store them below decks. The faded lines on the flight deck needed repainting occasionally. We didn't mind that. But anything to do with a padeye exasperated us.

Padeyes—tie down points for chains connected to aircraft—served a necessary function. But apparently, they could never have water in them. They could never have an inkling of metal shining through the paint. No, the haze gray paint had to be fresh. Each of us logged many hours with air hoses blowing rainwater out of padeyes. If they needed painting, we had to blow any water or debris out of them. It seemed a pathetic sight for highly trained flight deck personnel to be sitting on a chock with paintbrush in hand, painting one padeye after another. Someone once told us the flight deck had 1,300 of them. That sounded right. But when I blew water out of them, or worse, painted them, there seemed to be 13,000.

Times like these called for moments of entertainment. Moments of levity. Spalding and another newbie named Czarnecki served these needs on one particular Saturday of never ending padeye maintenance.

"Czarnecki, go down to supply on the ei…eighth deck and requisition a padeye wrench," Eppers said. He loved to prank.

Czarnecki cocked his head. "A what?"

I covered my snicker with a cough and kept painting my padeye.

"Don't you know what a padeye wrench is? Just go," Eppers said.

Czarnecki, following orders, hopped up and headed behind the island and down a ladder.

There may have been a supply compartment on the eighth deck. Every division on the ship likely had a supply compartment. Czarnecki surely had no idea where to go. If he found the eighth deck, he'd realize he had traveled to the bottom of the ship with twelve ladders to climb to get back on the flight deck. He surely didn't realize that a padeye wrench didn't exist. Similarly, no light bulbs for smoking lamps existed and there were no actual gig lines.

Before Czarnecki returned, Spalding came back from the trip I had sent him on for twenty feet of gig line. "Man, I never found supply on the eighth deck."

We lost it. Our laughing clued him in on the prank.

"You bastards," Spalding said, smiling.

He learned, as we had as newbies, that aircraft carrier flight operations occurred without the phantom padeye wrench.

Beckley had his own prank, but it was one we didn't find amusing.

Sailors with a rank below petty officer needed a liberty card to leave the ship at the end of the workday. Beckley collected them at morning muster and handed them out when he deemed the day's work complete. Many times, he'd hold a sailor's card, claiming he didn't work hard.

He kept them in his breast pocket and occasionally pulled them out, waving them. "You want liberty today? Then I'd better see you busting your butts."

The bullying tactic struck fear in many of the newbies. No one worked any harder, though, because everyone knew Beckley chose his victims at random.

AN Czarnecki worried every day knowing his wife and kids waited to pick him up at the pier at 1600, the time we normally knocked off. He had joined the Navy later in life, hoping to support his family. As our Med cruise departure day approached, we all valued our time on liberty, but especially the guys with family.

We gathered at 1600 as Beckley finished handing out the liberty cards. "Dismissed."

"Wanna go do something?" McGee asked me.

"Yeah, something. Let's just get off the boat. We might—"

"Petty Officer Beckley. What about my liberty card?" Czarnecki said, standing next to me.

Beckley stroked his mustache. "Do you think you deserve liberty?"

"He worked his ass off today," McGee said.

Beckley stared at McGee. "I don't remember asking your opinion, shipmate."

"Asshole," Li'l V said, his head down behind me.

Beckley turned his head in my direction. "Who the fuck said that?"

Several looked back, shrugging.

With no reply, Beckley returned to Czarnecki. "Go empty the trash in the division office and report back to me in the island."

Czarnecki took off in a run toward the division office located on the other side of the ship.

His wife and kids presumably sat in their car, wanting to spend time with him for the few days they had left before we headed to sea.

Beckley headed toward the island. He had the duty that day and was in no hurry to leave. He usually hung out in flight deck control, sitting in the handler's chair acting like he ran the show.

Most everyone took off for the coop to change clothes and

hit the beach.

Li'l V had the duty as well and headed for the island to find out what meaningless task Beckley had in store for him and his crew. Most duty section leaders gave guys the evening off while on duty, other than those they put on watch. Not Beckley. He always found busy work.

I followed Li'l V toward the island.

"Where ya going?" McGee said.

"This is bullshit. I'm gonna get Czarnecki's liberty card," I said.

"Dude. C'mon. He does this shit every day. He'll give it to him eventually."

"Not today," I said.

I'm not sure what came over me. I wasn't a crusader. But Czarnecki didn't deserve that treatment. No one did. I wanted to stand up for him.

"I'm outta here," McGee said, heading for the coop.

McGee's reaction was probably right. My efforts were likely fruitless. But I'd hoped I could at least reason with Beckley.

I walked into the yellow shirt shack and stood near the doorway to flight deck control. Several guys stood around the Ouija board talking to Beckley who sat in the handler's chair. I had no business there, but I wanted to wait and see if he'd give Czarnecki's liberty card to him.

Czarnecki entered the island fifteen minutes later out of breath. "Petty Officer Beckley...huh...I emptied the trash. Can I have my liberty card?"

Beckley held up his hand at Czarnecki, not even looking in his direction. Li'l V stood across from Beckley.

"I want the coop swept and swabbed before anyone on

duty goes to chow, understood?" he said to Li'l V.

"Understood," Li'l V replied, with obvious irritation. He walked toward me, rolling his eyes.

Beckley turned back to Czarnecki. "Now, what do you want, shipmate?"

"My liberty card."

Beckley obviously knew. He'd played this torturous game before.

"Oh. Yeah. It's in the division office. I left it there for you to get after you finished emptying the trash. See the yeoman."

Czarnecki dropped his head, turned, and exited the island. I followed him to tell him I was sorry Beckley was doing this. But he took off in a run back to the same office from which he had just come.

I walked back in the island to ask Beckley why he did that. For what purpose?

Beckley talked with two others while playing with a yellow liberty card. He laughed and said, "I guess Czarnecki will be back shortly."

One of the others laughed, and one didn't.

That bastard, I thought.

Anger arose in me. I walked into flight deck control. "You've had his card the whole time?"

Beckley's smile subsided. "It's none of your business, shipmate."

"You son of a bitch." I knew I crossed a line. I knew there'd be no return so I decided to forge ahead and make my stand.

"What the fuck did you call me, Donley?"

"You know he worked hard today. Czarnecki works hard every day. You know his wife and kids are waiting for him on the pier." Each of my statements became louder as I progressed.

Beckley jumped out of the chair. "Shipmate, I suggest you shut your fucking hole."

"You shut your fucking hole!" I said, pointing at him.

The guy that had laughed with Beckley dropped his mouth. The other looked away, likely seeking an escape. I heard others jostle behind me in the next compartment.

"It's bad enough you pick on guys for no reason and hold their liberty cards. Someone on duty could have taken out that trash. Hell, it could have been done hours ago."

"Shut up!" Beckley said, slapping Czarnecki's liberty card on the Ouija board and placing his hands on his hips.

"But this is worse. You had his card in your pocket and sent him all the way back to the division office knowing he wouldn't find it there. What are you going to say when he gets back? That it's in the coop?"

Li'l V walked in and put his arm across my chest. "C'mon, Brian. Cool down. Let's go."

Li'l V was the one that confronted people. He never feared getting in someone's face if they deserved it. Some thought him quick-tempered.

I was like Ralphie in the movie *A Christmas Story*, whaling away at the bully until his mom had to pull him off. Li'l V played the mom part.

"You son of a bitch! What kind of sick game is this?" I said, remaining defiant.

"Brian, shut the hell up," Li'l V said.

"Alright, Donley. That's it. I'm writing you up. You won't see liberty for a long time."

"I don't give a shit. You son—"

"Donley!" I turned to find Chief Fitch. He also had the duty that day. "Everybody except for Donley clear out. Beckley, you wait in the yellow shirt shack."

Beckley walked by me, grinning. I stared back, my hands in fists. I knew I crossed a line. Americans have long enjoyed the right of free speech, freedom of the press, and freedom to assemble. Not so for those in the military. We couldn't say whatever we wanted.

Fitch closed the door.

"Cool down, Donley," Fitch said, in a low tone.

"Do you know what he did? He—"

Fitch held up his hand. "I know enough. I overheard from the compartment next door and I've heard of Beckley doing this. You let me deal with Beckley, and I assure you he will not do it again. But you're never allowed to talk to a senior petty officer like that again. You understand?"

I paused, my eyes looking to the side. I turned them back to him. "Yes, Chief."

"Now listen. I know that Beckley can be a mean SOB, but he's also a pretty good LPO. I'm gonna have him come back in here. I want you to apologize. But don't worry, he won't be writing anyone up. Can you handle that?"

"Yes, Chief."

I thought it ridiculous to apologize. But Chief Fitch had earned the right for me to trust him.

Fitch opened the door. "Get in here, Beckley."

Beckley walked in with Czarnecki's liberty card in his hand; his grin remained.

"Donley," Fitch said.

"Petty Officer Beckley. Sorry. Won't happen again," I said.

Beckley folded his arms. "Well, shipmate, you—"

Fitch stepped between us and snatched Czarnecki's liberty card from Beckley's hand.

"Donley, go find Czarnecki and give him this."

"OK, Chief." I headed out the door.

The door closed behind us. I walked into a full yellow shirt shack. Several men stood ready to hear the next scene of this unfolding drama.

The screaming began immediately. Chief Fitch loudly conveyed to Beckley his displeasure at recent events. Fitch rarely used profanity, but he used the "F" word with a mastery unlike any I'd ever heard—succinctly placing the emphasis at key points.

Li'l V and I looked at each other, mouths open.

After several sentences, a second class petty officer pushed us out of the island. "Everybody out. That's none of our business," he said.

Czarnecki ran up to us as we walked across EL 2. "They didn't have my liberty card in the…the…division office."

I gave him the coveted yellow liberty card. "We got it."

Czarnecki snatched it. "Who had it?"

"Long story," I said. "Go see your wife and kids. I'll tell you tomorrow."

Czarnecki took off on another run, this time to the coop to change clothes and see his family.

"We didn't get it," Li'l V said.

I cocked my head. "Get what?"

"His liberty card. You said 'we got it.' But we didn't fight for it. You did. You got it. Took some balls."

I shrugged. "Well, I suppose Chief Fitch got it."

"He's the man," Li'l V said.

And thus, the era of Beckley withholding liberty cards ended. And he never said a word to me about it.

That liberty card incident would never have happened at

sea. No time for it, for pranks or busy work. The doldrums of port waned as the Med cruise began.

CHAPTER 17

A slight makeover occurs when a carrier goes to sea. Safety rails at various points near the catwalks come down. Our blue dungaree shirts and ball cap covers get stowed away as flight deck workers transition to a variety of colors for the duty assignment. The mess decks serve meals around the clock, supporting varying work shifts. The slight list of two or three degrees to port and starboard begins. As the land disappears from the horizon, we wait for the first few aircraft to fly along the starboard side for their approach.

Li'l V walked into the coop as I put on my red shirt.

I did a double take. "What? Why are you in a yellow shirt?"

He placed his hands on his hips and looked off to the side as if posing for a picture. The stencil across the chest read, "FLY 1."

He turned back and smiled. "They promoted me."

"When?"

"A little while ago. Right when we were pulling out. Chief Fitch called me to the division office and said. 'Go to supply. I'm making you a yellow shirt.'"

Li'l V waved his hands as if directing an aircraft. "I'll be spotting those CATs." He rubbed his chest. "Reminds me of my high school soccer jersey."

I cocked my head. "You played soccer?"

"Yeah. Why? A black man can't play soccer? I have to play basketball?" Li'l V said, in mock indignation.

"I just mean—"

"I'm kidding," he said, pushing me. "I was a damn good soccer player. I also kicked for the football team. I had a scholarship offer to some little school in Virginia, but I didn't want go to college."

Eppers, Garfield, and a few others walked up and congratulated Li'l V.

ABH3 Wright muttered, "Humph."

Wright had trouble making friends. As Beckley's pet, we didn't accept him as one of the guys. We'd caught him leaning in to listen to our conversations. Then he'd run to tell Beckley. No one trusted him. Except Beckley. He believed everything Wright said. Wright wore his black hair slicked back and parted in the center. Like Alfalfa, but without the point in the back. His upper lip tried desperately to grow a mustache, but it never quite reached fruition. He looked as though he needed to clean ash from his lip. His constant body odor didn't help him in making friends. He failed to shower daily like the rest of us did and would only go after multiple complaints.

Garfield heard his "humph" remark. "You got a problem, Wright?"

"Nope. Just figures."

"What figures?"

"That Li'l V would get promoted to yellow shirt even though we've been in tractors the same amount of time." Wright closed his locker and started to walk out.

Garfield blocked him. "What's your deal?"

"He's black. Chief Fitch is black. Get it?"

"Yeah," Garfield answered. "I'm black. You're white. What the fuck does that have to do with anything?"

The naive may have believed the United States Navy free of racism. It existed. But rarely. For guys that lived and worked together, race became an afterthought. I never thought of Li'l V in terms of color. I don't think he thought of me that way either. We liked each other. Respected one another. The black guys typically hung out together on liberty and the white guys did the same. But not always.

However, racism reared its ugly head on occasion. Ignorant souls like Wright had made comments in the past. Normally only around white guys, assuming we'd all agree. Most blew him off and few ever challenged him. I don't think Beckley shared his views. I hated Beckley but never knew him to screw people over based on race. He was merely an equal opportunity tormentor.

Wright tried to walk by. Garfield put his hand out and moved his face within inches of Wright's.

Li'l V grabbed Garfield's arm. "C'mon, man. We have to get on deck. Birds will be landing soon. Forget about that idiot."

But an audience had gathered around the confrontation.

Wright made a "move along" motion with his hand. "Go on, Garfield. Stick with your buddies."

"Shut the fuck up," McGee said.

Garfield, agitated, pulled away from Li'l V. Two others blocked Garfield as he pursued Wright.

"That's right. Hide behind them, you wuss!"

Garfield broke free and tackled Wright. They both attempted punches, but none landed. They rolled around and

Wright got on top. Like in the typical schoolyard battle, the two appeared destined for a protracted wrestling match. McGee reached down and pulled Wright up by his waist as if he were light as a feather. Garfield jumped up, ready for more. Li'l V held him back.

"What the hell is going on in here?" Beckley yelled as he walked up to the scene. The labyrinth of racks, lockers, and sailors blocked his view of what had actually occurred.

Fights rarely happened in the Navy. The promised severe punishment deterred most. We'd heard that participants would earn three days' bread and water in the brig before anyone asked what happened. Further punishment awaited the instigator. When fights did occur, they happened due to stress after a long time at sea, or in port when someone had one too many drinks. But mere hours into our Med cruise?

McGee's big body blocked Wright and his disheveled shirt. "Nothing going on here."

"Bullshit! Somebody was fighting," Beckley said.

Garfield stared down Wright as if he'd pounce any second.

"We were just horsing around," I said. "McGee claimed nobody here could body slam his big ass."

Wright started to speak, but McGee backed into him, pinning him against a rack.

Beckley put his hands on his hips—his shirtless beer belly protruding. "Shipmates! We don't have time for this horsing around. Get changed and get your asses on deck. We have recovery soon." Beckley stormed off, buying my lie.

A couple of guys manhandled Garfield and pushed him out of the coop to cool off.

"Beckley's gonna find out you lied, Donley," Wright said.

"No, he won't. Because you're gonna keep your mouth

shut." McGee poked his finger at Wright's chest.

"What's the big deal, anyway? All I said was that Li'l V got promoted because—"

"Shut up, Wright. Just shut the hell up. Everybody knew Randolph would make yellow shirt. Everybody knows he deserved it," I said.

"Man, I ain't no racist. I'm just saying—"

McGee waved his hands in front of Wright. "Oh my gosh, shut the fuck up."

We walked out of the coop, leaving Wright to ponder his views on race and reward.

The Bull cut through waters several miles off the coast of Virginia Beach. The flight deck quickly filled up with aircraft. I sat comfortably on the P-16 firefighting truck with a great view of all the action on deck. The crash LPO, Petty Officer Climer, had seen fit to assign me driving duties after a thorough testing of the equipment. Dusk approached on my third time out on deck that first day of the Med cruise. My two rescue men stood behind the truck, talking and joking. All routine. Even for a first day.

Huge stenciled lettering on the island structure read, BEWARE OF JET BLAST, PROPS, AND ROTORS.

An F-14 taxied onto CAT 3 for launch. The yellow shirt lined up the nose wheel with the CAT as he straddled the shuttle slot. He moved off the CAT, behind the foul line, as a green shirt from V-2 Division attached the holdback pendant. Another green shirt circled his finger directing the yellow shirt to advance the Tomcat a few more feet until the launch bar fit securely in the shuttle. The pilot locked his eyes on the yellow shirt, reacting to his direction. The pilot's partner in the back seat looked down and appeared to check instruments in the cockpit.

Two white shirt final checkers looked over the aircraft and gave a thumbs up. After a final check, the green shirt pointed forward, and the yellow shirt signaled the Tomcat pilot to come to full power. The holdback pendant held the bird while flames shot out of the exhaust. With a full complement of weapons, the F-14 needed afterburners for launch. The yellow shirt turned over direction to an officer from V-2 that made final checks and then touched the deck. An operator in the catapult pushed a button, the holdback pendant released, and the Tomcat left the carrier with a roar.

From our parking spot between the bow CATs, I watched Li'l V directing his first few birds onto CAT 1. A senior yellow shirt stood behind him, talking him through the process. He looked a bit awkward, but knowing Li'l V, he would master the process in a short time.

An F-14 taxied behind the JBD (jet blast deflector) behind CAT2. The JBDs protected the awaiting aircraft from the exhaust of the launching aircraft. Most aircraft listed the crew's names under the cockpit. After the steam from the CAT lifted, I noticed this Tomcat had Lieutenant Brad "Skeeter" Davies under the pilot and Lieutenant Roy "Cajun" Babineaux under the back seater. The plane captain, AN Willow, had his name on the side of the nose gear door. I saw this bird and those names every day, sometimes several times a day, but never knew the faces behind the names.

Master Chief Platt walked the deck making sure everything ran smoothly. No one had any doubt about who ran the Bull's flight deck.

Airman "Spalding" Worthington scrambled around aircraft, removing chocks and chains. For a newbie, he picked up new skills quickly and became a strong asset to V-1 Division. His endless energy left his contemporaries scrambling to catch up. Many sailors learned to never volunteer for anything. Spalding always volunteered. I assumed that his farm upbringing of baling hay and shoveling grain gave him a strong work ethic.

Our division officer, Lieutenant Tunball, also walked the deck, a little less confidently than the master chief. Tunball flew the E-2C Hawkeye for a living. Like many pilots, he was serving a required sea tour as part of the ship's company rather than a flight crew. His day entailed paperwork and V-1 Division business. In addition to those duties, he worked on the flight deck for a few hours each day.

Tunball had arrived three months earlier. On the North Atlantic cruise, he had jumped right in with the coolies, chocking and chaining. He impressed us with his hard work and dedication to learn every job in V-1 Division. When we weren't flying planes, he often jogged on the flight deck to keep himself fit. He constantly tucked and pressed his uniform either from an obsessive-compulsive disorder or an insecurity about his appearance. Always adjusting his belt buckle to ensure it lined up with his zipper. Persnickety. His direction of planes bordered on the nerdy side. He had probably read all the standard operating procedure manuals and wanted to follow them to the letter. On the few occasions he addressed us in the ranks—his high-pitched, raspy voice didn't exactly command confidence, but we could tell he really cared. That he really wanted to do a great job. Officers with the rank of lieutenant commander and below were sometimes called "mister." That certainly fit Mr. Tunball.

Returning from a previous launch, the first few birds made their "controlled crashes" as the pilots would say. Master Chief Platt gave a signal regarding the location in which he wanted each bird parked. He would "call the deck."

An F/A-18 caught the four wire, leaving it deep into the landing area close to an area called the crotch. As it started to taxi, I noticed fire in the starboard intake.

"Hey. Hey!" I said, waving at my two rescue men. I put the P-16 firefighting truck's gear in drive and started moving forward. Master Chief Platt halted the aircraft. He pointed to the starboard engine with his left hand, and made a figure-eight motion with his right. This signaled the pilot to restart the engine in hopes of burning out the fire.

One of my crew grabbed the CO_2 extinguisher and stopped next to the master chief.

Engine fires rarely occurred, but when they did, the engine restart typically extinguished the flames. If that didn't work, our crew would try the fire extinguisher.

Petty Officer Climer ran up. "Stay right there, Donley." My job required maneuvering the P-16 where its fire hose and water tank could offer a response of AFFF—a mixture of water and foam.

My heart raced. I tried to focus on my training. I thought about all those fires I fought in Millington with Sergeant Vasquez.

Don't panic, I thought.

The Hornet's pilot looked back and forth between his cockpit controls and the intake. Squadron guys in green and white jerseys ran up—all of them waiting on the pilot.

No one seemed to panic. Every one stood nearby and watched Master Chief Platt's calm signaling. After a few seconds, a small puff of black smoke blew out the back of the engine, and the fire was gone.

As a precaution, we shut down the engines and towed it out of the landing area. I moved the P-16 back to our parking spot. The master chief moved back to his spot to call the deck. Like nothing had happened. Like he dealt with engine fires every day.

It took an hour for me to calm down. Sitting in the crash shack, two other crash guys and I talked about the engine fire and pored over every detail multiple times. The most significant detail was that this event occurred on the first day of the six-month Med cruise. A bad omen perhaps?

"You men did good today," Petty Officer Climer said.

"Us?" I said. "We didn't do much of anything."

Climer took a drag off his cigarette. "You did your job. You didn't panic or do anything stupid. That's half the job."

We chuckled.

"You remembered your training. You remembered the procedures," Climer said.

Sniff.

"I'm glad the master chief was there," I said, sipping my coffee.

Climer sat down by us and pushed his glasses up his nose. "All those yellow shirts should know how to deal with an engine fire. But Master Chief Platt has probably done it a bunch of times. Hell, he was on deck for the Big E fire."

"The who?" one of the crash guys said.

"The Big E. The *Enterprise*. You remember that movie you watched about a fire on the flight deck during 'Nam? There were three big fires around that time. The *Forrestal*, the *Oriskany*, the *Enterprise*. Master Chief was on the Big E during

163

that fire. Killed like thirty guys."

"Dang. I bet he has some stories," I said.

"Don't ask him. He doesn't like to talk about it. His best friend was killed. I heard him talk about it once when he had a few beers. He said bombs and aircraft were exploding all around him. He was on a hose team fighting a fire near the fantail right next to his friend. The deck chief grabbed him to come help with something else. They started running toward the island. There was this big explosion that knocked him and the chief to the ground. He looked back and his friend and the hose team were gone."

"Gone?" I said.

"Into thin air," Climer said. "Except for some body parts. Those guys went through hell. Platt's been in the Navy a long time. Seen it all. But that had to be the worst."

"He was probably a coolie on a flattop in World War II," I said, smiling.

"I wouldn't say that to him. He might kill you." Climer said, with a serious look.

My smile disappeared.

"I'm kidding," Climer said. "He's definitely old school. Been in a long time. Probably forgot more about the flight deck than you know right now."

Two weeks into the cruise, my mind and body became accustomed to the rhythm of flight deck operations and life at sea. Twelve hours on, twelve hours off. A better schedule than other cruises where they'd tell us, "just go to your rack and we'll wake you when it's time to come on back." Most of us hated that, having no idea if we'd get two hours of sleep or six hours of sleep. The Med cruise carried a rhythm.

"You will shit, shower, and shave every day," Beckley once told us. Easy enough. All the stress stayed on the roof—another name for the flight deck. Shipboard life off the roof meant rest and relaxation. Reading or watching a movie. Laundry and haircuts. Writing a letter to our moms or girlfriends.

I liked to wake early and venture to the mess decks for a big breakfast with two eggs over medium, hash browns, bacon, and toast. My daily commute through this 6,000-man city at sea, took me past all the things you find in any city. I walked past sick bay, the post office, and the ship's store. One thing you wouldn't find on the carrier—women. None. Zilch. Nada.

I exited the catwalk behind the island for the planned 0712 start of flight operations.

"Donley!"

I turned my head to find Petty Officer Eppers.

"Master Chief wants you in flight deck control," he said.

I heard nothing good in that sentence. I hadn't spoken with the master chief since the day Li'l V and I received our mess cranking speech. I slowly turned and headed toward flight deck control. Like the long march to the principal's office.

Maybe that little weasel Wright told on me for lying to Beckley about the fight, I thought. Maybe he wanted to chew me out for yelling at Beckley.

I'd heard of guys going to see the master chief in the division office. He had a sign over his desk that read, LACK OF PREPARATION ON YOUR PART DOES NOT CONSTITUTE AN EMERGENCY ON MY PART. This man meant business. Flight deck business. Naval business. Military bearing on steroids.

I walked into the yellow shirt shack on the way to flight

deck control—my teeth on the verge of a minor chatter. My palms moistened. Yellow shirts donned their float coats and took the last few puffs of their cigarettes. Beckley sat there drinking black coffee. I fought through the smoke toward flight deck control. Like Li'l V and I had done, I paused at the doorway. But I didn't have Li'l V to urge me through. I looked behind for help, but no yellow shirt came to my rescue. They adjusted their headsets attached to their helmets and walked out one after another. I had to face this one on my own.

Master Chief Platt sat near the handler, his yellow shirt full of belly hiding his gold belt buckle.

"Sir, I can only do so many fucking things at once," the master chief said to the handler.

I missed the handler's comment that caused the master chief's response. The lieutenant commander simply nodded. I wanted no part of him either.

Master Chief Platt took a Camel cigarette from his pack and tapped it on the face of his watch, packing the non-filtered death stick. He lit it with his Zippo lighter, which had the chief's anchor emblem and two silver stars. The man didn't appear angry—or worse, hungry. He seemed emotionless. I'd be making no appeal. No excuses. The master chief spoke, and you obeyed. No questions. No hesitations.

I rubbed the toes of my flight deck boots on the backs of my pant legs in a fruitless attempt for a shine. Couldn't hurt, I figured. I reared back my shoulders and forged ahead. After all, I had "CRASH" adorned across my chest. I wasn't some little coolie anymore. I had earned a valued position in V-1 Division.

I approached him and he gave me a "what the hell do you want?" look.

"Master Chief, uh...Ep...Eppers said you wanted to see

me?" My stuttering matching Epper's."

He took a drag off his smoke. "Donley, right?"

"Yes." Surprised that he knew my name, I glanced down at my shirt to see if he had read my name on my jersey. We didn't stencil our names on our flight deck jerseys as we did on our dungaree shirts. He did know my name.

"Chief Fitch said you'd make a good yellow shirt."

"He did? Cool!" I cringed inside at my remark. Cool? No. No. No. A terrible response to the master chief.

"Well, is he right?"

"Uh...yeah...I mean yes. I can do it. I want it," a smile began forming on my face.

The master chief's stern demeanor, and lack of anything close to a smile, wiped the smile from my face.

"I have one rule. There's the right way, the wrong way, my way, your way, and the Navy way. We do things the Navy way. Got it?"

"Got it," I answered, matter-of-factly.

In reality, the master chief had many rules, which he always prefaced with "I have one rule." Some of his other rules were the "lack of emergency on your part..." one and the "keep your head on a swivel" one that many used. Classics such as "hope for the best, plan for the worst" and "think before speaking." And my personal favorite, "don't fuck up."

"I'm putting you in Fly 2 with Eppers. It can get pretty hectic there, but you stick with him, and do everything he says. He's a damn good yellow shirt. Any questions?"

"No, Master Chief." I had many questions but knew better than to ask him.

"Alright then, get to it."

I did a rough about-face and then did a fist pump passing

through the doorway. I looked up to find Beckley.

"Well. I hear they're making you a yellow shirt." He shook his head. "I don't see it." He folded his arms. "I remember when I made yellow shirt. Scary as hell. All those million-dollar planes moving around. One mistake can cost millions of dollars. Kill somebody. I don't think you can handle it. I think you'll wash out and then we'll put you back with your little crash crew buddies. Humph." He poured out his coffee and walked out.

Hardly a congratulatory or motivational speech from the division leading petty officer. I suppose he meant to scare me. To rattle my confidence. It worked.

CHAPTER 18

Petty Officer Climer offered a joking, yet encouraging tone. "I can't believe you're gonna abandon your crash crew, Donley. Where's your loyalty?"

"Yeah, man. Just when we get you trained, you run off to be a glorified traffic cop," Garfield chimed in.

I smiled and began emptying my locker. "C'mon, guys. I—"

"We're messing with you, Donley," Climer said. "You'll make a good yellow shirt. You'll also make a good on-scene leader. I expect you to run up and be the first one to raise your hands on fire drills. You got the training."

"Sure," I said, extending my hand to Climer.

I headed out the door for the twenty-second walk to the yellow shirt shack. No welcoming committee greeted me. I found an empty locker and stowed my gear. Critical items, such as cigarettes, a coffee cup, and a novel for downtime. We didn't carry anything in our pockets on deck, for fear it might fall out and foul an aircraft's intake. In a small sheath strapped to my belt, I carried a folding knife and a Dzus key, used in pilot rescue for quick access to cockpits.

I rubbed the front of my newly stenciled yellow shirt with the words "FLY 2" across my chest and then put a lanyard, connected to a whistle, around my neck. When moving aircraft with tow tractors, we used whistles to signal a stop for the plane captain riding the brakes in the cockpit. I'd also been issued a pair of wands—flashlights with cones for directing aircraft at night.

Eppers, Li'l V, and a few yellow shirts walked in for a break.

"Whooo. Yes, sir. Look at you," Li'l V said. "Just like I said in boot camp when we got our orders. I said we'd be yellow shirts."

I began buttoning my yellow float coat. Unlike my yellow shirt, this life vest and cranial helmet appeared to have years of experience. The float coat had numerous black marks and fading. I made sure the tiny CO_2 cartridges showed no punctures and that the internal inflation bladder had no holes. The cranial helmet's white reflective stickers had rubbed off in the corners. My helmet had no radio headset, known as "Mickey Mouse Ears." No one would want to hear from me on the radio. Not from a newbie.

"You ready to get st…started?" Eppers said, with an unlit cigarette dangling from his lips."

"I guess," I said, hands in the air.

"You guess?" Li'l V said. "You ain't a little nervous, are you?"

I poured myself some coffee. "A little. Yeah."

The coffee offended me. I added the requisite amount of sugar and cream to overcome its harshness. Most crews were issued one cloth filter per month with their large can of coffee. The coffee got nastier as that month progressed. I understood why no one stole coffee, but they did steal coffee filters.

After one sip, I poured it out. "OK, Eppers. I'm ready," I

said, strapping on my helmet.

"Well, I'm not. We have a yellow shirt briefing first," he said, gulping his black coffee.

The yellow shirts gathered around the Ouija board in flight deck control before each launch to learn which birds needed to launch first, where some would park after landing, and any other instructions from the handler.

I walked into flight deck control with the other yellow shirts, two hours after my most recent visit with the master chief. He sat in the same location, nursing his non-filtered Camel cigarette. I listened carefully to all that was said, nodding, and acting as if I knew what it meant. Acting as if I belonged. Li'l V nodded and probably understood everything. I had no experience. I had nothing to contribute. But I wore a yellow shirt. I'd now be considered a "leader" on the flight deck.

The briefing ended and we filtered out one-by-one. I followed Eppers to the landing area in front of the six-pack.

Eppers leaned over and yelled to overcome the noise of the starting aircraft. "I'll give you some easy ones to direct until you get the hang of it. Just stick by me."

A brown-shirted plane captain stood by his F-14 Tomcat and gave a thumbs up. This told us it was ready for launch. Eppers rubbed his arms and pointed his thumbs out, signaling the coolies to remove the chocks and chains. I stood behind Eppers as he motioned the F-14 to come forward until it cleared the Six-pack. He then pointed to a yellow shirt in Fly 3 near the arresting gear wires. That Tomcat eventually found its way to CAT 3 for launch.

An A-6 Intruder pulled out from EL 1 next to the island.

Eppers stood behind me at the top of the six-pack. "You're

going to do this one and then pass it to him," he said, pointing to Li'l V who stood near JBD 1, the jet blast deflector for CAT 1.

I turned to look at him. "Wait. What?"

"You ca...can do this," he said, patting my shoulders. "Get your arm up."

I held my right arm straight up, notifying the other yellow shirt that I was ready to receive the aircraft.

I swallowed hard and adjusted my protective eye goggles with my left hand. The other yellow shirt glanced to his left and noticed me. He turned the aircraft in my direction and looked at me again quickly, then pointed at me. The pilot jerked his head from over his left shoulder and looked directly at me. I began waving my arms from the sides of my head to my shoulders directing the plane forward. Eppers had said he would tap my side if I needed to turn the aircraft. He offered no touch, so I kept flapping my arms, keeping the A-6 on a straight path.

Does this pilot know that I don't know what I'm doing? I thought.

The Intruder seemed like a house on wheels coming directly at me. The pilot and bombardier/navigator in the seat next to him sat nearly ten feet up. A pilot with a million dollar education in a twenty-two-million-dollar airplane relied on me, a nineteen-year-old kid with a high school diploma.

I noticed an aviation ordnanceman in a red shirt walk by out of the corner of my eye. I heard an S-3 take off CAT 2. A brown shirt on EL2 held up his hand, signaling that his bird was ready. Flight deck operations didn't stop because I was directing this A-6. Everyone's routine continued. But nothing seemed routine about this for me. I had asked for this. I wanted my yellow shirt. It was terrifying.

Eppers grabbed my right earpiece and pulled it slightly

away from my head. "Get ready to pass it!"

I looked to my left. Li'l V held up his hand ready to receive the bird. I awkwardly pointed with both hands toward Li'l V, like the kid in little league basketball that doesn't know what to do with the ball and quickly throws it to the nearest teammate. Li'l V directed the aircraft toward him with confidence. A bit of swagger, perhaps. He wanted the aircraft like a teammate that wanted the ball. He wanted to take the game-winning shot.

This was no ball, though. It was a naval bomber with experienced pilots. Those men in that machine trusted the yellow shirt to guide them around a crowded flight deck, sometimes within inches of another aircraft. They trusted us to direct them near the deck edge where, from their view, they saw nothing but water on one side of them. They trusted the deck crews' training and experience to get them either to the CAT, or to their parking spot. In addition, they depended on hundreds of other experienced and dedicated squadron workers to keep their aircraft in peak operational condition.

I'd performed the most basic of maneuvers. Directing a plane in a straight line. The second and third times were no less terrifying, but I slowly developed some confidence. After recovery, I walked in the yellow shirt shack with a few aircraft moves under my belt.

Eppers stood up, a cigarette dangling from his mouth. "Hey, ya'll, here's Do...Donley directing." He proceeded to mock me with a furious waving of the arms and a frightened look.

The room looked at him, pointed at me and laughed. I laughed with them. I'm sure I didn't look as ridiculous as Epper's exaggerated imitation, but every pilot and deck worker probably knew I was a yellow shirt newbie.

Two weeks later, I had directed, moved, and parked every bird for every spot in Fly 2—either taxiing pilots or with a tow tractor. I no longer looked like a newbie and settled on a directing style that was within regulations. Some had more flair, but I stuck with the basic motions.

At the end of our pre-launch yellow shirt meeting in flight deck control, I began to walk away, having understood everything in contrast to my first meeting.

Chief Fitch grabbed my arm. "I want you to spot CAT 3 on this launch."

"What? Me?" I said, pointing my thumb to my chest.

"Yep. You have to learn sometime. I'll stand behind you."

For the past week, I had buttoned my flight deck vest and strapped on my cranial helmet with confidence. Now, I walked out of the yellow shirt shack, nervous. A little less confident. The fears of that first day of directing crept back in.

All the aircraft direction I had done involved a few basic principles. Spotting an aircraft on the catapult involved numerous principles, safety issues, and interaction with other individuals.

I walked over to CAT 3 with Chief Fitch. "The most important thing is to get the bird lined up straight on the CAT. The last thing you want is a spin-off."

Pilots hated spin-offs, meaning when we directed them off the CAT and to the back of the line for launch. Pilots wanted to fly, not sit on the deck. Most spin-offs happened due to a malfunction of the aircraft on the deck. Then they'd spin-off for a parking spot. Yellow shirts could not help that. But a yellow shirt lining up the aircraft crooked on the CAT causing a spin-off drew the ire of the pilot, the squadron crews, the air boss, and pretty much everyone on the aircraft carrier.

I stood on CAT 3 next to the chief while a helo took off behind us before launch. I had stood behind Eppers several times while he spotted CATs so I knew the basic moves and order. He talked me through much of what he did, but between his stuttering and the deafening noise, I heard little.

"Get ready," Chief Fitch said, tapping my shoulder. "I'll let you know if you need to adjust left or right."

I nodded.

We straddled the CAT for two reasons. As the aircraft approached, the shuttle would move from the end of the CAT, between our legs, and to the launch position. The straddle also aided in lining up the aircraft.

A Fly 3 yellow shirt standing between the arresting gear taxied an F/A-18 Hornet. He looked over his shoulders to see if I was ready. I raised my hand as nervously as I had on that first day I wore the yellow shirt. He passed the bird to me. I kept it at a forty-five degree angle over the lowered jet blast director, until I determined the right time to turn the Hornet toward the CAT. I made the turn and guessed correctly, only needing a slight adjustment left and then back right to keep the nose gear lined up with the CAT slot.

Steam rose under my feet and floated across the deck.

Chief Fitch grabbed my shoulder and leaned in. "Spread his wings."

I had forgotten that basic step, but quickly spread my arms and opened my hands, signaling the pilot to unfold his wings and open his flaps. I made a fist to stop the aircraft. Chief Fitch patted my right arm, motioning us to move to the other side of the foul line. A green shirt knelt down next to the nose gear and motioned for me to move the bird straight forward. Once the green shirt ensured that the launch bar and holdback pendant were in place, he signaled me to put the aircraft in full power. I looked fore and aft, making sure we had a clear deck and pointed my right arm forward with my left arm folded up. The pilot went to full power, and I passed the aircraft to a V-2 catapult officer, called the shooter. He performed the final checks and ordered a worker in the catwalk to push a button, releasing the F/A-18 down the catapult and into flight.

Unlike during that first day two weeks before, I wanted to run back to the catapult for another. The adrenalin rush of an aircraft launching in full power, only feet from me, offered a thrill greater than any amusement park ride. It's exciting if one is only a bystander, but to play a small part in it added to the excitement. I spotted eight more birds that launch with Chief Fitch offering the occasional pointers.

I walked toward the six-pack with Chief Fitch. "Can I keep spotting?" I asked, like a little kid wanting some candy.

He smiled. "Yeah, I guess. Just don't fuck up," he said, offering the universal admonition given in the Navy when one embarks on a task.

I spotted well over a hundred birds on CAT 3 over the course of a few days. The operation had become second nature to me until one new element was introduced. On certain days, some of the aircraft carried nuclear weapons. We knew them by the marines with rifles that guarded them and the red safety pin that hung under the wing next to the bomb. As the aircraft lined up for launch, I held my hands in the air signaling the aircrew to hold their hands in the air so they didn't accidently touch any controls they shouldn't. AOs (aviation ordnancemen) removed the safety pins and we resumed with the launch. Those red safety pins told a story of the serious business that an aircraft carrier performed. They alerted me to the important job

I held. The responsibility the Navy had placed on me. All the little attention-to-detail things our CCs put us through in boot camp made sense. Chief Smith's missile lectures ran through my mind.

All the aircraft required the pilot to engage full power for launch. None fueled that rush more than the F-14 Tomcat in afterburner. The extra power needed to propel a Tomcat off the flight deck shot flames from the exhaust. At night, it lit up the deck. The only ones that didn't like it were the one or two guys standing near the JBDs. They had to cover their faces due to the heat.

I always noticed the pilot's call signs and wondered where they came from. I spotted a Tomcat with "Diver" stenciled on the side. I assumed this pilot liked to swim or perhaps almost drowned once, and his fellow pilots had given him that name for mocking reasons.

The F-14 engaged full power. After I passed direction to the shooter, I glanced at the rear of the aircraft. Two white shirts, called final checkers, walked the length of the Tomcat and knelt at the rear of each side at launch. These were senior men in their squadrons who made a final inspection of an aircraft before launch. They offered thumbs up if all was ready. The white shirt on the starboard side of this F-14 dropped his arms and pushed his neck in to look at something on the aircraft. I noticed a small panel pop down on the Tomcat. The shooter stopped shaking his two fingers for continued full power, and began to kneel to shoot the bird. The final checker put his arms up in a cross pattern to halt the launch. I began to signal the same but realized that neither the shooter, nor the green shirt in the catapult about to press the button, saw the foul deck signal.

I lurched forward, grabbed the shooter's arm, and yelled,

"Foul deck! Foul deck!"

There really wasn't a foul deck, but he knew what I meant. He threw his arms up in a cross pattern as did three others. He waited to power down the Tomcat until he ensured there was no chance of an inadvertent launch. If the holdback pendent released and the shuttle pulled the aircraft at low power, the Tomcat would end up in the water. The shooter stepped toward the aircraft and pulled back on his thumb signaling the pilot to throttle down.

A squadron chief walked up to the final checker, waving his hands in indignation for causing this launch to abort. After twenty seconds of hands on hips and pointing at the aircraft, the chief circled his finger in the air letting everyone know this F-14 would need to spin off. No launch for the aircraft. The pilot unsnapped his oxygen mask and mouthed something we could not hear. I assumed it to be laced with profanity.

I walked over to the final checker. "What was wrong?"

"Let's put it this way. That pilot will thank me later."

Attention to detail may have saved that pilot's life and was even more important when things became second nature. When someone got cocky. When complacency set in. When a bird fell from the sky.

CHAPTER 19

The shores of France disappeared in the distance as we headed to sea after a few days in port. The Riviera offered us some unpleasant weather, and I kept switching from wearing my foul weather jacket to going without it. I had no complaints, though, because I knew the guys below decks craved the fresh air we experienced above on a daily basis.

A few birds began moving about the deck as we prepared for the first launch of the day. As the carrier turned into the wind, flight deck personnel leaned a few degrees forward to overcome the air being forced over the deck. I noticed a wall of water ahead—a strong rain shower that would soak us. As we pushed through it, a few guys took cover under wings. I didn't have that luxury since I stood in a position to direct aircraft behind the JBD (jet blast deflector) for CAT 2.

A few drops hit my face as the wave of rain shower came over the bow. I turned aft, and what felt like a water hose hit my back and legs. It passed so quickly that my front side remained dry. One of those odd things that happens at sea.

I taxied an F/A-18 toward JBD 2 and instructed the pilot to spread the fighter's wings. Everyone on deck waited for the H-3 Sea King helicopter to take off from Spot #3 near the crotch, the location where the landing area ends and the bow begins.

The H-3 provided support for pilot rescue or if a sailor went over the side. Typically, two H-3s flew near the carrier during flight operations. They were always the first to launch and the last to recover. They produced little prop wash compared to the massive six-bladed rotors of an H-53. More than once, I reached for a padeye while those big helos blew at my body.

I stood about fifty feet away, holding a closed fist in front of my chest, notifying the pilot to hold his brakes and maintain position. Eppers held his fist in the same way, holding an A-6 on CAT 3. Spalding, wearing a blue shirt, ran from stacking chocks next to the island, and stood ready to break down chocks and chains from an F-14 at the top of the six-pack near me. Rather than turning aft in the rain shower, his front side was soaked, and as he turned, I noticed his backside was dry.

Blue shirts removed chocks and chains from the helo and the pilot received signals to begin his ascent. As the helo rose about twenty feet, the tail section ripped apart from the main fuselage. The tail rotor kept turning and the helo swung wildly up and left. It floated a brief moment and started coming back down to the deck. The main rotor blades dug into the deck, spraying small pieces of rotor in every direction, but mostly aft.

Eppers jumped up to get the attention of the A-6 pilot on CAT 3. He moved his hands back and forth under his neck, telling the pilot to kill his engines. Spalding looked at me, arms extended, as if asking what to do. I gave the pilot of the Hornet whom I had been directing, open hands: an unofficial signal that "I'd be right back" and "don't move." He didn't see me, as he stared at the helo, now fully crashed on deck, but in one main piece. I ran toward the crash site where Chief Fitch had already assumed command of the situation. Two teams dragged fire hoses to the site, although we saw no fire. Both team leads kept their hands on the nozzle ready to release the water.

I looked aft and noticed about thirty men had hit the deck, presumably protecting themselves from the rotor debris that had shot down the deck like bullets.

The helo's starboard side door opened from the inside, a welcome sign of survivors.

"Go take chocks to that A-6," I yelled at Spalding.

I worried the A-6 on CAT 3 needed securing after Eppers shut down the engines.

Chief Fitch walked around every inch of the downed aircraft looking for fire. One by one, the helo crew emerged, bruised and slightly broken. Only one required a stretcher.

Petty Officer Climer ordered the large 20K forklift to push the helo upright so a tractor could tow it to EL 1 for a trip to the hangar bay. Several squadron guys followed, carrying a few of the larger pieces.

All aircraft held their positions, as we conducted two full foreign object damage (FOD) walkdowns, searching for anything that an aircraft engine intake could suck in. These FOD walkdowns occurred two to three times per day as we looked for screws, trash, pieces of the flight deck surface, or anything that did not belong on the deck. As a little over 100 men walked along, we found numerous pieces of the rotor blades, which we placed in bags.

A few pieces of rotor blade were found in the intake of the A-6 that Eppers had shut down. His action saved many man-hours of work and thousands of dollars by preserving one or both engines. For Epper's quick thinking in a stressful situation, a rear admiral gave him a formal letter of commendation.

The long-delayed launch that day resumed after a different H-3 Sea King safely launched from Spot 3 and flew into position. Miraculously, no one was injured. No one took a piece of rotor blade to the face. No hunk of metal knocked anyone down.

"How the hell did we get out of that clean?" Master Chief Platt said to Chief Fitch as he walked by us.

Another day in that dangerous environment. Another day on the flight deck.

Unlike the engine fire on day one of the Med cruise, the helo crash seemed like another day at the office. Sure, we talked about it over the next several days, but no one held any grave concern. No talk of a bad omen.

"That's our accident. You have one every cruise. Now we got it out of the way," Beckley said, walking through the yellow shirt shack and into flight deck control.

"Don't li...listen to him," Eppers said. "We might have ten more crashes. I've seen it."

Everyone knew better than to believe what Eppers had seen in the past. He embellished half his stories, and the other half he made up from scratch. We'd hear him tell a story to one person only to offer a wildly changed variation to someone else. Every story entertained us, but they were never true. We loved his Vietnam War stories because that war ended when he was only twelve years old.

I egged him on. "Really, Eppers. You've seen ten crashes in one cruise?"

"Yep. Back in 'Nam. We had these planes always coming ba...back with a wing on fire or a pilot shot or something. They'd land...land rough or go off in the port catwalk. Happened once a week."

Li'l V coughed, "Bullshit!" his cough masking the interjection.

Eppers lit another smoke, ever the chain-smoker. "It ain't bullshit. Ask any of the old guys. Planes flying missions and getting shot at by the Japs."

"Japs?" Li'l V said. "You mean Vietnamese?"

"Yeah. Vietmanese. That's what I said." Eppers always mispronounced Vietnamese by switching the N and the M.

No less than eight yellow shirts roared with laughter.

"This one pilot landed and was so out of it, I had to climb up, open the cockpit, and put on the brakes." Eppers stood and acted out the scene.

More cried, "Bullshit!" and some laughed as we headed on deck for launch.

Huffer starting units blew aircraft engines to life, and plane captains asked us to send their birds to the CATs.

I noticed Li'l V spotting CAT 2 while standing off to the side of the CAT. On occasion, the catapult crew asked us, for our safety, not to straddle the catapult slot while retracting the shuttle. That forced the yellow shirt to spot the CAT without the benefit of standing in line with the nose of the aircraft. Not an impossible task, but one requiring some experience. Li'l V, of course, picked this up easily.

After numerous times spotting the CAT, I'd had no spin offs. Yet.

A green shirt catapult worker came over to me as I raised my hand to spot an S-3 Viking on the CAT. "Hey, need you to stand off the CAT while we look at something."

I nodded as if to communicate "no problem," but inside, I hesitated.

I worked the S-3 into position as everyone started their normal functions. As the Viking nose gear reached the stopping point, I realized I had the bird misaligned. The catapult crew looked at it, a few senior flight deck workers in khaki pants looked at it, and worst of all, Master Chief Platt looked at it.

Platt immediately raised his finger and twirled it in the air. "Spin it off."

He walked by me shaking his head. "Get this one right."

Fortunately, the S-3 was the last plane to launch from CAT 3 so the spin off and respot happened quickly. And the second time I lined it up perfectly. I cringed at the crap I'd take in the yellow shirt locker after recovery.

After the last bird launched, I headed over to the six-pack area, readying for recovery.

"It's always fun to see you yellow shirts screw something up," AE2 Jakes said, smirking.

Jakes wore a green shirt for one of the F-14 squadrons and maintained the aircraft's electrical systems. We'd had several conversations since the start of the cruise while waiting for his birds to get parked. He'd always initiated the joking.

I folded my arms. "Yeah, Jakes, it's not easy having the hardest job on the flight deck. If I flunked out of high school like you, I could have been a wire puller. Isn't that what you do all day?"

He scoffed. "Shit, I turned down offers from Harvard and Yale to make sure these Tomcats protect your sorry ass. Somebody has to do the brainwork. You're just a glorified parking attendant."

"What do you do every day? I see you walking around these Tomcats acting like you're doing something," I said. "Then do you go down to your squadron shop for Coke and Smoke? I mean, do you do any real work?"

"Hell, I—"

Slam!

An F-14 Tomcat landed, interrupting our conversation.

"I guess you better get ready to pretend like you're working," I said.

I walked down to the aft end of the six-pack where we typically parked the first F-14 during a recovery. A near empty deck made that an easy parking spot. A lone EA-6B Prowler that failed to launch due to a maintenance issue stood on EL1. Master Chief Platt made a cutting motion with the pretend blade of his left hand to the inside of his right arm, signaling his order to park the Tomcat in the six-pack. Eppers received direction of the bird from the gear puller and then passed it on to me. I gave the Tomcat a wide berth with the room I had, making for an easy spot. We parked Tomcats on the six-pack tightly so they'd all fit.

I made two mistakes. First, I assumed that since I had done this so many times, my depth perception was on target. Second, I failed to have someone give me a thumbs up at the rear of the aircraft, indicating an "all clear." I taxied the Tomcat to a stop, gave the command to insert chocks and chains, and shut down the aircraft.

Three squadron workers from the EA-6B came toward me, two with hands in the air, and one shouting what I assumed was his displeasure with me, but I could not hear him over the flight deck noise.

Unbeknownst to me, the rear of the Tomcat had scraped the nose of the Prowler. The sinking feeling disappeared quickly as I ducked under the Tomcat to spot the next one. Parking the aircraft took precedence. After recovery, I looked at the damage I'd caused. The Tomcat squadron guys, especially Jakes, gave me mocking applause. The squadron chief for the EA-6B gave me a butt chewing.

"Do you know what you've done?" he said.

"Sorry, Chief. Looks like a bad scratch," I said. I knew any crunch was bad, but I assumed a little paint would fix the scratch.

"Do you realize the electronics that are inside this nose? Do you realize how long it will take to make sure those systems are not damaged?"

"Sorry, Chief."

He dismissed me with his hand. "Just get the fuck outta here."

I noticed him having a lively discussion with Master Chief Platt. My sinking feeling returned, tenfold.

I walked into the yellow shirt shack to thunderous applause.

"Yeah, King Crunch," Eppers said.

We called any non-flight aircraft accident a crunch.

I shook my head, knowing my cockiness, lack of attention to detail, and overall complacency caused the accident.

Several others chimed in.

"Man, that squadron chief was chewing your ass."

"Nothing Master Chief hates more than crunches."

"He's gonna have your ass."

"Dude, you're fucked."

While every comment was true, that last one summed it up, nicely.

A few others chimed in, some laughed, and I lit a cigarette. Master Chief Platt walked in, and the room quieted down.

He walked past me and stopped at the threshold to flight deck control. "Donley...come here."

Those may have been the last three words I had ever wanted to hear. Few individuals have the power of a master chief, who can end your life as you know it.

I stubbed out my freshly lit cigarette and faced my destiny. I expected a rapid explosiveness of the F word would cause others to flee flight deck control. Fortunately, my bladder was empty, because uncontrolled urination seemed like a certain result.

The master chief sat down and lit his Camel.

I approached him like a dog with its tail between its legs that had crapped on the carpet. "Master Chief."

"Donley, there's nothing I hate more than getting my ass reamed from a squadron chief. It's even worse when they're right. You had two fuck ups today. Not one, but two. Can you explain this to me?" He leaned his head back, his eyes burning a hole through of my skull.

He had yet to raise his voice. I imagined him holding that back for the worthless and feeble answer I would give. I thought of saying, "no excuse," or something simple. I knew that some long explanation of what happened would only exacerbate the situation. I decided on honesty. It's always risky, but I forged ahead.

"I got cocky, Master Chief. I just got cocky. It won't happen again."

I stood firm, almost at full attention, but inside, I cowered in a corner waiting for the powerful blows that were sure to come.

He looked at me without speaking, drawing out the torture. After several seconds, I glanced off to the side and considered making a run for it.

He took a long drag off his non-filtered death stick and blew smoke past me. "Alright. Get the fuck out of here. Don't let it happen again," he said, and turned to talk to Chief Fitch.

I backed away slowly and cautiously. I walked into the

yellow shirt shack, somewhat in shock.

"What did he say," Li'l V asked.

"Don't let it happen again," I said, sitting down.

Li'l V threw up his hands. "That's it? You lucky bastard."

"Yeah, I guess."

Realizing my fortune, I wanted to jump for joy at successfully emerging from the high-pressure situation. However, that seemed like another act of cockiness.

After a short break, we began suiting up for the next launch. Wright, Beckley's stooge, stuck his head in the door, smiling. "Donley. Mr. Tunball wants to see you. You have to go see the old man."

I dropped my head.

"Whoa," Eppers said.

"Holy shit," Li'l V said. "Now you really are fucked."

I'd heard of guys seeing the captain of the ship, or the old man as we all called him, after a crunch. I thought it a myth.

How did he find out so quickly? I thought.

Ten minutes after surviving the master chief, I again made my way into flight deck control where Division Officer Tunball stood, tucking in part of his flight deck jersey and smoothing back his hair.

"Sir," I said.

"Donley. I know you've already spoken with the master chief. However, the captain witnessed your crunch and wants to speak to you about it. Let's go."

I didn't need to ask why or what would be said. I knew.

I wasn't in any condition to see the Old Man in regards to appearance. I shaved at the end of my shift so whiskers darkened my face. My boots held no shine. The dungaree pants and yellow shirt I wore carried a day's worth of exhaust and flight deck grime. I could feel that my hair pointed in multiple directions from wearing my cranial helmet.

What a fine first impression I'll make, I thought.

I followed Lieutenant Tunball up five ladders within the island structure toward the bridge. These areas, from the flight deck to the bridge, were known as the Captain's Passageway. Some sailors did their temporary duty keeping these areas immaculate for the many dignitaries that the brass led through them. They cleaned and painted them constantly. I looked and felt out of place in these passageways. I noticed the words "Officer's Country" stenciled on several doors. These spaces were off limits to us enlisted peons.

We reached the threshold to the bridge.

"Permission to enter the bridge," Lieutenant Tunball said, standing at attention.

I mirrored him.

Lieutenant Tunball may have been a nerd, but he seemed a good man to have at my side at this particular moment. He knew how to wade through the pomp and circumstance of meeting the captain. Officers were gentleman; we enlisted were something one rung below that. They used strong interjections; we cussed. They drank wine; we drank beer.

The officer of the deck turned, "Permission granted."

I had seen the captain twice before. Once while he walked across the flight deck in port with some men in uniforms from another country. The other was during a general address he gave the entire Air Department at an assembly.

The quarterdeck literature offered his biography. Captain William J. Cochran graduated from the Naval Academy in the 1960s, third in his class. He flew F-4 fighters in Vietnam under the call sign "Warlock." Rumors suggested that he evaded capture after getting shot down behind enemy lines. The man oozed naval business. The business of war.

I saw his lanky body filling the large captain's chair to the left of the bridge. A sailor, wearing inspection-ready dungarees, stood at the helm steering the carrier. Several others busied themselves with gadgets or talking on phones. Tons of activity but little noise.

"Captain! I'm reporting with Petty Officer Donley," Tunball said.

The captain turned and looked at us. He curled his finger for us to approach.

We stepped over, me a half step behind Tunball, trying to hide behind him.

"Donley," the captain said. He cleared his throat. "How much money in electronics is there in the nose of a Prowler?" His deep voice commanded respect.

I started to say one thousand dollars, then thought of going big and saying one million. Maybe the question was rhetorical. I chose truth again.

"I...I'm not sure, sir."

"Well, it's a hell of lot more than you make in one year. There's nothing more important to me than safety on the flight deck, but after that comes protecting the equipment the American taxpayer has provided us."

Tunball stood silently.

I thought of various punishments he'd give me. Three months of making bug juice again. Reduction in rank and working as a coolie. Maybe he'd send me to some dark, deep hole in the ship, scraping rust.

The captain looked out to sea and looked back at me. "Do you think you can be more careful?"

"Yeah...yes, sir!"

"Carry on," the captain said.

I didn't move, unsure of proper protocol. Lieutenant Tunball motioned with his eyes for us to leave. I bolted out of the bridge, Tunball three steps behind me.

We made our descent to flight deck control.

Tunball put his hand on my shoulder. "Let's not ever do that again, OK, Donley?"

"Yes, sir."

CHAPTER 20

I walked into the hangar bay with McGee for a liberty boat ride to Alexandria, Egypt. We had purchased tickets for a bus to Cairo to see the pyramids.

"Damn!" McGee said, noticing the line to board a boat. "We'll have to wait three hours."

"Nah. Maybe half that," I said, feeling optimistic.

After weeks at sea, I would have waited eight hours to get off the ship for the day. To walk on dry land. To eat food not slapped on my tray in the mess deck. To see something I'd only read about in books. To break the monotony of our daily job.

Aircraft carriers rarely pulled into a pier in foreign ports due to the carrier's size, or due to the country we visited feeling uneasy about the nuclear weapons on board. So, the carrier anchored about a mile offshore and several liberty boats transported us back and forth. No one enjoyed the wait, but the liberty boat ride offered a chance for a cool breeze and a nice view of the land. Drunk sailors in a bouncing boat presented another experience altogether. Two kinds of sailors made the return trip from the pier to the ship: those who were drunk, and those who were holding the drunk over the side as they vomited.

Fortunately, our wait lasted under two hours. Once on

shore, we boarded the bus and took in the sights and sounds of Egypt. Horns honked incessantly. Merchants peddled their wares to sailors. Women walked in tennis shoes but covered themselves in the traditional garb of the Middle East.

The Great Sphinx stood guard as we approached the pyramids of Giza. I noticed camels moving about the area. I'd assumed the pyramids to be made of steps we could climb. However, some of the massive stones were as big as houses.

A camel driver approached us. "Hey, American. You want to ride? Five dollars."

"Oh, hell yeah," McGee said, offering up the five dollars.

The camel driver shouted a command, and the camel lowered itself so that we could climb aboard. A nasty, white foam oozed from the camel's mouth. Hardly inviting. Another command, and he led us around the pyramids for a bumpy ride.

When we finished the trip, the camel driver looked up at us. "OK. Ride over."

Noticing we were several feet up, I said, "Alright. Tell the camel to get back down."

"Five dollars to bring camel down," he said.

"What? You son of a bitch," McGee said, agitated.

"Just chill," I said, giving the camel driver five dollars.

He lowered the camel and we hopped off.

Every liberty port offered some trap for sailors and many paid a high price. We learned our lesson and decided to call it a learning experience. Five dollars for a funny story and a break from the flight deck routine.

An aircraft carrier is longer than three football fields and nearly as wide as one—covering 4.5 acres. I'd walked or run nearly every foot of it and learned to park aircraft in most of the spots on deck. As we reached the fifth month of the Med cruise, I had managed to trade with Li'l V a few times and work Fly 1. I liked standing on the bow late at night all alone, taxiing an F/A-18 to its parking spot. Even with all the aircraft and personnel, that unique situation put me with one aircraft on the bow, alone. A surreal experience.

I made a similar swap with a Fly 3 yellow shirt and worked as the gear puller for a few recoveries. I liked spotting the CAT, but I loved working as the gear puller with the responsibility to signal a clear landing area. Pilots brought their aircraft into a level approach, caught one of the four arresting gear wires, and then came to a very abrupt, but safe landing. I'd raise my hand as the first person to direct the pilot after his controlled crash.

I stared into the endless ocean and enjoyed its beauty. The Mediterranean Sea offered a comforting presence when smooth-as-glass waters met the adjoining sky. Lost in the quietness of the moment, I thought of home and the time remaining on that long cruise. And what I'd do when I got home.

That entire sequence raced through my head in a split second as I shifted my focus to the F/A-18 Hornet on final approach to land at near 150 MPH, approximately fifty feet from me.

The howl of the Hornet grew louder as it slammed on the deck and went to full power. Excessive noise and excessive power. Hallmarks of naval aviation. After the pilot throttled down, I instructed him to release his brakes, and I waited for the green shirt tailhook runner to signal that the tailhook cleared the arresting gear wire. Then, the pilot raised his tailhook and taxied out of the landing area. I waved my hands, signaling to Chief Fitch, who'd tell other yellow shirts where to park it.

Unlike the Hornet, the C-2 aircraft seemed to land at a snail's pace. Its enormous propellers turned so fast, they appeared as a blur. As other aircraft shut down their engines, the flight deck noise reduced to the humming of the C-2. Most aircraft taxied within only a few feet of me. For this one, I moved several more feet away giving the propellers a wide berth.

Its official name is the C-2 Greyhound and is used to transport personnel and cargo. We called it a COD, for carrier onboard delivery, but some called it a Hummer, like the E2-C, due to the sound the propellers make. We welcomed the C-2 aircraft because it typically brought mail. Other than the occasional phone call from a port, mail was the sailor's lifeline to his life back home. We always hoped for bulky orange bags to emerge from the rear of the aircraft. Orange meant mail.

My dad would catch me up on sports. My mom would ask me if I was eating enough. My little brother would ask if I was bringing him a souvenir from some faraway port. Every sailor on board waited for those sweet words over the 1MC loudspeaker, "Mail Call."

Chief Fitch ordered the COD to an open spot near the island. Safety personnel guarded the perimeter, ensuring workers avoided the spinning propellers.

I noticed two A-6 Intruders to my left, one banking to enter the approach pattern. Airman Schmidt, a plane captain, walked along the C-2 as it slowed to a stop. He carried several tiedown chains, and I noticed the bright red gloves that he always wore. An F-14 appeared far off the fantail as the next aircraft readied to land.

I looked fore and aft and waved my right arm up and down signaling a clear deck.

The C-2 hummed. An F/A-18 pilot climbed down from his cockpit. Eppers walked toward the top of the six-pack. All routine.

Thud!

In an instant, Schmidt was dead.

PART THREE

Into the Valley of Death

CHAPTER 21

When the C-2 propeller took Schmidt's head off, the gory debris sprayed Airman Apprentice Sipka. He screamed at first, and then went into shock. A day later, he transferred to the hangar bay. We understood. No one thought any less of him. But he was done with the flight deck.

Donley questioned his own return to the flight deck, but only for a moment. He knew his place. He knew he couldn't resist the rush that the flight deck provided. He knew he'd never forgive himself if he left his fellow roof rats. Medical released him two hours after the incident, and he immediately returned to his flight deck duties.

An eeriness remained for two weeks following Schmidt's death. The captain ordered a steel beach picnic—a day off from the normal routine where mess cooks served grilled burgers, and a makeshift band played classic rock. Some guys tanned, some jogged, and others slept in their racks. The picnic provided a welcome break and a fresh start after an engine fire, helo crash, a man blown over the side, and the horrific propeller incident.

The day after the steel beach picnic, flight operations were to begin later than normal, at 1300. Squadron crews had the opportunity to perform needed maintenance without concerns about the aircraft flying that morning. The coordination and expertise to keep all those planes running in peak condition on a daily basis rivaled that of any maintenance crew in the world. V-1 Division worked at cleaning and painting areas of the flight deck and catwalk that needed attention.

Donley leaned against McGee's tow tractor near CAT 3. Two blue shirts, Spalding, and Airman Apprentice Terry Parks leaned on the tractor as well. Parks had arrived on the ship at the same time as Spalding. They had been running buddies for liberty in the days leading up to their arrival to the *Bull*. A short man like Spalding, Parks's blond hair could blind a person if the sun hit it just right. He never smiled. Always serious, Parks worried about everything.

"What time is the last launch?"

"When can we go to chow?"

"What happens if I can't do it?"

He never stopped asking questions.

A lone F-14 Tomcat sat on CAT 3. Lieutenant Brad 'Skeeter' Davies was stenciled under the pilot and Lieutenant Roy 'Cajun' Babineaux under the backseater. Of the near ninety-five aircraft assigned to the Bull, Donley noticed their names, especially their call signs—Skeeter and Cajun—most often.

Like most of the flight deck workers, Donley had seen the film *Top Gun,* giving him a glimpse inside the lives of these fighter pilots. While it's certain that many pilots had great haircuts and amazing flying skills, many of them seemed more on the academic side. The valedictorian type with the needed smarts to get these flying jobs. Skeeter had swagger, though, and Donley assumed him to be more the Maverick or Iceman type in *Top Gun.* Cajun, the backseater, appeared to be the brains of the operation.

Another Tomcat sat on CAT 4 about thirty feet away. These two aircraft served as the alert five, meaning they had to launch in five minutes should the need arise.

McGee sat on his tractor ready to engage the huffer unit to start the Tomcat. The two coolies would remove the chocks and chains. Donley stood by to taxi the bird for its shot down the catapult. Several other workers would emerge from their shacks to finish the process.

The two pilots sat in the cockpit fighting the sun and boredom. Skeeter, the pilot in the front seat, sat back with his helmet and sunglasses on, possibly sleeping. Cajun, the officer in the back seat, served as the RIO (radar intercept officer). Although he had no flight controls, the RIO served as an integral part of the team, partnering with the pilot to make the F-14 Tomcat a force in air warfare. Cajun read a Tom Clancy novel, pausing occasionally to stare out to sea.

Unlike during flight operations, few noises carried across the flight deck. An A-6 engine performed a low maintenance turn on the patio, an area aft of EL 3. A plane captain washed his helo in front of the island. McGee, as usual, talked.

"Ever tell you guys about winning the state high school football championship?"

"Yes," Donley and Spalding said in unison.

Dismissing that, McGee launched into his story anyway. "We were undefeated and had won every game by like three touchdowns that year. No one could even come close to beating us. We—"

"Hey, did you hear we're near Libya right now?" Spalding said.

McGee threw up his hands. "Hey, I'm right in the middle

of a story."

"Yeah, yeah. You lead your team to victory in the state championship. Heard it," Donley said, swiping his hand at McGee. He turned back to Spalding. "What did you hear?"

Rumors were standard operating procedure in the Navy. They even had a special name—scuttlebutt. Rumors about the time flight operations would begin, what some drunken sailor did in a port, some news event back home, or anything difficult to immediately refute.

"What's the scuttlebutt?" someone might say.

"I heard..." the other would reply.

Spalding stood up from leaning against the tractor and pointed out to sea. "When I was in line at sick bay yesterday, I heard some officer say we are near Libya and are gonna cross the Line of Death."

"The Line of Death?" Parks said.

"Yeah. You know Muammar Gaddafi, the head of Libya? He's a dictator. He said that if any American ships or planes go into the Gulf of Sidra, he'll shoot at 'em. If they cross the Line of Death and come into the gulf."

"That's it. We're going to war," McGee said.

"What?" Parks eyes widened.

"Calm down. Don't listen to this idiot," Donley said, pointing his thumb at McGee. "We ain't at war with nobody."

McGee folded his arms. "Oh, yeah. Then why do these planes sometimes come back with no bombs or missiles? Who do you think they fired them at?"

Donley folded his arms, mocking McGee. "Training. They have to practice. They probably just shoot 'em into the ocean or have some target set up on the shore."

"You don't know what you're talking about, Donley. We

are at war all the time," McGee said.

Spalding and Parks looked back and forth as if watching a tennis match.

Donley rolled his eyes. "Really, genius? How do you—"

"Launch the alert five. Launch the alert five," boomed over the 5MC flight deck loudspeaker.

Skeeter sat up and began adjusting his gear. Cajun stowed his novel. Several guys in green and white jerseys emerged from the catwalks and islands. McGee started his tow tractor and began backing up to start the Tomcat.

"Get ready to break it down," Donley told the blue shirts, pointing to the chocks and chains under the Tomcat.

Within four minutes, Donley taxied Skeeter and Cajun's F-14 forward and gave the signal for more power. The shooter took over and opened his left fist three times, instructing the pilot to use afterburners. The shooter saluted the pilot, touched the deck, and pointed forward. The Tomcat roared off the deck, followed by their wingman thirty seconds later.

Was there a real threat or was the launch for training? The deck crew didn't know.

Donley, McGee, and the two coolies felt relieved that they no longer needed to stand by the alert aircraft. They could finally take a break before the main launch. On the way to the island, Donley glanced back at the two F-14s disappearing in the distance and wondered if they were headed for training. Or for war.

Skeeter knew that two Libyan fighters were no match for the F-14s. He learned that their proximity to the carrier exceeded the captain's comfort level. He and his wingman were tasked with diverting the Libyans away from the carrier if they came closer than 150 miles to the ship. U.S. standing orders held that pilots could not fire unless fired upon.

Skeeter had the two Libyan MiG-25s in view—189 miles from the carrier. He made multiple attempts to communicate with the opposing pilots. "Attention, unidentified aircraft. State your intentions."

The MiGs failed to respond by radio and instead headed straight at Skeeter and Cajun.

An alarm in the Tomcat's cockpit signaled missile lock. Skeeter looked up. A projectile shot out from one of the MiGs.

"What the hell?" Skeeter yelled. "They fired a missile at us."

Cajun rose up for a better look. Skeeter gave the Tomcat more power and banked hard left. The missile zinged by them.

"Damn, that was close," Skeeter said.

Cajun looked over his right shoulder. "I felt something. I think it clipped us."

The two MiGs separated. Skeeter's wingman achieved missile lock on the MiG that had fired at Skeeter. The F-14 Tomcat's Sidewinder missile made contact at the MiG's exhaust. The explosion lit up the sky. Skeeter repositioned to attack the other MiG but it accelerated and headed in a direction away from the carrier. Skeeter's wingman rejoined his side.

Skeeter and Cajun performed protocols, assessing their aircraft. As they flew back toward the ship, their aircraft failed to respond to certain basic controls.

"What do we got?" Cajun said.

Skeeter rotated his stick. "I don't know. Something doesn't seem right. We need to call Air Operations and go through the checklist. And we need to get back on deck."

After the FOD walkdown, the flight deck came to life in preparation for the 1300 launch. Typically, the flight deck crew parked several aircraft on the fantail, but the landing area had to stay clear for the two alert five Tomcats that had launched. The handler told all the yellow shirts in flight deck control that one of the Tomcats had a malfunction and needed to land immediately, rather than after the birds on deck had left the CATs.

Donley walked with Li'l V from the island.

"Looking forward to Israel?" Li'l V asked.

Donley shrugged. "Trying not to think about it. Still two weeks away. I heard they might let us take a tour to Jerusalem. That might be cool."

"Let's do it. See where Jesus walked and all that," Li'l V said. "See all those places I've read about in the Bible." Li'l V glanced out to sea. "You ever read the Bible?"

"Some. You know. Went to Sunday School every once in awhile with a kid who lived up the street."

Both of them looked up at the two Tomcats flying over the starboard side. One broke left to enter the landing pattern.

Li'l V headed toward CAT 1 where he'd parked an E-2C Hawkeye earlier that morning.

Several F-14s lined the four row, an area on the bow along CAT 2.

Garfield, wearing silver proximity pants, leaned against the P-16 firefighting truck parked on the bow. Petty Officer Climer, the crash LPO, stood with his hands resting in his flight deck vest, talking with Garfield. Another crash crew sat between parked helos by the island structure.

Master Chief Platt walked along the six-pack, hands behind his back, as if conducting an inspection. Lieutenant Tunball trailed him as they headed for their position to "call the deck."

Several officers in white vests and sunglasses assembled on the LSO platform. The landing signal officers (LSO) were known as Paddles, a reference to the days when they held actual colored paddles to aid the pilot's landing. These experienced pilots assisted the airborne pilots during recovery and graded every landing. The Fresnel Lens lighting system had long ago replaced the handheld paddles.

Donley stood at the top of the six-pack and watched the F-14 headed for landing. A Fly 3 yellow shirt walked by him, taking his position along the foul line as the gear puller. He looked fore and aft and waved his arm up and down, signaling a clear deck.

Just another day on the flight deck.

"How we looking? Cajun asked.

Skeeter slightly moved his stick. "Something's bent about this. Not sure. We went through the checklist, but I'm having to put in more rudder than normal."

The Tomcat leveled off twenty seconds from landing. One of the paddles crew talked to Skeeter by radio.

"Power," Paddles said.

The Tomcat's right wing kept dipping down.

"Power," Paddles said.

"I've got a problem!" Skeeter said. "I can't, can't..."

Six seconds from landing.

Paddles hit the button for flashing red on the lens, signaling Skeeter to wave off. Paddles talked in his phone, his voice rising with each command. "Wave off. Wave off. Wave off! Wave off! Wave—"

CHAPTER 22

Donley watched the Tomcat's unusual approach. It seemed a little low, but he'd seen aircraft land in many different ways. Smooth, rough, and banking to one side or another. The wing dipping to its right side seemed odd when it was only seconds from landing. While some aircraft will have several slight movements as they land, Tomcats usually came in smoothly.

That's not right, Donley thought. That's not right. Why don't they wave it off?

"Oh, no," he said. "Oh, no. No! No! No!"

The Tomcat dipped right then hard left and slammed into the round down on the fantail of the carrier—a ramp strike in aircraft carrier jargon.

Donley started to run but couldn't decide which way to go. He crouched.

A large chunk of the aircraft headed toward the LSO platform. The rest of the aircraft slid toward the island, smashing into three helicopters and one E-2C Hawkeye. An instant before, the pilots ejected as the Tomcat had started rolling up. Cajun, the backseater, ejected starboard past the island. Skeeter, the pilot, ejected into the island. A piece of metal screamed down the foul line, hitting the gear puller and Master Chief Platt.

A small fire shot out toward the sea from the finger, a small area forward of the LSO platform. A huge ball of fire rose in front of the island. Donley looked left and right at each fire, unsure of which way to go.

Li'l V ran by him toward the island.

The shipboard announcement system rang out. "Fire, fire, fire. Fire on the flight deck!"

Chief Fitch sipped coffee in the chief's mess with another chief. The announcement of a fire on the flight deck sent him to his feet and out the door.

Several men blocked his way in the tight passageway.

"Make a hole!" Fitch yelled.

Sailors backed up against the wall as Fitch ran by.

He climbed four ladders and entered the catwalk behind the island. A wave of heat struck him—driving him back for a moment. Chaos ensued aft of the island. He noticed three bodies on the deck, two still and one barely moving. He moved forward in the catwalk and ran to the front of the island.

Men had dragged a fire hose across the deck from the corral, the area between EL 1 and EL 2. McGee came from under an aircraft, grabbed some of the hose, and pulled it toward the island. A purple shirt, responsible for fueling aircraft, crawled, his shirt ripped and face bloodied. The E-2C Hawkeye, previously parked in front of the island, now lay against an F-14 in the bottom of the six-pack. Its port propeller rested on the ground with flames licking its edges. Fitch ran toward the top of the six-pack for a better vantage point of the fire in front of the island.

He found Donley, motionless, staring at a clump on the deck. The gear puller's torso, head, and right arm lay in a mess of blood, entrails, and yellow fabric. His lower half lay ten feet away in the landing area—the left arm missing.

Master Chief Platt lay prone on the deck. No blood. No apparent injuries. The same piece of metal that cut the gear puller in half had struck Platt in the head, killing him instantly. Lieutenant Tunball knelt at his side, providing compressions to his chest in a hopeless effort to save him.

"Donley!" Fitch said.

Donley continued to stare at the gear puller's remains.

Fitch walked toward Donley. "Donley!" Fitch grabbed his arm and turned him around. "Donley! Listen to me. I need you leading fire hose teams. Go down to EL 4."

Donley stared back at Fitch. Emotionless.

"Now's the time to run toward fire, not run from it," Fitch said.

Donley emerged from his catatonic state and slowly nodded. "OK," he said quietly. Then more animated. "OK!" Donley ran toward EL 4.

Terry Parks, a blue shirt, ran up to Fitch. "Chief! Where do I go? What do I do?"

Fitch pointed aft. "Follow Donley. I'm going to the island. There's nothing I can do up here."

Farther down the deck near EL 4, Eppers led the effort to extinguish the fire on the finger. At the ramp strike, the Tomcat's port wing had clipped off toward the LSO platform where the paddles crew stood. Three of the officers had jumped into the catwalk the moment before the ramp strike. The wing had struck those remaining and crashed into the F/A-18 parked on the finger.

Eppers directed a fire hose on the Hornet's right side where

211

the fire's base seemed to be. Another hose crew attempted to cool the Mk-82, a 500-pound bomb hanging underneath the Hornet.

Li'l V worked frantically, urging fire hose crews to move their water sprays closer to the fire at the island. A crew of mixed-colored shirts would move two steps toward the fire only to be pushed back by a wall of flames that shot up. Aircraft resembled a jumbled mess of metal and fire. Rotor blades from the three helos crisscrossed over one another. The F-14 had flipped and topped most of the helos. A Sidewinder missile, attached to the starboard wing, pointed toward the bow.

A white, box-shaped piece of metal lay at the edge of the crash site. Underneath, three members of the crash crew lay dead. These three men, highly trained to respond to this type of situation, were some of the first ones killed by the sliding Tomcat.

Flames had reached vulture's row, an area on the port side of the island for viewing flight deck operations. Every vulture's row bystander, likely yearning for fresh air and the excitement of flight deck operations, had been thrown to the ground from the tornado-like inferno that shot up.

No one had received any communication from flight deck control. The Tomcat had shoved one of the helos into the flight deck control side of the island. The handler and four others all lay unconscious.

A voice from the primary flight control yelled into the handler's radio handset. "Control! Control!"

Young Airman Spalding had returned to sick bay for a stomach ailment that would not go away. He had tried to work through the problem, but Donley sent him down after the alert five Tomcats had launched. This time, the corpsman ordered him to a rack in sick bay after the contents of his stomach ended up on the examining room floor. Vomiting helped a little, but he felt weak, and a 101-degree fever confirmed the ache in his head.

When the announcement of a fire on the flight deck rang out, Spalding sat up.

"What are you doing? Lie down," the corpsman said. "It's probably a drill."

Spalding pointed at the speaker. "They didn't say it was drill."

The corpsman gently pushed him down. "Lie down, man. You're in no condition to help anyway."

Spalding complied, unaware of the nightmare unfolding on deck.

Petty Officer Beckley staggered to his feet. He reached up to feel his forehead and pulled his hand away, blood covering his fingertips. The impact on the island reached into the yellow shirt shack on the other side of flight deck control, knocking him off his seat and into a locker. Alone, he stumbled into flight deck control and noticed the wrecked room and bodies laying about. A wave of heat caused him to cover his face.

"Anybody...anybody alive?" his words slurred.

No one in the room answered.

He heard a muffled voice. "Control? Control?"

He stepped over a body and pried the handset from the handler's hand. "Hello?"

"Control. What's your status?" the unidentified voice said.

Beckley looked at the handset and then put it up to his head. "Help. Please, help us."

Another wave of heat pushed him over as flames climbed up the other side of the bulkhead. He dropped the headset and ran out of the back of the island. He looked forward toward EL 1 and saw men running back and forth. He looked aft as a ball of black smoke poured around the island. Then he looked straight and headed for the catwalk.

Crash LPO Climer ran behind the P-16 firefighting truck that came from the bow. Typically, he'd have two P-16 teams, a driver, and two rescue men on each. Remaining crash crew stayed in their shack in the back part of the island ready to respond if needed. However, one of the helos had been pushed up against the crash shack door with flames shooting out of each end—the crash crew trapped.

He saw the distinctive white truck under the wreckage and realized one of his P-16 teams had perished.

Garfield and the other rescue man donned the remaining portions of their proximity suits.

Climer grabbed Garfield's arm. "Go help Eppers," he said, pointing to the smaller fire on the finger.

"Work the base of the fire," he said to the P-16 driver, who had turned on the fire nozzle attached to a tank on the truck.

"Which one?" the driver asked, throwing his hands up in the air. "Which fire?"

"Right there," Climer said. He pointed to the upside-down F-14 Tomcat.

Li'l V ran back and forth between two hose crews that had responded to the fire—one from the corral and the other from across the landing area.

"Move in!" he yelled to the landing area crew, then ran over to the corral crew.

Wright, Beckley's pet, took the lead on the corral hose team.

"Wright, move in," Li'l V said.

"We can't. It's too hot," Wright said.

Li'l V looked up at the tall flames. "But you're too far back. The water's hardly hitting the flames. You've got to get closer. Move in a little!"

"Fuck you, Li'l V. You move in. We're staying here."

Li'l V threw his arms up, his eyes widened. "Get off the fucking hose then." Li'l V looked at the fire and then back at Wright. "If you don't get some water on that Tomcat, it'll explode." Li'l V looked around for others to help and noticed Climer.

The landing area hose team moved in, only to be thrown back by the flames.

Li'l V ran up to Climer. "This isn't working. What do we do?"

Climer looked up and down the deck. "You're doing fine. You keep telling them to move in. We need more hose teams though. I'll go—"

Boom!

The explosion knocked Climer and Li'l V to the ground. A ball of fire rose into the air. Climer looked over at the hose team from the corral but couldn't see them. Wright's hose team had disappeared. Completely consumed by the explosion. Several feet from the island, the remainder of their fire hose swung wildly with the nozzle blown away.

A burst of water hit Climer in the face. "The sprinklers!"

Hundreds of sprinkler heads lay level with the flight deck and offered a blanket of water mixed with foam. No one needed to man a hose. Trained personnel in several sections of the ship could activate the sprinklers.

The water shot up around Climer in several sections but not around the island. Not where it was needed most. The water around Climer quickly died down to a trickle.

"What the hell?" Climer said. "Why did it stop?" Climer stood up. He threw his arms out and looked up toward the island at the bridge. "What the hell!"

The F/A-18 Hornet on the finger stood in flames after the Tomcat's wing had struck it. The pilot leaned over in the cockpit, unconscious. Several bodies in white vests—most of the LSO crew—lay dead and dying. One of the LSOs leaned against the platform as if taking a nap, his head skewed to the side, nearly severed.

Two Intruders were parked on EL 4 forward of the Hornet. One of them had been modified as a KA-6D tanker for in-flight refueling and held several full fuel tanks. All of the pilots on EL 4 had managed to climb out of their aircraft.

Garfield ran up to Eppers and pointed at the pilot in the Hornet. "I gotta get that pilot out of there."

"How?" Eppers said. "There's no one to dr...drive the forklift and get you up there."

Garfield looked back at the enormous 20K forklift behind the island. One of the helos partially rested on top of it. On a typical pilot rescue, the rescue men rode in a cage attached to the forklift.

"I'm gonna blow the canopy and climb up the ladder,"

Garfield said.

The F/A-18 had a device allowing rescue personnel to trigger and blow the canopy.

Eppers looked at the cockpit. "Wait until we get the fire down on the right side."

"No. I gotta go now," Garfield said. "But I'll need help getting the pilot down."

"I'll get someone," Eppers said.

Garfield opened a small compartment with a handle and lanyard. He grabbed the handle, turned, and ran. The canopy blew off the Hornet and out to sea. He pulled the ladder down on the left side of the aircraft and put his foot on the bottom step. Flames continued on the opposite side of the aircraft.

Donley and Parks ran up to Eppers. "Where do you want us?" Donley asked.

"Parks, go in the catwalk and make sure that hose is pulled out all the way," pointing past EL 4. "Donley, Garfield's gonna get that pilot. Go get the other crash guy to help."

"OK," Donley said.

The carrier maintained a heading into the wind, forcing the black smoke aft, offering the flight deck crew some visibility.

Donley ran across the deck from the finger toward the island to retrieve the other rescue man who was wearing a proximity suit. That rescue man was about to enter a helo, presumably to pull a pilot from the wreckage.

Ten feet from Climer, who was near the island, Donley stopped. Wait a minute. I'm trained for this. I was a crash guy. I can help Garfield, he thought.

Donley turned to see Garfield at the top of the ladder

next to the cockpit. A flashback entered his mind of watching Garfield do this many times on the mock aircraft at Millington firefighting school. Climbing up on a burning aircraft had become routine.

Just like training, he thought.

However, the training aircraft didn't have full fuel tanks and had no bombs hanging from the wings.

So many times they talked about those fake rescues over chow or on their way to the barracks. Now, they faced the real thing.

Boom!

The explosion knocked Donley onto his backside.

He looked up. "Nooooo!"

The orange and yellow flames rolled high into the air, edged by black smoke. The most forward A-6 on EL 4 propelled into the air similar to a helicopter taking off. It came down hard on the same spot. The other KA-6D sank as if swallowed by a hole. The F/A-18 ceased to exist—as did Garfield. Vanished into thin air. In an instant, Donley's friend was no more.

Climer placed his hands under Donley's armpits and lifted him up. "C'mon."

"But...Garfield?" Donley said. "What about Garfield?"

Climer looked back. "He's gone."

Donley, shaken, followed him toward the new fire on EL 4. The A-6 that had jumped up and down burned brightly.

Eppers lay face down several feet into the landing area. Donley ran toward him. He grabbed Epper's arm, but paused, fearful of what he would see. Donley flipped him over. Epper's face, blackened from smoke, didn't move. Suddenly, two white eyes appeared. "What ha...happened?" Eppers said.

Donley dropped his head in relief and looked back. "You

OK?"

"Yeah. I th...think so." Donley grasped his bicep and helped him up. Eppers looked at EL 4 and took off in a run. Right back into the action.

Donley followed. He looked at the finger and thought of Garfield. He'd seen the flight deck claim a life. Now it claimed his friend.

Is this really happening? he thought.

CHAPTER 23

The 500-pound, Mk-82 bomb hanging underneath the Hornet had detonated, causing the neighboring KA-6D tanks to explode. Garfield and the F/A-18 pilot left no remains. A few of the wounded from the LSO platform and two hose crews perished. The explosion created a hole under the finger and part of the elevator. The fiery wreckage of the tanker rained down to the hangar bay. The Hornet's debris scattered in hundreds of pieces on the flight deck, the hangar bay, and the ocean. The remaining A-6 on the elevator caught fire—its bombs cooking. Three fires now existed. Two on the flight deck and one in the hangar bay. None of them under control.

Moments before the detonation, Airman Apprentice Parks had jumped in the port catwalk near the landing area. He pulled out the remaining section of fire hose for the crew that trained their stream of water on the Hornet that Garfield had climbed up. Parks took two steps up the ladder out of the catwalk when the blast propelled him over the side, sending him tumbling toward the water. Fortunately, he hit feet-first. The seventy-foot fall sent him deep into the ocean. He gulped in a mouthful of seawater, opened his eyes, and sensed light above him. He moved his arms and legs—rising toward the surface. The closer he came, the brighter the light. He broke the surface, surrounded by fire.

Every sailor must pass a swimming test in boot camp—no exceptions. The swimming test, conducted in a chlorinated, indoor swimming pool, offered little difficulty for those with basic swimming skills. The recruits jump in from a four-foot diving board, tread water for five minutes, and swim to the other end of the pool.

Parks found himself, shocked and disoriented, trying to swim in four-foot swells. Everywhere he turned, he found fire fueled from the burning liquid that floated on the water. Remembering his boot camp training, he looked for a clearing and planned to swim under the fire. If he needed to break the surface for air, he'd wave his arms wildly to move the fire out of the way and take a breath. Then, he'd dive back down and keep swimming.

The carrier had cruised by him. He looked up as the huge fantail moved further away. He noticed a clearing and dove under. He tried to hold his breath as long as possible to avoid coming up into fire. He pushed himself as far as possible and broke the surface, waving his arms to move the fire out of the way. No fire. He had cleared the unsafe area by several feet. He pulled the lanyard on his float coat and broke the seals on the two tiny CO_2 canisters to inflate his vest. He turned toward the fire and paddled backward, moving further and further away.

Small chunks of metal floated near him. He noticed something brown and grabbed on, hoping to gain a little more floatation. The object rolled over, revealing a dead plane captain, his face burned beyond recognition.

"Ahhh!" Parks screamed, pushing the body away.

Parks turned each way, making three revolutions. He found no shipmates. Only a carrier in the distance. Small fires on the water. And miles of ocean. He'd never felt so alone.

Airman Spalding ached all over. He didn't mind missing normal flight deck operations, but his sense of duty beckoned him to the fire on the flight deck. He lay in a rack surrounded by several empty ones, other than one holding some poor guy with a cast on his left leg and another on his right arm.

What the hell happened to that guy?

"Hey, dude. What happened to you?"

"Uhhhh." The broken sailor failed to form any words.

Spalding looked at the ceiling. Bored and sick.

A corpsman ran into the room, frantically rifling through cabinets for supplies.

"Hey, what's going on?" Spalding asked.

The corpsman didn't look at him and put supplies in a bag. "Mass casualties. We've got mass casualties coming."

"From where?"

The corpsman looked at Spalding. "The flight deck." He grabbed his bag and ran out of the room.

Spalding sat up, quickly. The blood rush to his head forced him back down.

I've got to go. I have to.

He sat up again and put on his boots. He stood at the doorway waiting for his chance to sneak out unnoticed. Several other corpsmen worked to move sick sailors out of the area, presumably to make room for wounded ones. Spalding made his break out of sick bay and headed down the passageway toward the mess decks.

No one sat at tables eating. Several sailors moved tables and chairs out of the way to make room for a mass casualty staging area.

Spalding ran up one ladder and looked through an open hatch toward the hangar bay. Several men ran back and forth. He poked his head in and noticed the fire in the aft end of the hangar bay where EL 4 traveled down. He took several more steps toward it.

Is this the fire? I thought it was on the flight deck.

Several aircraft filled the hangar bay, either for maintenance or parking. Yellow and blue shirts from V-3 Division were charged with movement of aircraft in the hangar bay and had even tighter movements than those of the flight deck crew. Where the flight deck crew (roof rats) moved their aircraft within feet, the hangar deck crew (bay rats) did it within inches.

He stepped back toward the hatch to head toward the flight deck.

A V-3 Division yellow shirt, noticing Spalding's blue shirt, grabbed his arm. "C'mon, help us. Go man a hose."

Spalding ran toward the fire. A large chunk of steel, and what appeared to be an upside down A-6, lay on the edge of the opening where EL 4 lowered.

Each elevator had a large opening from the hangar bay to the outside, surrounded by the elevator track. Huge doors could close off the hole for protection during extreme weather or enemy attack. The doorway across from the fire began to close. The door next to the fire had closed a few feet and stopped. In addition, the hangar bay had doors that could close and divide the hangar into three sections. As Spalding ran toward the fire, the giant doors began their tortoise-like path toward closing to contain the fire and keep it from spreading to the remainder of the hangar bay.

Spalding noticed a hose team with only two men, who

struggled to hold on with the high water pressure exiting the nozzle. He grabbed on, offering them some relief.

"I thought the fire was on the flight deck!" Spalding yelled to the guy in front of him on the hose.

"It was. Or is. Part of the flight deck and elevator exploded and that A-6 came crashing down. It sort of flipped down into the hangar. I think—"

The fire surged, pushing the team back.

One yellow shirt and two blue shirts attempted to hook up a spotting dolly, a hangar bay tow tractor, to an F-14 Tomcat, hoping to move it away from the fire. They had little room with the hangar bay packed full of aircraft. Flames from the burning A-6 seemed to jump toward the F-14, threatening a larger fire.

"Move in!" a yellow shirt said.

Spalding complied and looked up. He couldn't see it, but looked toward the flight deck, fearing what his friends and shipmates were experiencing on the roof.

Other aircraft carrier business occurred. While the barbershop, post office, and dental clinic closed their doors, sailors continued to perform vital tasks. Those below decks kept the carrier's propulsion reactors running. They made sure plenty of water was pumped to the flight deck fire hoses. Communications notified nearby ships in the fleet to proceed toward the Bull to aid in water rescues, firefighting, and first aid.

Damage Control Central (DCC) coordinated all emergency activities on the carrier. Repair parties from each department notified them of damage, flooding, fire, or malfunctions. This gave the captain the best information available to assess the situation and take corrective action, though, he didn't need DCC to inform him about the flight deck. It was unfolding before his eyes as he looked down from the bridge. The fire near the island warmed the bridge, coming dangerously close.

The reason for the failure of the flight deck sprinkler system remained unanswered. Had the header pipe that supplied the water become clogged? Could there have been an electrical failure in activating the system?

A crew fighting the fire from inside the island found extensive impact damage but little fire. They had managed to extinguish all the flames and remove the wounded from flight deck control. The aft end of the island remained inaccessible due to the smashed and burning helo shoved against it. DCC ordered the firefighting crew to remain on site as a precaution at every level of the island from the flight deck to primary flight control at the 010 level.

The other F-14 that had launched with Skeeter and Cajun's had never landed. They still flew near the carrier, running low on fuel. Aircraft were haphazardly moved off CAT 1 to make room for a KA-6D tanker to launch and refuel the Tomcat. Ultimately, the flight operations crew found no alternate airfield close enough, even with the proposed refueling. No one considered landing in Libya a viable option. The Libyans would confiscate the Tomcat, imprison, and possibly torture the pilots. The closest naval air station was NAS Sigonella in Sicily, and the closest safe landing field was in Malta. Still, they were too far. This situation, known as Blue Water Operations, meant that if the Tomcat could not land on the carrier, the crew would have to eject and ditch the aircraft. A helo would pick them up from the water. The captain made the difficult decision and ordered that action.

Flight deck corpsmen conducted triage, directing the wounded toward EL 1. From there, aircraft elevator operators lowered them to the hangar bay. The most critical would travel down the bomb elevator, delivering them close to sick bay. Several had severe burns and some had grievous wounds from the shrapnel that had splintered about the deck. Lieutenant Tunball had left the master chief and attended to a green shirt who crawled along the deck. One sailor sat on his backside, hands around his knees, rocking back and forth.

The fire near the island burned out of control. Three hose teams worked to beat back the flames that reached several feet into the air, blackening the port side of the island. Chief Fitch pointed for the hose team from the aft section of the flight deck to aim their nozzle at the base of the F-14 Tomcat. Li'l V controlled the nozzle of another hose team, while directing a third team to follow him.

Chief Fitch ran up to Li'l V. "Bombs and fuel tanks. Keep the water on 'em. Keep 'em cool."

Fitch began to run aft and stopped. He noticed a cart sandwiched between two aircraft in the midst of the fire. A cart loaded with one bomb. Two aviation ordnancemen lay near the cart, apparently dead. The bomb remained alive, surrounded by fire.

He ran back, grabbed Li'l V's arm, and pointed to the bomb. "There. Keep that cool."

Li'l V nodded, moving toward the bomb cart near the burning wreckage, and pulling the reluctant hose team with him.

The boot camp CCs chose Victor "Li'l V" Randolph as the leader of that company for good reason. He oozed leadership. He epitomized control under high stress. Nothing rattled him.

He saw no obstacles—only opportunities. There are two kinds of military leaders. Those who men will follow blindly into battle. And those who will get a lot of people killed due to their incompetence. Li'l V was the former.

A hectic eighteen minutes had passed since Donley had witnessed the ramp strike. He made sure the hose team standing in the landing area kept their hose on the burning A-6 Intruder on EL 4. Amidst the chaos, he noticed an incredible sight. Six different colored jerseys manned the hose team. A white shirt manned the nozzle, followed by men in blue, purple, red, green, and brown. Every color represented. An incredible testimony of flight deck teamwork.

All those men had survived boot camp firefighting training. They'd all survived the hell of the smoke-filled building. They had all experienced additional aircraft firefighting schools. Their core training kicked in. If any of them ever complained about too much firefighting training, their appreciation for those instructors now knew no bounds.

It's not just a job, it's an adventure.

That phrase entered Donley's mind, if only for a brief second. He remembered that day at the high school college fair when he knew he wanted to join the Navy. The recruiter in his uniform. The picture of the Tomcat. He desired that adventure.

The men on the USS *William Halsey* did much more than a job during the fire. They experienced adventure. Beyond adventure. The ultimate test. Many had already died for their country. Lost limbs. Their flesh burned to the bone.

Climer walked back and forth before the A-6 on EL 4. The fire had drawn down to a controllable level. It looked to be nearly extinguished. He ordered hose teams to keep cooling the bombs, which hung ominously.

Donley's team kept a steady stream of water on the left side of the A-6. He glanced over to the large, raging fire next to the island. One huge fire rolled up from the upside-down Tomcat. Several other fires burned around helos and the E-2C Hawkeye.

He saw Li'l V on a hose team and Chief Fitch near him, leading the fire fight.

If they could just get that fire out, he thought.

Donley ran over to Climer. "How 'bout we move my hose team to the island."

Climer looked at the inferno next to the island and then back at the A-6. He nodded. "OK, do it. I'll keep these other two teams to cool the bombs."

Donley ran back to his team. "We're gonna move this hose to that fire. You stay back and make sure the hose feeds all the way out," he said to the last man on the hose team.

Li'l V grabbed the guy behind him to man the nozzle. He ran back thirty feet where the hose had gotten caught around an aircraft's nose wheel in the six-pack.

Chief Fitch ran over to that hose team and pointed toward the island. He put his arm on the back of the man on the nozzle as they walked toward the fire. While they wore blue dungaree pants, Fitch wore khaki pants—a sign of leadership. Their jerseys a blend of colors.

CHAPTER 24

The explosion was not the largest one that day. But the bomb detonating on the cart was bad enough. Chief Fitch and the rest of the hose team were annihilated. Their body parts littered the deck. Their fire hose lay silent where it fell—the nozzle somehow closed.

Donley's hose team had traveled only a few feet before the detonation. He stopped. His hose team stopped. They merely looked on in horror as a leg dropped down in front of them as if falling from the sky. As if it were raining body parts. The limb wore a khaki-colored pant leg.

The detonation didn't seem to make the fire worse, only to encourage it on. The fire rolled in a violent, tornado-like rotation. Black smoke pointed its path toward the sky.

Li'l V stood up slowly from behind the nose wheel where he had untangled the hose. The entire flight deck seemed to stop at what had just happened.

The Tomcat that caused all this destruction lay upside down at the base of the fire. The AIM-9 Sidewinder missile hung under the right wing, atop the wreckage. Its nose peeked through the fire as the flames moved back and forth.

The missile left a trail of smoke as it launched from the Tomcat—roaring past Li'l V. He turned and followed its path as did Donley and his hose crew. It struck the third of six F/A-18 Hornets parked on the four row on the bow near CAT 2. Six Hornets fully fueled for their launch. Loaded with missiles and bombs. The fourth fire on the Bull that day had begun.

Climer and Eppers ran toward the center of the flight deck where Donley stood.

"Eppers, make sure that A-6 fire is out. I'll take this one," Climer said, pointing toward the island. Then he pointed toward the bow. "Donley, get Li'l V and take that one."

He said this as matter-of-factly as if he were handing out cleaning assignments. As if saying, "You sweep the deck, and you go clean the head."

Donley nodded and ran to Li'l V. "C'mon. Climer wants us on the bow."

Moments earlier, they had strolled toward the bow discussing a port visit to Israel. Now they ran toward the same bow. This time, at an inferno.

"Help! Is anybody here! Help!" Airman Parks had screamed that repeatedly but heard no reply.

He leaned over a piece of floating metal the size of a surfboard with the number 321 stenciled on it. With the carrier wake gone, the swells reached three feet. He rose up to see miles of ocean and then dropped down—surrounded by the walls of water—to a strangely claustrophobic feeling. His feet dangled underneath in a dark abyss.

Sharks? Are there sharks?

As a swell raised him up, he turned a different way each time, looking for a larger piece to float on. Something to get him out of the water. Away from predators that lurked below.

His life vest remained inflated. His strobe light worked, but he decided to save the battery for nighttime. He trembled at the thought of nightfall occurring before rescue.

Am I gonna be stuck out here all night?

Despite the lukewarm water, he shivered. That water would turn cold at night. Hypothermia a potential result.

The strobe light had Velcro glued to the side so that it could attach to his cranial helmet and guide rescue crews to his location. He opened the dye marker packet to create a bright green trail in the water around him. He had everything available to him that the Navy had issued for survival in the water. Except his whistle, which he must have lost when the explosion blew him over the side.

His voice became hoarse from his constant pleas for help. "Help! Anybody! Anybody."

The last plea trailed off to a whimper. The next three times Parks rose up on a swell, he kept his head down. The first two times for rest, the third in defeat.

He thought of a day six months earlier when he walked in the woods near his house with a couple of friends. He had barely turned eighteen and wanted to spend his last day of freedom with them. They had managed to score a six-pack of beer. His friends drank a toast to his decision to join the Navy. He had felt proud. Life was simpler then. Safe. When he had returned home late at night, his mother could smell the beer on his breath. She let it slide, knowing that her boy had become a man. Parks missed her, most of all. A grown man that only wanted his mother. He needed the one person who had always been there for him. Who would say the right thing to comfort him. Who had always been his protector.

"Hey! Anybody here!" a voice said.

Parks lifted his head, anxious for the next swell to raise him up to a vantage point.

"Who's there!" he asked, but saw no one.

"I'm coming!" the mysterious voice said.

Parks rose again and saw red. The red of a cranial helmet and inflated life vest swimming toward him.

"Hey!" Parks yelled, waving.

The next swell joined the two sailors, and Parks's new best friend grabbed onto the hunk of metal.

The sailor in red put his hand on Parks's shoulder. "I'm Chief Michaels, " he said, breathing heavily. "Are you... injured?"

Parks smiled. "No...uh...no. I'm fine."

Parks cocked his head curious about his red jersey. He's not in crash. Must be ordnance, he thought.

Michaels looked left and right as they rose up. "I bet you're pretty scared out here all alone."

"Yeah...kinda," Parks lied.

"What's your name, shipmate?"

"Parks. Terry Parks. V-1 Division."

Chief Michaels looked directly at Parks. "Listen. They've got helos in the air. They'll be looking for anyone in the water. They'll run a man overboard roster and figure out who's missing. I see you lit off your dye marker. That's good. That'll help."

Parks wiped away a spray of water that hit his face. "Have you seen any other survivors?"

"Nope. Just you. How'd you end up in the water?"

"I was coming out of the port catwalk and boom!" Parks lifted his hands up. "Next thing I know, I'm in the ocean. By the time I got above the water and looked around, the boat was already passing by. Then these big waves from the fantail rolled me around. Thought I was gonna drown. How about you? Did you get blown over the side?"

Chief Michaels looked around as they rose up on swell. "We need to look out for helos or other ships. If you see one, turn on your strobe light and attach it to your helmet. They might see it, even in the daytime." As they came back down, the chief looked at Parks. "Listen. I know you're scared. But you're gonna be fine. They will find you."

Parks cocked his head. "You mean us, right? They'll find us?"

"Rescue is coming," Chief Michaels said.

Parks nodded, reassured of his survival.

Li'l V ran up to Tunball on the bow, Donley a few steps behind.

Lieutenant Tunball had helped a wounded sailor to EL 1. He ran over to the new fire on the bow, ready to lead. But there was no one there to follow him. Most of the flight deck crew had run aft to fight those fires. Mostly wounded men and medical personnel remained on the bow. A few pilots who had abandoned their aircraft when the ramp strike occurred, joined Tunball—ready to aid the effort. While Lieutenant Tunball represented the senior yellow shirt on the flight deck, he had little experience. He had the technical knowledge, but lacked the practical skills to lead the firefighting.

Donley noticed a body on the deck. The sailor with more experience than anyone, Master Chief Platt, lay dead fifty feet from the new fire. The other man with ample experience, Chief Fitch, lay in pieces.

Where's Beckley? he thought.

Too many yellow shirts lay wounded on EL 1. Too many senior squadron guys suffered injuries. Too many men in khakis were incapacitated. Every division and squadron experienced heavy casualties, but none more than V-1 Division.

Tunball grabbed Li'l V by the arm. "Randolph. You're the on-scene leader. Tell me where you need me."

Randolph looked around. A slightly frantic Tunball and three pilots looked at Li'l V for direction. A plane captain and two squadron white shirts pulled a fire hose from the starboard bow catwalk. They opened the nozzle and poured water on the flaming Hornet in the four row.

"Ahhhh!" a blue shirt screamed, rolling on the ground and reaching for a bloody stump where his foot used to be. His flight deck boot, with severed appendage, lay three feet away.

Li'l V turned to Tunball. "Keep helping the wounded. Get them to safety."

"Brian, I need a hose from up there," Li'l V said to Donley, pointing toward the port bow.

Donley nodded and waved for three other guys to follow him.

The wind pushed the fire seaward rather than up in the air, giving it the appearance of a smaller, less threatening fire. The bombs that hung from the burning Hornet, and the birds next to it, told a different story. The men on the Bull had experienced the danger of unexploded ordnance more than once that day.

Donley's hose crew poured water on the Hornet as a third crew, mostly green shirts, approached from the port catwalk, just aft of the burning Hornet. Three teams fought the Hornet fire with their one-and-a-half-inch hoses of AFFF firefighting agent mixed with water.

Three more men joined Donley's hose crew with Airman Czarnecki second in position on the hose.

Li'l V waved for Donley.

"Take the nozzle," Donley said, handing the nozzle to Czarnecki.

Czarnecki nodded.

Donley headed aft to Li'l V's position in the center of the scene.

"You're my crash crew," Li'l V said. "Search for pilots or anyone else that needs help near the fire. Anyone that needs rescue."

The wind blew the majority of smoke aft so Donley headed there, the thick, black smoke darting up, down, and sideways. He looked aft and noticed Climer leading the effort on the island fire, which seemed to have drawn down. The fire on EL 4 had reduced to white smoke— apparently extinguished.

If we can just get this fire out, Donley thought.

Donley had seen many die that day. Garfield and Chief Fitch hurt the most. He'd experienced countless other emotions that day. Fear, anger, shock. The new ball of fire that flew up near EL 4 frustrated him.

What the hell is that? What now?

The fire appeared to come from the sea. Nothing on the flight deck burned. It came from below.

The hangar bay doors closed behind Spalding—insulating the remaining two-thirds of the hangar bay and several birds. But now, Spalding and several of his shipmates fought the fire in a giant box, trapped in unbearable heat. Black smoke billowed out of the partial opening for EL 4 that protected the firefighters from smoke inhalation. But the blaze caused their faces to wince. The V-3 yellow and blue shirts managed to move the Tomcat away from the A-6 Intruder that had fallen from the flight deck. But they only moved it ten feet away. The hangar deck, packed with planes, offered little room to maneuver aircraft far from the lone burning Intruder.

Spalding served on one of three hose crews pouring water on the fire. The hangar deck sprinkler system had come on for six seconds and then stopped abruptly, similar to what had happened with the flight deck sprinkler system. Spalding kept looking up in anticipation of its return.

A flame darted out from the aircraft directly at Spalding's hose team. The front two men fell backward. The front of the hose whipped around from the water pressure exiting the nozzle.

"Ahhhh!" The man that had operated the nozzle, covered his face. "My face! My face!"

The other crawled away.

Spalding reached with one hand to help the man but turned back to the hose. He moved up and wrestled for control of the nozzle. He took two steps toward the aircraft as a wave of heat assaulted him.

Undaunted, he pulled on the hose. "C'mon! Move in!" he yelled.

The other hose teams held their positions rather than moving toward the fire. One held their hose at a high angle from a distance too far to be effective. The other team knelt down underneath the nose of a nearby F-14 Tomcat, shooting the water at the base of the fire.

The corpsman that had treated Spalding and told him to wait in sick bay now treated a downed man near the burning

Intruder. He held a bandage on the man's chest as two stretcher-bearers lifted him. Another lay near him with intestines hanging out of his stomach.

Boom!

The 750-pound Mk-117 bomb reached cook-off temperature and exploded. The flames shot directly up toward the flight deck.

Spalding's corpsman, the two stretcher-bearers, and the wounded man in the stretcher were blown into Spalding's hose team. Their bodies lay on top of one another. Spalding, already weak from fever and vomiting, mustered the strength to climb out of the pile. The rest of his hose crew survived, protected by the other bodies receiving the blast damage.

"Help! Get 'em off of me!" one of the survivors screamed.

Spalding reached down and pulled the legs of the dead man on top. Both of the legs came off sending Spalding to his backside.

"Ahhh! Ahhh!" The surviving sailor—covered in blood—scooted back in terror at the grisly sight of the legless torso.

The rest of the team pulled their hose out from underneath the bodies and forged ahead toward the Intruder.

The hose crew that had fought from far away now stood trapped in a corner, fighting to protect themselves. The hose crew under the F-14 Tomcat were crushed against the bulkhead, their appendages poking out from behind the Tomcat.

The remaining portion of the Intruder burned with a new fury as if no water had been poured on it. Flames climbed up the bulkhead and reached the overhead—threatening to spread the fire to other spaces.

Few men stood upright after the explosion. Spalding, the newbie blue shirt, led the effort to extinguish that fire. He pushed toward the fire, swinging the nozzle left and right. The three men behind him had no choice but to follow. The wind pressure at the hangar opening pulled the huge ball of fire outward toward the sea, taking much of the heat with it.

"C'mon! C'mon!" Spalding yelled. "We can do this!"

A group of sailors rushed in from the side hatches and a new hose team developed. Spalding pointed for them to aim their hose to the left. "There! Right there!"

Spalding and others in the hangar deck could not see what lay below the A-6—a gaping hole in the deck. The Mk-117 bomb had wreaked havoc through three decks below the hangar. Several sailors performing their emergency duties from their below-deck stations died instantly. Shipboard firefighting crews responded quickly, many wearing oxygen breathing equipment due to the enclosed spaces.

DCC received several calls from newly damaged areas. Six men in a second deck maintenance compartment reported being trapped in their space. Large pieces of bulkhead blocked their only exit. Smoke began to fill their room.

Wounded men cried for help from beneath the damage. Rescue crews ordered cutting torches to slice their way toward the injured.

DCC offered the captain grave news. Seven fires on five different levels. The USS *William Halsey's* fire on the flight deck had become a ship on fire.

On the bridge, the captain gave his order. "All stop."

The Bull slowed and came to rest in the water.

CHAPTER 25

"Move in! Go! Move in!" Li'l V yelled as he motioned for all three hose crews to approach the F/A-18 Hornet burning on the bow. Two of the teams half-stepped toward the fire. The third team that approached from aft fought through black smoke to offer help. They stood against the combing, the curb-like section along the edge of the deck.

"C'mon! Go, go!" Donley said as he walked up from behind them.

The team leader, a squadron white shirt, nodded at Donley and pushed forward. The other three on the hose behind him followed.

Li'l V ran up to the aft team, "That's it! Move in!"

The three teams, attacking from three angles, managed to keep the fire from spreading to aircraft next to it.

Donley ran up to Li'l V. "I didn't find anybody. We need to—"

Boom!

A small explosion shot out from the right side of the Hornet—knocking Li'l V and Donley to the ground. They jumped right back up to find the aft hose team missing. The other two hose teams, pushed back by the explosion, returned to their position.

The hose from the aft team swung wildly in the air, banging against the neighboring Hornet. With the nozzle open, the high water pressure made the hose a menacing weapon— another danger on the flight deck.

Li'l V navigated around the wild hose to find the missing hose team. Donley took a less direct route around two aircraft and jumped into the catwalk.

Li'l V jumped in from another direction. "Where the hell are they?"

"Heeeelp!" a voice cried.

Li'l V leaned over the edge of the catwalk. "There!"

Donley joined him. Two of the men from the hose team floated in the water, one flapping his arms, the other face down. One man lay unconscious in the flight deck safety net, a wire mesh that protruded four feet out from the deck. A painful landing the sailors called "halfway to hell," but it was better than falling in the sea.

The scream for help had come from a man that hung precariously on the round bar forming the edge of the net. He wore a white jersey and had been the one on the nozzle.

"Help!" One hand let go of the net. "Ahhhh!"

One slip and he would fall to the sea.

"I'm coming!" Li'l V jumped down into the net. He approached cautiously to avoid knocking the sailor off.

Donley climbed down to the section of net next to him.

As Li'l V reached to grab the man's arm, the man's fingers slid off the bar. Li'l V grabbed his wrist, inches below the net, just before he would have fallen seventy-five feet into the ocean.

Although one could certainly survive a trip into the sea, too many perils existed. With the ship stopped, rescue crews could use small boats to find men floating in the water. But only if the sailor made it to the surface. The fall from that height risked breaking bones—a broken neck, perhaps. Hungry sharks might attack. Debris from the ship might fall; or spilled, floating petroleum might burn on the water. And the best of swimmers, when injured, could drown.

Li'l V strained to hold on.

"Don't let go!" The white shirt looked down at the water and then back up.

"I...won't," Li'l V struggled to say.

The white shirt kicked his legs and pulled Li'l V further down. His waist had reached the edge of the net—a precarious position for Li'l V now. Donley made his way into the net and grabbed Li'l V's feet.

Sitting on his backside, Donley leaned back. "I got ya."

All three men inched further toward the sea.

"I'm...losing him!" Li'l V's grip came off the man's wrist and slid to his palm.

Donley reached down and grabbed Li'l V's belt.

"Uhh," Li'l V grunted. "I can't—"

Another man, wearing blue, jumped into the net. He grabbed Li'l V's belt with his right hand and then reached down and grabbed the arm of the squadron white shirt. With one powerful tug, he lifted both of them into the net. They all collapsed, exhausted.

It was McGee. The big ex-football offensive lineman had shown up at just the right time.

"Huh...huh...thanks," Li'l V said.

McGee nodded.

"Yeah, thanks," the squadron guy said. He looked at Li'l V. "Thanks to both of you."

Two stretcher-bearers arrived and lifted the unconscious sailor out of the other net.

"Took you long enough," Donley said to McGee, as they climbed out of the net and into the catwalk.

McGee grinned, slightly. "We gotta get that hose." He pointed to the wild hose that continued to whip around, spraying water in every direction.

"Be careful," Donley said.

McGee approached the hose in a crouch, as if sneaking up on his prey. He moved his head around with the hose's movement. Timing his attack, he pounced on the hose and wrestled it to the ground. He turned off the nozzle and stood with the hose at his side. He opened the nozzle back up, and moved toward the fire all alone—a one-man firefighting team.

A trail of blood and the smell of burnt flesh worked its way through the ship from the flight deck to sick bay. Fifty-four minutes after the ramp strike, wounded sailors covered the mess decks. Those who could walk rode down EL 1 from the flight deck to the hangar bay, and then made their way one level down toward sick bay, next to the mess decks. Most of them had minor burns or cuts from flying debris. A few had psychological trauma—a sort of flight deck shell shock. The most critical rode down the bomb elevator. Doctors triaged burns of all degrees, deep gashes, compound fractures, and amputations. The lone operating room stayed full.

Corpsmen ran back and forth, from the mess decks to sick bay. They applied bandages, calmed the frantic, and gave information to the doctors.

The light-blue painted mess deck, swept and swabbed

twice daily, had streaks of blood down the makeshift aisles that had formed. Most of the men sat calmly, waiting their turn for treatment. Every time the bomb elevator door opened, they turned to see the next critically wounded sailor. Some came through unconscious, but some came through screaming. Men missing arms or legs. One man had a large chunk of metal stuck in his head through his cranial helmet.

In a corner, stretcher-bearers began carrying the dead in body bags to cold storage. They waited as a chaplain administered last rites over one of the bodies.

The flight deck crew had trained for mass casualties numerous times. Sailors were tagged with phantom injuries, such as sucking chest wounds, amputations, and burns. Donley and Garfield had received extensive training at Millington Firefighting School. They had learned to seal off a sucking chest wound. To use a donut bandage for compound fractures. To mark a letter T and the time of an applied tourniquet on the injured man's forehead. Most of the flight deck crew knew the basics.

Those not busy with fires managed to stabilize the wounded to prevent an injury from getting worse, or to calm them down and deliver them to sick bay quickly. Flight deck corpsman, wearing white flight deck vests with the red cross symbol, ran from one body to another, assessing injuries. One corpsmen, working furiously, walked backward toward EL 1, not realizing it had just been lowered with wounded. An aviation ordnanceman quickly grabbed him before he fell forty feet and added himself to the growing list of dead and wounded.

The fire on EL 4 was fully extinguished and the bombs cooled. The squadron commander ordered the A-6, damaged beyond repair, to be pushed over the side. Eppers led an effort to clear space in the landing area for helos. Nearby ships could deliver medical personnel and also transport some of the wounded to operating rooms on other ships.

Other ships in the fleet responded to the captain's request for assistance with rescue, treating wounded, and aiding in firefighting efforts. Some ships could come close enough to spray water on the fire if needed, although two ships traveling close together posed a collision risk.

The first helo landed as fires continued to burn on the flight deck at the bow and next to the island. Four medical personnel hopped out of the helo carrying supplies and bags of blood. They rode down EL 1, headed for sick bay. Three of the wounded were loaded onto the helo as it took off for a ship four miles away.

Petty Officer Beckley had wandered to the fourth deck, several levels below the hangar bay.

No less than three sailors, noticing his yellow flight deck jersey, stopped and asked him, "What's going on up there?"

"It's terrible. Terrible," Beckley responded. "I'm looking for help." He kept touching his forehead where the blood had dried.

One sailor grabbed his arm. "You OK, buddy?"

Beckley looked at him, eyes wide. "It's terrible."

"Let's get you down to sick bay," he said.

Beckley pulled his arm away. "No. I gotta find help." He backed up and tripped over a knee knocker—the lower portion of a passageway opening that separated two compartments during flooding. Another element of a ship's watertight integrity.

The sailor dismissed him with his hand and walked away.

Beckley rose and ventured deeper down into the ship. On the fifth deck, a young sailor ran by him with no shirt.

"Shipmate! Where the hell is your shirt?" Beckley barked.

"Uh…there's a fire. I was told to go help."

"Young man, you are in the United States Navy. You need to be in the proper uniform. Go get your shirt on!"

The young sailor backed up. "Yes…yes, sir," he said, and ran back the direction from which he came.

Beckley put his hands behind his back and walked in the other direction, far away from the fires.

Parks and Chief Michaels floated several miles from the carrier. The swells had lowered to one foot, offering better visibility. They could see for miles but saw nothing other than ocean until it met the sky. The occasional cloud formation offered a brief reprieve from the sun. They floated, helplessly, their legs dangling in the water—a tempting target for sharks.

Parks looked left and right, scanning the horizon. "Seems like we've been out here for hours. Will they ever find us?"

"Actually, it's only been about an hour or so. They've got helos and other ships out there looking. Hey, where you from?" Chief Michaels said.

"Huh? Oh…West Virginia."

"Ah. Mountain boy?"

Parks cocked his head. "How'd ya know?"

"Just a guess. Keep thinking about those mountains. About going home. What's your favorite memory from back home?"

Parks looked up and to the side. "I know. Back when my dad lived with us, he would take me camping. We'd go deep into the mountains. He taught me to start fires with a bow and spindle.

"'Like the Indians,' he'd say.

"We caught rabbits in noose traps, skinned them, and cooked them on the fire. We fished for trout in the river with gear we made from stuff we found in the forest. He showed me how to make a spear and told me what to do if I saw a bear.

"'Make some noise and the bear will go away. If they come at you, don't run. They can run faster and climb better. Just lie down and play dead. They might claw at you a few times, but they'll probably just go away.'

"My dad took me camping on my twelfth birthday.

"He put his hands on my shoulder and said, 'You take the lead this time.'

"A half day into the trip, I realized I'd walked for five minutes without talking to my dad. I turned but didn't see him. I saw nothing but thick forest. I backtracked my steps and called for him but he didn't answer.

"I started to panic and yelled, 'Dad! Dad!'

"Then I stopped and searched for the mark I'd left on a tree. My dad had taught me to mark my path by leaving stones in certain patterns, breaking ground brush in the direction I was headed, or using my knife to mark an arrow on trees toward my path. This time I had marked the trees. I walked for two hours finding each marked tree. All of a sudden, I came to the road where we'd left our truck. But still no sign of my dad. Then he just walked out of the woods.

"'Where were you?' I asked.

"'Right behind you. I wanted to make sure you could find your way out. Not panic. You did good, son. I'm proud of you.'

"'You mean a test?'

"'Yep. A test. And you passed.'

"At first I was mad but then realized the confidence that

it gave me. That was our last trip. I heard him and my mom arguing one night. The next day he left. Mom said he was messed up in the head from Vietnam. He just sort of checked out of our lives. I wish he were here now. He'd know what to do."

Chief Michaels smiled and patted Parks's arm. "I think he kinda is. I mean, I think he's taught you well. You don't look like you panicked. You didn't drown. You're using your float coat vest. You found this hunk of fuselage to float on. You have good instincts. Trust them. You can't mark trees. But you can keep trying. Keep thinking. Keep believing."

Parks scanned the horizon, looked back at the chief, and nodded.

CHAPTER 26

Donley grabbed onto the hose behind McGee as they moved toward the F/A-18 Hornet burning on the bow. The image of Garfield in a silver proximity suit on the Hornet popped into his head as well as the explosion that ended his life.

A conversation from many months before ran through Donley's mind.

He and Garfield sat in the back of a firefighting truck at Naval Auxiliary Landing Field Fentress during their firefighting training. The experienced guys in the front fought boredom as an EA-6B did a touch-and-go on the runway.

"Could you really do it?" Garfield said to Donley.

"Do what?"

"Rescue a pilot. That's why we're out here. To rescue a pilot and put out the fire."

Donley held up his hands, palms up. "Heck yeah. That's what we've been training for all this time."

Garfield nodded. "Yeah, I know. But when the shit really goes down. Will you climb up on a burning plane and rescue a pilot? We're trained for it. We think we'll do it. But have you really thought about it?"

They both sat silently for a moment.

"I guess. If I'm honest, the thought scares the crap out of me," Donley said.

"Me, too. I guess if it really happens, you don't think about it, you just do it. Kick it into a higher gear, you know?" Garfield shifted a mock gear. "My dad did it once. Saved a kid in a burning house across the street. The second story had flames shooting out of the windows. The lady in the front yard yelled, 'My baby girl! I can't find her! I think she's inside.' My dad took off and ran inside. He came out thirty seconds later with the girl. He didn't have any training. He just acted. Like it was natural."

"Dang. Maybe you inherited it," Donley said.

Garfield nodded. "I hope so."

"Hey, you two fuckers quit being so serious. You'll do your job when the time comes, or I'll kick your ass." The guy in the passenger seat had heard our entire conversation. He turned. "Anybody that says they wouldn't be scared is lying or crazy. Why do you think you're here? To train. To train over and over until it's second nature. Because when the shit goes down, the scared ones will respond because of their training. And the crazy ones won't take unnecessary risks. Just do what they're trained to do." He turned back and continued his conversation with the driver.

Garfield had answered his question with a resounding "yes." He had no hesitation when it came to rescuing that pilot. He may have been scared, but his training kicked in. He found that higher gear. He gave his life for a shipmate. The ultimate sacrifice.

Donley's reflection entered and exited his head quickly. He had no time for mourning. The fire before him, despite strong efforts from the hose teams, had spread to the next F/A-18.

Both aircraft burned as one. One large ball of fire putting off unbearable heat. Black smoke whipped up and then port as the winds changed. One hour and nineteen minutes had passed since Skeeter's Tomcat struck the ramp.

Climer looked over his right shoulder toward EL 4. That fire posed no further threat. The mysterious ball of fire that rose up near that location from below decks was gone. He had no idea where it came from and quickly focused on the fire in front of him at the island.

As the crash and salvage LPO (leading petty officer), Climer had sailors working in rotations under him when the ramp strike occurred. Six formed two of the P-16 firefighting truck crews. The others had assignments to operate equipment such as the crash crane, 20K forklift, or helo salvage kit. Above Climer, the crash chief, and an officer called the air bos'n, headed up the group responsible for aircraft firefighting, pilot rescue, and clearing the landing area of wreckage.

Most sailors worked in crash for a short time and then returned or advanced to yellow shirt. Typical of most, the air bos'n and crash chief had worked in crash early in their careers but had spent most of their time as yellow shirts. Climer was a crash and salvage lifer. He loved every minute of it. With sixteen years of service under his belt, he planned to finish his twenty years, retire, and join the local fire department in his hometown of Bangor, Maine.

Climer knew that one of his P-16 crews lay dead under the island fire. Garfield had perished attempting to rescue the pilot on the finger. Two of his crew fought the island fire with him. But where were the rest of his crew? Where were the crash chief and air bos'n? What Climer didn't know, was that those in the crash shack suffered a similar fate to that of those in flight deck control, where the handler and several others had died or experienced severe injury.

The crash shack lay at the aft end of the island with two compartments. One served as the crew's break area with lockers and an assignment board. The other housed the leadership's office, training documents, and some of the rescue gear. Although crash was a part of V-1 Division, they operated with some independence.

When Skeeter and Cajun's Tomcat struck the rear end of the island, those in the forward end, such as flight deck control, experienced a massive jolt. They'd either had a piece of furniture strike them or were thrown into the bulkhead. Those at the aft end, the crash shack, suffered a far worse fate. The air bos'n, crash chief, and other crash crew members died instantly on impact. Their remains lay cooking in the oven-like environment.

From the 08 level, near the bridge, a firefighting team poured water from their hose down on top of the Tomcat. No bombs or missiles remained to cook off. Every fuel tank had exploded. Nothing else to reinvigorate the island fire. The black smoke slowly turned to gray as the flames subsided.

The P-16 firefighting truck had exhausted its water tank.

Climer walked over to the driver. "Take that hose crew and check every inch of this area," he said, spanning his pointed finger from the fore to the aft end of the island.

The P-16 driver nodded and joined a hose crew, which had been constantly pouring water out of their nozzle for the past twenty-two minutes.

For the first time since the ramp strike, no fire was visible in, on, or around the Tomcat and surrounding aircraft.

The dent in the back of the island, thirty feet up, seemed unexplainable. Had a missile struck it but failed to explode? The ejection seat and remains of Skeeter on the deck below the dent provided the answer. While the RIO of the Tomcat, Cajun, had ejected over the island and safely out to sea, the tiny rockets on Skeeter's ejection seat drove him into the island, killing him instantly. It looked like a bird strike. Aircraft will sometimes hit birds, denting the airframe and occasionally piercing the metal. Every squadron guy has a story of digging the carcass of a bird out of a wing. But this was no bird strike. Skeeter was a highly skilled pilot that tried to land a damaged plane.

The island looked scarred and abused. Debris lay about the deck mixed with puddles of water from the firefighting efforts. Hospital corpsmen moved in to treat the wounded but could do nothing for the severely burned bodies—absent of life.

Climer, exhausted, looked toward the bow, thankful for Victor "Li'l V" Randolph.

Li'l V had resumed his position on the bow as on-scene leader—directing the three hose crews. The bombs and missiles hanging from the Hornets pointed directly at him. Firefighting crews were trained to approach a burning aircraft at an angle away from the missiles' direction. With one Sidewinder fly by under his belt, Li'l V knew the missile could release at any moment. But, amidst the chaos of burning planes, hose crews, and dead bodies, Li'l V had no optimal position. He put himself in the location where he could best lead the situation. Directly in the line of fire.

"Keep water on those bombs," he yelled to one of the hose crews.

He would run ten yards, bark a command, and return to his

original spot.

Like Garfield, he acted almost robotically as his leadership and bravery worked in concert with his training. His perseverance to beat the fire knew no bounds. He owned those unique qualities that allowed him to excel at anything. Had he pursued college, he'd have made the dean's list and served as the striker for the soccer team. Had he attempted to learn a foreign language, he'd attain fluency. Had he chosen to enter the ministry, congregants would fill the sanctuary to hear him preach. Had he joined the army, he'd lead an infantry squad. While others spent most of their spare time on liberty drinking beer, Li'l V completed courses to hasten his promotion. To enhance his knowledge as a yellow shirt.

McGee's hose team worked from aft, one team worked from the top of the bow, and one team, full of ordnance men in red shirts, came from across the bow as the F/A-18 Hornets burned. The last fire on the flight deck. The fury of the fire made the hose team's efforts seem fruitless at times, but they kept pouring on the water. They kept battling.

After the last explosion that had propelled the hose team into the catwalk and the ocean, the two flaming Hornets appeared as one hunk of burning metal. No one could see what bombs remained on the bow aircraft. What fuel tanks remained unexploded. The fire obscured the view of what remained under the mangled Hornets' wings.

Donley ran up to Li'l V. "I'm gonna move closer and see what we got."

"What do you mean?" Li'l V said.

"Bombs. I don't know if they all went up or if there's one left in there."

Li'l V slapped Donley's back. "Be careful."

Donley approached the Hornets, hunched over, as if walking under a helo's rotor blades. He covered his face in vampire fashion due to the heat. McGee moved his hose spray over Donley's head, providing cover.

Boom!

The explosion lifted the nose of one of the Hornets into the air and propelled it aft. It came down on the folded wing of a non-burning Hornet next to it. The impact tore off the folded portion of the wing as the Hornet nose rested, precariously, on the wing's remaining section.

McGee's hose crew, knocked to the ground, slowly stood up.

Li'l V ran up to McGee. "Where's Donley?"

McGee struggled to get the nozzle securely in his hands. He looked at the area where Donley had stood. "I don't know! He was right there!"

McGee opened his nozzle, pushing the smoke and fire back.

Li'l V grabbed the nozzle and pulled it to the right. He pointed toward the Hornet. "There!"

Donley lay yards away from the fire, unconscious, and directly under the wing. The same wing upon which another Hornet's nose teetered back and forth. Thousands of pounds of aircraft threatening to fall on Donley at any moment.

"Make a hole!" a voice yelled. The sailor bumped Beckley as he jumped over a knee knocker.

Sailors looked liked hurdlers whenever they rushed down ship passageways, timing their jumps over each knee knocker.

As Beckley wandered down the passageway, the

commotion intensified. Sailors ran back and forth, many wearing firefighting gear. One sailor removed his OBA mask and dropped to his knees. He struggled to rise, panted hard, and continued to move down the passageway, coughing and rubbing his eyes.

Beckley turned and looked to the other end of the long passageway that ran fore and aft. Little activity emanated from that direction. He turned back toward the chaos. The old sailor pondered his next move.

ABH1 Simon Beckley fancied himself a seasoned sailor. An old salt as one might say. He had enlisted during the Vietnam War and had served on four other carriers, including a small carrier that flew only helos for transporting marines. He'd driven tractors and operated elevators. He'd worn a blue, red, and yellow shirt. He'd worked in the hangar bay almost as much as on the flight deck. He'd served at several air fields in support roles. He remained in that awkward position of being a senior petty officer with no likelihood of advancing to chief. Senior V-1 leadership tolerated his authoritarian methods to some extent, but he had long ago lost the loyalty of those under him. They considered him a cruel taskmaster. A Simon Legree.

Beckley was a capable aircraft director. He knew his SOP (standard operating procedures). He knew the rules, but failed in their application. He missed the big picture. He used the rules to lord over underlings. He saw everything in black and white. His methods hindered his ability to adapt during unusual situations. He failed to react when faced with adversity. He couldn't think on his feet. He had seen his share of accidents as had anyone with that much time on deck. But he'd never experienced a fire on the flight deck. The shock overwhelmed him.

Unsure of the commotion down the passageway, he moved forward to investigate. Beckley stepped over one knee knocker and hugged the bulkhead. His left hand palmed the bulkhead and his right hand grabbed wires that ran down from the overhead.

"We need more help!" one sailor yelled.

"Corpsman! Somebody get a corpsman!" yelled another.

The voices grew louder as Beckley drew closer. Beckley began to step over another knee knocker but pulled his leg back and hugged the bulkhead as two men came running and hurdled through the knee knocker. Beckley stepped through again as the smell of smoke and the heat of fire overpowered his senses.

A hose crew shot water far down a passageway toward a fire that ran from the deck to the overhead. Smoke obscured some of the men on the hose crew. The ones he could see wore OBAs. The vast amounts of water used to fight the fire had drenched every man in the area.

Sparks flew from a cutting torch as a welder worked to remove a beam that had blocked a passageway.

Beckley grabbed the arm of a sailor near the scene. "How big is the fire?"

The sailor looked down the passageway. "Which one?"

"What do you mean which one?"

"There are fires from here all the way to the hangar." The sailor grabbed a portion of the fire hose and pulled it around the corner to give the hose crew more slack. He looked back at Beckley. "And there's a bunch of guys trapped in a compartment down there. We're trying to cut our way in."

Ping! Ping!

"What's that noise?" Beckley asked.

"The guys that are trapped are banging on the bulkhead.

Like SOS or something. They don't know we're trying to get to them. It must be like an oven in there."

Beckley looked down another passageway that ran from port to starboard. He saw little activity. He took one step toward his next escape. Another path to avoid danger and uncertainty.

The same sailor approached Beckley. "Hey, you're a yellow shirt. Don't you work on the flight deck? Is that fire out?"

"Uh…yeah…uh…I'm down here to help."

"Give us a hand," another sailor said, waving Beckley toward an unconscious man on a stretcher.

Beckley reached down and picked up one end of the stretcher. "Let's go, shipmate," Beckley said, as they lifted the wounded man.

CHAPTER 27

Thump. Thump. Thump.

"Hey, do you hear something?" Parks said to Chief Michaels.

The two men had floated on the hunk of aircraft fuselage for over ninety minutes. Chief Michaels scanned the horizon. "Yeah. Listen."

Thump. Thump. Thump.

"There!" Parks said. "A helo! A helo!" Parks reached for the strobe light on his float coat and turned on the flashing light. "Maybe they'll see the flashing."

Both men waved their arms. "Hey! Over here! Hey!" Parks yelled.

"They see you," the chief said. "They're turning this way."

Chief Michaels put his hand on Parks shoulder and smiled. "You made it."

"Yeah, we made it," Parks said, mirroring the chief's smile.

"When they drop the harness in the water, you go first, OK? You've been out here longer."

"OK, Chief." Parks looked at the helo and then back at the chief. "Thanks. I don't think I would have made it if you hadn't been here. I would have freaked out and drowned."

"You did fine, Parks."

The H-3 Sea King flew in low and made a sharp turn so that the starboard side faced the two men in the water. The door opened wide. The prop wash from the rotor blades swirled the waves and sprayed water. A rescue swimmer hung his legs over the side and jumped into the ocean twenty yards from Parks. He wore a wetsuit, flippers, and a mask. The rescue collar began lowering from the helo. One of helo crew leaned out as the collar hit the water between Parks and the swimmer.

"Are you injured?" the diver asked Parks.

"No. I'm fine."

"Alright. We're gonna get you in this collar. You hold on tight, and we'll get you home."

Parks nodded.

The large yellow collar was made of flexible material. The opening spanned twenty-eight inches and had an adjustable strap to secure around the person needing rescue.

The diver lifted the collar and placed it over Parks's head and down his torso. Parks pushed his arms through and locked them around the front of the harness.

"You ready?" the diver said.

Parks nodded. "Yep."

The diver raised his arm and gave a thumbs up to the hovering helo. The line from the collar to the helo became taut as the helo's winch turned, and Parks left the water after nearly two hours. Under any other circumstances, most sailors would enjoy the ride. Before he reached the helo, Parks looked left and right over the water noticing floating debris, much like the piece that had been his lifeboat, as far as he could see.

The line stopped as Parks came even with the helo door. A crewmember in a flight suit and helmet reached out and grabbed his hand, pulling him into the helo. After removing the collar, the crewmember lowered it back toward the water. A sailor in green flight deck gear sat in the helo, holding a bandage to his head.

"They just pick you up?" Parks asked, raising his voice to overcome the noise of the helo's propellers.

"Yeah. About ten minutes ago. Got blown off the deck when that plane blew up on EL 4. Don't know when I got hit in the head. Hurts like a son of a bitch."

Parks smiled. "Thank God they found us."

"Yeah. The big man upstairs was looking out for us, I suppose."

The reeling line reached its endpoint. Parks watched as the crewmember operating the winch reached out and pulled the diver in.

Chief Michaels? Parks thought.

"Hey! Where's the chief?" Parks said.

The diver cocked his head. "What?"

"The chief. He was right there next to me in the water." Parks moved quickly toward the helo door and looked out. The winch operator and diver put their arms out, blocking Parks from falling.

"What are you talking about?" the crewmember said, throwing up his arms. "We didn't see anyone else."

"Chief Michaels. He had red on. He was floating on that hunk of metal with me almost the whole time."

All three men looked at the metal riding up and down on the waves. Several other pieces floated nearby.

"Where did he go?" Parks leaned out again, dangerously close to falling out of the helo.

"We only saw you when we made our approach," the diver said. "If he was there, he's gone now. He must have drowned.

We'll keep looking for a little bit, though. You need to sit back. You've been through a lot."

Parks sensed their patronizing tone. He noticed the diver twirl his finger next to his ear as if suggesting Parks was crazy.

The crewmember spoke into his mic. "Be advised..."

Parks sat back down next to the green shirt. His post-rescue elation waned as he wondered what had happened to the chief. The man had comforted him—perhaps saved him—during that traumatic time.

Two-thirds of the hangar bay enjoyed a relative quiet thanks to the fireproof doors separating the hangar. Several dead and wounded covered the deck of the chaotic aft end. Spalding's hose crew had reduced to three when the man behind Spalding noticed his buddy calling for help. He abandoned the hose for his friend. A squadron green shirt led the new hose crew that had formed.

"Pull!" the green shirt said, grasping far down on his fire hose and encouraging the two men behind to help.

Spalding looked at the green shirt and nodded as both men led their hose crews closer to the burning A-6 Intruder. The water and flames collided with little effect. The green shirt's hose team inched by Spalding's team as if in a slow race.

Spalding stopped his team due to the heat. The blaze whipped around in a fury.

What's he doing? Spalding thought, looking at the squadron sailor moving past him.

The green shirt moved dangerously close to the A-6 and dropped to one knee. The rest of the hose team mimicked his action. He trained his hose in an upward direction attacking the base of the fire. Spalding's team and another hose crew had their nozzles pointed so that water dropped down on top of the aircraft. The green shirt swept the nozzle at the base of the fire. Firefighting 101. The flames slowly drew down, as if someone were turning them off. Within two minutes, the A-6 fire had been extinguished. Gray smoke billowed out of the EL 4 opening.

"Keep the water on it! We gotta make sure," the green shirt said.

Spalding nodded.

After another two minutes, a squadron chief moved his hands in front of his neck, motioning for the crews to turn off their hoses. He walked around the A-6 with another chief inspecting the bird, careful to avoid the huge hole the aircraft lay across.

"It's out!" he proclaimed.

Two corpsmen triaged the area. Seven sailors lay dead. Stretcher-bearers carried off the critically wounded. Uninjured sailors led the walking wounded through a starboard hatch.

Spalding laid down his hose.

He walked over to the green shirt and extended his hand. "Man, I'm glad you came along when you did. What's your name?"

"Lejeune. Like Camp Lejeune, North Carolina," he said, with a southern drawl. "Check out that big hole."

Spalding and Lejeune walked over to the hole. As far as two decks down, sailors looked back up at them. No fire burned, but the blackened bulkheads, pieces of metal, and furniture confirmed the aftermath of a bomb detonation.

After the hangar bay reported "all secured," DCC received a similar report from every other deck—except the flight deck.

The sailors below decks, after inspecting every compartment, began the grisly task of removing the dead, many burned beyond recognition. Several bodies lay crushed under metal. They wouldn't see their final resting places until work crews reached them.

The welders with the cutting torches removed enough of the bulkhead for rescue crews to reach the six trapped sailors. Five had died from smoke inhalation. One sailor, unconscious and barely breathing, lay against the bulkhead with a metal bar in his hand. Presumably, he was the one that had continued to bang on the bulkhead, signaling for help. Thrilled at finding a survivor, stretcher-bearers quickly delivered him to sick bay.

Nearby, a sailor squatted, leaning against a bulkhead. His OBA mask hung around his neck, his head lowered, and his arms resting in his lap.

A corpsman walked up to him and put his hand on his shoulder. "Hey, you alright?"

The squatting sailor looked up and nodded, his mouth open as he breathed hard. "Just...huh, huh... tired."

ABH2 Whitley, a Fly 3 yellow shirt, sat on the mess deck, awaiting his turn in medical, while more crucial patients were treated. A large bandage surrounded his left elbow.

When the plane had exploded on EL 4, a piece of metal had struck him. He'd glanced at the injury when it happened and noticed the skin had been cut to the bone. He'd quickly looked away.

The corpsman that finally bandaged him said, "Oh, shit,

dude!"

Hardly the kind of bedside manner Whitley needed. The corpsman's remark told him the seriousness of his injury. He had pulled up his arm as if in a sling and had not been able to move it since. Although he knew he needed medical care, he feared what the doctors would find when they removed the bandage, but the initial excruciating pain had become bearable.

Beckley arrived at the mess decks toting a stretcher with a partner. The wounded man held his right thigh with blood trickling out. They set the stretcher down next to Whitley. Beckley looked over the nearly seventy men sitting or lying in various states of injury. Some moaned and groaned, but many sat quietly, holding their injuries. Two men swabbed the deck—their swab bucket full of red-tainted water.

Whitley looked up. "Petty Officer Beckley?"

"Whitley. What's wrong with you, shipmate?"

Whitley looked at his arm and then back up. "My elbow's all busted up. What about you? Where were you?"

Beckley reached up and touched his forehead. The small patch of blood had long since dried. "Can't you see? I'm wounded. I don't need to tell you where I've been."

Whitley slightly shook his head. "I just meant where were you on deck when the Tomcat hit? Is there still a fire up there?"

"Oh...yeah...It's terrible. Lots of fire. I got knocked out. Came to medical to make sure I didn't have a concussion."

Beckley sat down next to Whitley.

A man next to them had a bandage around his eyes. "Hey, who's there?"

"Don't worry, shipmate. They'll come get you soon," Beckley said. He turned to Whitley. "Did you make sure the catwalks were secure before flight ops?"

Beckley referred to the yellow shirt procedure of walking their area of the flight deck and catwalks, ensuring equipment was stowed properly and everything was in place. A legitimate question, any other time.

Whitley cocked his head. "What?"

Beckley looked across the deck at the wounded again. "We've got a lot of painting to do when we get back to port," he said, matter-of-factly.

Whitley slowly diverted his eyes from Beckley and looked off to the side. What the hell? he thought.

CHAPTER 28

Climer, confident the fire at the island posed no further threat, ran toward the bow to help Li'l V. The explosion's boom stopped him in his position—forty yards away from the fire on the bow. He turned aft to protect himself, then turned back and continued.

As he approached, he noticed three hose teams. One far up the bow with four red-shirted aviation ordnancemen. Despite the explosion, they maintained a strong position working their hose left and right. A hose team with two white shirts, a pilot, and a shirtless guy walked their hose from the starboard side of the bow. McGee's hose team rose from the deck and reassembled as Li'l V ran up to them.

One F/A-18 nose lay on the remaining wing of another F/A-18—looking as if it would fall at any moment. Both aircraft burned, but the large ball of fire from the explosion had reduced to a few small flames. Black smoke covered the area.

Climer came within twenty yards as Li'l V took off toward the two Hornets on fire. McGee handed the nozzle to the man behind him, leaving four men on that hose. McGee followed Li'l V.

Climer reached the hose team McGee had abandoned. Climer stopped and noticed McGee and Li'l V as they reached down toward a yellow shirt that lay prone on the deck.

Screech!

The Hornet nose slid off the wing toward the three men.

Climer cupped his hands around his mouth. "Look out!"

A large puff of black smoke blew through the area, obscuring Climer's view.

Bang!

The Hornet crashed down to the deck, but had no effect on the fires as they continued to burn.

Climer took three steps toward the scene, but stopped. He saw no trace of the men.

"Move in! Move in!" he yelled, waving both hands from back to front.

Two of the hose teams walked toward the fire. The aviation ordnancemen hose team ran. The fire jumped and darted in every direction. They swept their hose furiously over the fire as black smoke turned to gray. Little by little, the flames subsided.

Climer turned in a circle, looking for fire, but none existed.

The courageous men of the USS *William Halsey* extinguished the final fire on the flight deck, one hour and twenty-seven minutes after the ramp strike.

Climer walked toward the wreckage. No way they survived, he thought.

Twenty yards away from where the Hornet had fallen, Climer noticed one man carrying another.

Li'l V had emerged from behind an F/A-18 Hornet parked three positions down from the ones that had burned. Using the fireman's carry, Li'l V carried Donley toward a safe location near the JBDs.

Climer ran over and helped him lay Donley on the deck.

Donley, groggy, opened his eyes. "What happened?"

Li'l V sat down next to him, exhausted.

Climer grabbed Donley's chin, moving his head back and forth looking for injuries. He turned toward Li'l V. "Yeah. What happened? Where's McGee?"

Li'l V looked up at Climer and shook his head.

Donley sat up. "What happened to McGee?"

"When the bomb went off it knocked you out. That bird was kinda leaning on top of the other, about to fall down on you. I ran in there to drag you out. As I started to get you on my shoulders, McGee ran up. The bird started slipping and was coming right down on us. McGee pushed us out of the way and took the whole thing on himself." Li'l V looked toward the wreckage. "He...he saved our lives. I couldn't even see him except for one arm sticking out. I knew it killed him the second it happened."

"The fire didn't seem too bad, but we were surrounded. Both birds had sort of collapsed. Even the catwalk was all blocked with debris. I thought we were gonna have to jump in the water. I looked aft and noticed a little space between the exhaust and the combing." Li'l V looked at Donley. "I dragged you through there and then got you on my shoulders."

"McGee sacrificed himself for us," Donley said. "And you saved my life, Li'l V. I shouldn't have—"

"You'd have done the same for me," Li'l V said.

Climer stood up and walked back toward the wreckage. "Shut 'em off." Each of the three hose teams had kept their water flowing for three minutes to make sure the fire had been fully extinguished.

Donley stood up and shook his head. He touched various parts of his body but found no injuries. "My head hurts."

"You mean like a headache?" Li'l V said.

"Yeah, like 'someone wacked me with a two-by-four' headache." Donley looked back toward the Hornets. "I can't believe McGee did that. I can't—" His bottom lip started to quiver.

"Don't go there, Brian. Don't go there. We gotta stay strong."

Donley noticed Climer walking around the wreckage. The pilot that had worked one of the hose crews stood next to him pointing. Corpsmen knelt over downed men, and stretcher-bearers transported the wounded toward EL 1. One man sat up in the stretcher, screamed, and passed out.

Li'l V stood up and walked toward the island.

The carrier stood fast; her only motion was a slight rocking back and forth caused by the waves. A helo launched from the landing area with wounded men. Eppers gave the pilot signals as it departed for another ship in the distance. Another helo flew toward the carrier, preparing to land.

Donley looked aft. A few men darted back and forth, but most walked slowly. Some staggered like zombies. Debris covered the deck. Pieces of metal, strung out fire hoses, and used medical bandages revealed the aftermath of battle against the enemy—fire. Nothing was dry, as if it had rained for days.

Aside from a few muffled voices, Donley heard something rare on the flight deck. No A-6 Intruders roaring off the catapult. No humming from an E-2C Hawkeye. No high-pitched whirring from an F-14 Tomcat. No slamming from an F/A-18 landing. He heard silence. A terrible quiet.

PART FOUR

The Refinement of a Sailor

CHAPTER 29

My dad always told me that you could tell a person's character in times of trial. In a little under two hours, I had survived the greatest trial of my life. I'd lost two friends and a chief I'd greatly admired. I had other friends whose fate remained uncertain. I felt embarrassed that Chief Fitch had to shake me into responding when the ramp strike happened. Time for reflection would come. Right now, I wanted to rest, if only for a few moments. McGee's death and Li'l V's risking his life for mine seemed too surreal to comprehend.

I saw no unattended wounded. No one screaming. I saw no fires to extinguish. I saw no pilots to rescue. A tremendous amount of work lay ahead, but I chose to follow Li'l V toward the island. I wanted to sit for a few minutes. Not talk to anybody. Not look at anybody.

One green and one blue shirt stepped off the helo that landed amidst the nearby rubble.

A blue shirt stepped off the helo. Parks?

"Hey, Parks. Over here."

He ran up to me, all wet. "Donley! How long has the fire been out?"

"Not long at all. Where've you been?"

"I got blown in the water. I was out there the whole time."

Parks pointed out to sea. "The helo picked me up about twenty minutes ago. I was out there with this ordnance chief and then all of a sudden he—"

I put up my hand. "Save it. You can tell me later. We're all gonna have some stories. I'm exhausted. Mentally exhausted. And...McGee—" I looked to the side. "He was killed just a little bit ago."

Parks's jaw dropped.

"I can't even wrap my head around it. I don't know what's real right now." I started to walk toward the island. "If you're alright, go up and see if Climer needs you. Unless you really need to go to sick bay, but most of us can wait."

Several guys stood in vulture's row, pointing at various places on the flight deck, just as they did during flight operations. Voyeurs to the hell of the last two hours.

I walked by an F-14 Tomcat, with canopy open, parked at the top of the six-pack. Not a scratch on it. The pilot had long abandoned it, but it remained there, waiting to launch, as if nothing had happened. I noticed a few other birds like that, but many sat askew, upside down, or collapsed. About eight squadron guys picked up hunks of metal on EL 4 and stacked them on a cart. Someone had constructed a temporary barricade around the hole in the deck at the finger and EL 4.

The carnage around the island looked like a wrecking yard. I couldn't tell where one aircraft ended and another began. Almost as if they'd melded together. A group of three filled body bags became four, as the corpsmen continued their grisly duty.

I walked by the last Tomcat in the six-pack and heard whimpering. As if a lost child were nearby. A tow tractor had slid against the main mount obscuring the person behind the voice.

I moved closer. "Czarnecki?"

The blue shirt looked up at me. His goggles rested on top of his cranial as he sat on the deck. Tears flowed from eyes.

I moved in closer. Another blue shirt's head rested in his lap.

"Odie didn't make it," Czarnecki said.

Airman Steven Odell had come onboard with Czarnecki. Guys commonly ended up bonding with those they had traveled with and shared first experiences. Czarnecki and Odell, or Odie as we called him, did everything together. The married Czarnecki took Odell home with him many nights. His wife put out an extra plate for Odie and they appreciated the way he played with their kids. The two friends had racks across from one another, and they'd lie there talking late into the night.

Odie's entrails lay on the deck next to him, barely connected to his body. His eyes remained wide open—void of any life.

Czarnecki had his left hand under Odie's arm, and his right hand on Odie's head. "I'm sorry, Odie. I'm sorry I couldn't fix you."

Shocked at the sight of Odie's body, I put on a brave front and leaned down. "Nothing you could have done, Czarnecki."

"He was still alive when I found him. He only mumbled and said 'Is it bad?' I didn't know what to say. I just said, 'We'll be home soon. My wife will make that chicken that you like.' He sort of smiled a little, and then he stopped breathing."

I stood up and waved over a corpsman.

"C'mon, Czarnecki. We'll let the corpsman take care of him now."

Czarnecki looked up and then back down. "See ya, Odie."

The corpsman and two helpers came over. They laid out a body bag.

I put my arm around Czarnecki and led him over to EL 1, which was filled with other wounded.

"You just sit here for a minute." Twelve guys sat or lay in pathetic condition. Some with bandages but some like Czarnecki had wounds that weren't outwardly apparent.

I walked over to the corpsman conducting triage. "I think he's spent. He doesn't need to be up here right now."

The corpsman looked over at Czarnecki and nodded to me. He wrote something on a tag and tied it to Czarnecki's flight deck vest. Czarnecki put his hands around his knees and began slowly rocking.

Why wasn't I rocking? I thought. I should have reacted like Czarnecki. Was I so cold that I felt nothing? Didn't I care?

I headed into the yellow shirt shack. Lockers had fallen over. Mine leaned against another set of lockers. I pushed them back, worked the combination on the lock, and reached for my pack of cigarettes.

I looked at the Marlboro and lighter. After all that fire and smoke? I shrugged.

I lit it anyway. I took a long drag and turned to see Li'l V sitting on the floor in the corner, smoking as well. He looked up at me and shook his head. He had given everything. He had put himself in harm's way repeatedly, led without hesitation, and saved my life. We said nothing. We both sat in total quiet.

After my smoke, I walked into flight deck control, accidentally kicking a few Ouija board aircraft templates strewn about on the deck. Two blue shirts moved other templates on the board, one talking into a sound-powered phone.

"What are ya'll doing? Do we really need the Ouija board

right now?" I said.

One of them held up his hands. "Mr. Tunball told us that after the corpsmen remove the bodies, we need to get everything back in order. He said to act as if we have flight ops tonight."

Back in order? I thought.

The Ouija board seemed to be the only thing undamaged. The glass wall behind the board where sailors recorded lists of aircraft in grease pencil had shattered. Severed cables and wires darted out in numerous directions. The handler's massive chair stood upright, but two feet from its normal location. The oddest thing was the set of lockers used by the chiefs. It stood in the same place but turned 180 degrees. The bars used to hold the locker in place lay on the floor—neatly sheared off. It was like those weird happenings you hear about with tornados. Stranger still, the television worked.

Two cameras recorded all flight operations. One embedded in the landing area and one operated by a sailor on a platform at one corner of the island. We could also view them live from several televisions. The flight deck control television showed the scene on the bow where we fought the final fire. It pointed toward the exact location where McGee lay. I shook my head, turned, and walked out.

Li'l V had left. I walked out of the back of the island and found him, standing toe-to-toe with ABH1 Beckley. I don't know what, if anything, had been said before I walked out. Neither spoke. I enhanced the awkwardness by standing there and not speaking.

Lieutenant Tunball ran up. "Beckley. There you are. Listen. The air boss wants us to get the landing area ready as soon as possible. CAT 1 should be good for launch. We probably won't use any of it, but he wants it ready. Let's get tractors and forklifts, and move the wreckage any place you can stick it for now."

I looked at Tunball, nodding. Li'l V and Beckley never wavered.

Beckley finally responded. Without leaving Li'l V's stare, he barked, "Yes, sir!" and walked aft. "C'mon Donley. You come with me."

Tunball put his hand on Li'l V's shoulder and turned him forward. "You go to CAT 1 and make sure—"

Tunball's voice trailed off as I walked aft of the island. The crash crew typically parked much of their equipment there, so we called it the junkyard. In the midst were two helos that the crashing Tomcat had shoved over. Beckley and I had to climb over pieces of equipment and metal to get by. One helo pressed against the crash shack hatch.

Beckley stepped beyond the wreckage and into the landing area. He stopped and slowly looked over the whole deck, his mouth open.

"What is it," I asked.

"It's terrible. Just terrible. I didn't know it was this bad."

I cocked my head. "What do you mean, didn't know? Where were you this whole time?"

Beckley whipped his head toward me. "You heard the lieutenant. Let's get these birds moved." He pointed at a few aircraft near the island that had been knocked into the landing area. "Get a tractor driver and push them back."

I had last seen Beckley smoking in the yellow shirt shack when Li'l V and I walked out for recovery of the Tomcat. During the entire ordeal, I had forgotten who was on deck and who wasn't. Until we conducted a proper muster, I wouldn't know who had sustained injuries or who had been off duty and come from the coop or other areas below decks. As I thought back, I could not remember Beckley at any of the fires.

As I walked away, I turned and looked back at him. Where the hell had he been?

I wanted to resolve this. Resolve the last two hours. Try to understand why my friends had died. The last thing I wanted to do was perform the same mundane task I had done so many times. I knew it needed to be done, though. I knew that aircraft carriers continued functioning despite accidents. Even with our carrier in that condition. The United States Navy would clean up the mess and get back to business. I resolved to do my job and mope later.

Off to our port side, two ships floated near us. Except during vertical replenishment, where another ship supplied the carrier with fuel and goods, the smaller ships usually cruised out of view. The frigate and cruiser rocked back and forth. Several sailors, small from my vantage point, looked and pointed at our ship. A helo hovered over one of them, about to land on its fantail.

Stretcher-bearers loaded two men on a helo in our landing area. Eppers had continued to direct helos during the fires and after they had been extinguished. He walked toward me as I prepared to move a Tomcat back.

"That's the la...last helo for awhile. I'm gonna go sneak a smoke."

He said this as he had many times before. As if he had performed some routine task and wanted a simple smoke break. He should have needed that smoke to decompress, to get away from the hell we had experienced. Nothing rattled Eppers.

I noticed something sticking out near his right shoulder

blade. "Hey, Eppers, wait." I walked over and looked closer. "Dude, you have a hunk of metal sticking out of your back."

The silver-dollar sized piece of metal protruded through his clothing.

Eppers looked over his shoulder, but was unable to see. "Damn. I wondered why my back hurt so much." He shrugged and continued toward the yellow shirt shack.

Hours later, the sun began to dip below the sea. The Bull pulled anchor and began to cut through the waters. The muster showed three men unaccounted for from the flight deck crews, and the frigate would continue the search for them.

Medical personnel had cleared the deck of dead and wounded. Several unusable aircraft remained parked on the deck, but the many small broken pieces had gone below. We conducted three FOD walkdowns. The air boss determined that CAT 1 and CAT 3 could launch aircraft and that the landing area could recover them. The flight deck remained a blackened stain, but now showed some semblance of order.

Li'l V parked the alert five Tomcat on CAT 1, and I parked another on CAT 3. The carrier had to maintain a defensive position as we cruised through dangerous waters.

Lieutenant Tunball called V-1 Division for a muster behind the island. "Listen, men, I know you don't want to hear a speech right now. We've had an unbelievably terrible day. We've lost friends and we'll mourn them soon. We'll keep a skeleton crew up here tonight. The rest of you go to sick bay if you need it, get some chow, or go to your rack. Back on deck at 0700."

A blue shirt threw up his hand. "Where we going, Mr. Tunball?"

"Word is, we're headed to Naples for repairs. Or at least band-aids. Probably be there a couple of weeks and then we'll finish the last month of our cruise. They won't fix everything. But we can finish our time on this cruise. Then we'll probably be in the shipyard for awhile."

No one spoke in the coop. No one turned on the TV. No one played cards. No one listened to their Walkman.

I showered off the grime and smoke of the day's events.

Eppers walked in and broke the silence.

Burp!

"They're serving chow if any of you boys are hungry."

Two guys headed toward the mess decks at that announcement. A few others began whispering as if they now had permission to talk. They had likely felt as I did. Too shocked to speak.

Spalding rolled into his rack under mine. "I feel like crap."

He had offered me a quick version of his experiences with the hangar bay fire.

"Maybe you should head back to sick bay," I said.

"They're overloaded. They don't need me taking up a rack." Spalding closed his curtains.

I began to crawl into my rack when Parks walked by.

"Hey, Parks. So what was it like out there in the ocean?"

Parks gave me all the details of his ordeal at sea and the mysterious disappearance of Chief Michaels. Parks looked over his shoulder and whispered. "Here's where it gets weirder. I checked with a bunch of squadron guys and even went to the air wing office. There's no Chief Michaels. No chief is even missing or unaccounted for. I was only out there for a couple of hours. But I think I might have…might be—"

I shook my head. "Look, it's been a crazy day for all of us. Just go hit your rack."

As I stowed my soap and shaving kit and closed my rack, I noticed something different about my rack area. McGee's big butt wasn't in my way. I turned and thought about him primping. I rolled into my rack and shut my curtains.

My mind raced. Although I was exhausted, sleep didn't seem possible. I kept seeing images of the gear puller's mangled torso. Of arms and legs apart from bodies. But mostly, I pictured Garfield, on top of the Hornet as it exploded. And McGee, crushed under the nose of another Hornet. My lower lip quivered and the tears flowed. I'd been broken.

CHAPTER 30

The doctor called it a blast injury. I had slept off and on for a total of two hours the night of the fire. I woke the next morning with a headache. I had no appetite and headed on deck for the 0700 muster when I leaned over the catwalk and vomited. I assumed I had caught whatever Spalding had. Some type of virus. Like Spalding, I didn't want to take up space in sick bay needed by someone who was seriously wounded.

Lieutenant Tunball had witnessed my offering to the sea. As I walked up toward muster, he stopped me. "We're already short, and I don't want you getting anyone else sick. Go to sick bay."

I took the ladders down from the flight deck a little slowly—stopping a couple of times with dizzy spells. I walked through the mess decks. One section had men eating, while five sailors cleaned another section which had earlier been used for triage. I assumed sick bay would have a line out the door, however, only a few guys waited for treatment.

I signed in at the check-in station. "Hey, seems kind of empty down here. I figured you guys would have more wounded to deal with."

The clerk looked up, his eyes red. "We did. We've been up all night. A lot of the wounded were treated and sent to their racks and some were sent to other ships. We just kept the critical cases."

After a forty-five minute wait, my headache had lightened and my stomach felt fine. I started to get up and walk out when the doctor entered.

He held a light to my eyes and asked me a series of routine questions. He clicked off the light and folded his arms. "Tell me more about the explosion that knocked you out."

"Well, there was this big explosion and it knocked me out." I held my hands up searching my mind for details.

The doctor nodded.

"Next thing I know, I'm lying on the deck after my buddy had carried me away from the fire."

The doctor clicked his pen and began writing. "I don't think you're sick. You have a blast injury. You're lucky your symptoms aren't worse. Sometimes people experience internal injuries. Stay off the flight deck and come back tomorrow morning. We'll check you, out and you'll probably be fine by then."

He gave me a light duty note, but I threw it away. After what others had experienced, I wasn't about to go lie in my rack while we were short on men.

I walked on deck feeling much better than I had two hours earlier. Several guys passed me, headed the way I had come.

Li'l V saw me. "Hey, man. You coming with us?"

"Where?"

"The fo'c'sle for a chapel service."

I looked forward. "I guess we don't have flight ops or any moves?"

Li'l V shook his head. "Nope. They basically gave us the day off. Mr. Tunball said we could go to the chapel service and then come back on deck in case we're needed. We're not flying. We got too many wounds to lick."

We entered the large compartment to a standing-room-only crowd. The chaplain led us through prayers and then cleared his throat.

"We don't know why God allows such tragedies. You're probably asking yourself why you lost a friend. Let me give you comfort with these words from Scripture. Psalm 139 says…"

My mind drifted away from the sermon. I had little church experience, but Li'l V grew up in church and nodded the whole time. He embraced every word of it. I wasn't a skeptic, but I fixated on those questions. Why did it happen? Why did they die?

Those questions flooded my mind. Li'l V brought it back to God. "Just trust Jesus," he said. "He's got a better plan than you do."

Li'l V had experienced the same brokenness we all felt. But he bounced back much faster. The faces of Chief Fitch, Garfield, and McGee haunted me. They'd pop in my head without notice. I couldn't let them go. I couldn't let them rest in peace. I remained unsettled.

We anchored off the coast of Naples, Italy. We had gone there three months earlier for liberty, but this time we worked, cleaned, and prepared the ship. Senior Chief Perez had come from below decks when the fire started, like Chief Fitch had. Within minutes, a piece of flying metal had knocked him out, but he'd recovered after three days. He took over leadership of

V-1 under Lieutenant Tunball. Perez made Li'l V the Fly 1 PO, putting him in charge of the bow area. He made me the assistant in Fly 2.

The senior chief gathered the entire division for muster. "We'll be in Naples for nine days. We won't have as many birds. We'll still have a hole on the finger and El 4 will be down. When we pull out of here, we're gonna fly every day. We've lost a lot of men, but we'll get the job done the rest of this cruise. Work your ass off, and then we'll hit the beach in Norfolk."

I didn't consider it the greatest pep talk I'd ever heard, but it worked.

The remaining yellow shirts gathered in our shack. With coffee and cigarettes in abundance, we continued to ask the difficult questions. How many had died? Why did the Tomcat crash? Why did the sprinkler system fail?

Lieutenant Tunball poked his head in from flight deck control, having overheard us. "I know you guys have a lot of questions. I'll try to get you some answers. But let's not dwell on the negative. I want you focused on your jobs. Standard operating procedures."

Eppers didn't get the message. "Hey, Mr. Tunball, why did that Tomcat hit the ramp?"

"Well, it apparently had a run-in with a Libyan MiG. I don't know much more than that, but it was likely a wounded bird."

He stepped into flight deck control and came right back. "And before you ask, we won't know about the sprinkler system until they can get into the guts of the ship, but it looks like the main pipe was damaged during one of the explosions. So, it could have been the busted pipe or an electrical control issue. It'll get fixed, though." Tunball stepped back out.

I considered them reasonable explanations, both above my pay grade. The numbers of those we lost were more important to me. The captain sent a memorandum for the entire ship with a motivational speech and details of the tragedy. We had lost thirty-nine sailors with one hundred and four wounded—the vast majority from flight deck crews of the Air Department and squadrons. Rescue crews found two men in the water of the three that had been unaccounted for. One, however, was never found and was listed among the thirty-nine dead. V-1 Division lost nine men with twenty-eight wounded. Four of those wounded sustained permanent injuries, ending their naval careers.

Every color jersey on the flight deck was represented among the dead.

That final month of the cruise ended without incident. Not a single accident. The day before we pulled into port, Lieutenant Tunball called me into flight deck control.

"Donley, we've received a special request. You don't have to say yes, but just think about it. McGee's parents asked if you could drive his truck and belongings to their home in Baltimore."

My eyes widened. "Wh…what?"

Tunball nodded. "I know. That's a lot to ask. But they were insistent. Since you're planning on taking leave, you could just fly home from there."

The thought of seeing them in their grief terrified me. But I knew I couldn't say no. I owed it to them—and to McGee.

I checked the map numerous times before exiting the freeway for McGee's working-class neighborhood. His family's wraparound porch stood out on their home's corner lot. I pulled into the driveway. My flight departed from Baltimore the next day, so I planned to pay my respects, then take a taxi to a hotel. My teeth began to chatter. I took a few deep breaths, opened the door, and began to reach for McGee's seabag.

"Brian!" McGee's dad walked out of the front door followed by all three brothers. "It's about time you got here. You get lost?"

"Uh...no, sir."

His dad gave me a bear hug. "You boys help with the bags." He put his arm around me and escorted me to the house. "Mrs. McGee's cooking dinner. I'll bet you're hungry."

"Oh. You don't have to feed me anyth—"

"Nonsense. You're staying for dinner."

I entered the living room, and McGee's mom walked out from the kitchen with an apron wrapped around her waist.

She put her hands on my cheeks. "Let me get a look at you. Were you injured?"

"No, Miss Carol. Well, a little. But nothing serious."

"Oh, thank goodness."

Beep.

The beep sent her back to the kitchen.

I expected awkwardness caused by mourning. Or anger since McGee died because of me. I certainly felt guilt. This was the opposite. The family seemed almost gleeful.

I sat with Mr. McGee in the living room as the boys carried the bags upstairs. I noticed they had my seabag. I held up my finger to object but pulled it back and decided to worry about it later.

Mr. McGee leaned in. "Listen, Brian. Don't think we aren't grieving. We've cried plenty of tears for Willie and will probably cry many more. His mom refused to change anything in his room. We were hoping you could tell us what really happened. The chaplain that came here said he was a hero and all that, but we wanted to hear it from you. One time. And that will be the end of it."

"Let's eat!" Mrs. McGee called from the kitchen.

The brothers barreled downstairs. The table looked set for Thanksgiving with no less than six dishes, bread, and cherry cobbler for dessert. I ate until I hurt, having gone without home cooking for so long. They shared stories about Willie, and I shared some as well. We laughed over how I called him McGee in my stories, and they called him Willie in theirs.

The whole family moved to the living room as I told them the story of the fire. I told them about the ramp strike, the explosions, and the unending flames. I spared them the parts about blood, body parts, and charred bodies. I spared them the sight of a man running on fire, screaming, and falling down in flames. When I came to the part about McGee, I gave as much detail as I could, beginning with him pulling Li'l V and the squadron guy into the net and ending with how the Hornet crushed McGee.

McGee's mother gasped.

"The problem, though, is that the last time I saw him, he was on a hose. But Li'l V saw it all and told me everything. You can trust that whatever Li'l V told me is exactly what happened."

Mrs. McGee's tears flowed. I tried to maintain composure but failed.

My head dropped into my hands. "He shouldn't have done it. He shouldn't have risked his life for mine."

"No. You stop that right now," she said, putting her arms around me.

The brothers slowly left the room.

Mr. McGee left the room and came back with two beers, handing one to me. "Here."

I looked up, wiped my eyes, and took the beer.

"Brian, we're very proud of you. We're very proud of Willie. He gave his life for his fellow sailors and for his country. And it hurts. It hurts real bad. But we understand. And we're OK with it."

Mr. McGee walked over to the mantle and picked up a frame with a black-and-white picture of a soldier. "You see this? It's my oldest brother, George. He served during World War II. A chaplain came to our house in 1943 and told my parents that he was missing in action. I was too little to remember, but my parents were sick over it. Not knowing what had happened to him. Six months after the war ended, they received a letter from someone that knew him. Said he was captured and taken prisoner by the Japanese. Horrific conditions. He lasted a long time but died from beriberi in the jungle a month before they were all rescued. It still hurt for my parents, but they finally had closure. They could let him rest."

I then realized they hadn't really needed me to drive his truck home. They needed closure. It gave me closure as well. I could let Willie McGee rest. I could say goodbye to Chief Howard Fitch and Kellen Garfield as well.

I suggested I leave for a hotel, but they would have none of it. I slept in McGee's bed that night. The best sleep I'd had since the fire.

After a hearty breakfast, Mr. McGee dropped me off at the airport. He opened the door to get back into his car. "You give us a call now and then. We want to stay in touch."

I nodded. "Yes, sir."

For some reason, the fire spared me. I came through it a different person. I had confidence that I could handle anything life threw at me. I was no hero. No Victor "Li'l V" Randolph. But I was a stronger person. Like a precious metal, the fire had refined me and made me stronger.

As I waited to board my flight, I cranked up my Walkman with my Chicago VI cassette and listened to "Feelin' Stronger Every Day." That's how I felt. Stronger every day.

CHAPTER 31

I'd heard that a few guys had gathered on the twentieth anniversary of the fire. By 2012, the Internet and social media allowed many of us veterans of that terrible day on the Bull, to keep in touch. We decided to gather at a hotel in Norfolk for the twenty-fifth anniversary. All the V-1 Division guys we could find. There'd be no tours of the Bull. She anchored in a shipyard, awaiting scrapping.

Li'l V failed to respond to the invites but I kept sending them. I'd not seen him since my discharge, two years after the fire. While googling his name, I found his bio on a page for a Christian school in upstate New York. He had served twenty years in the Navy and retired a senior chief. He earned a degree, taught science, and coached the football and soccer team. I also found his Navy Commendation Medal citation:

FOR HEROIC ACHIEVEMENT WHILE SERVING AS AN AIRCRAFT DIRECTOR ON THE FLIGHT DECK OF THE USS WILLIAM HALSEY. DURING AN AIRCRAFT FIRE ON 04 MAY 1987, ABH3 VICTOR MARTIN RANDOLPH DISTINGUISHED HIMSELF AS AN ON-SCENE LEADER OF SEVERAL FIREFIGHTING CREWS. HE REPEATEDLY PLACED HIMSELF IN HARMS WAY TO LEAD FIRE HOSE TEAMS. ON TWO OCCASIONS, PETTY OFFICER

RANDOLPH RISKED HIS LIFE TO RESCUE FELLOW SAILORS FROM CERTAIN DEATH. FOR HIS DEDICATION TO DUTY AND LEADERSHIP, PETTY OFFICER RANDOLPH REFLECTED CREDIT UPON HIMSELF AND IN KEEPING WITH THE HIGHEST TRADITIONS OF THE UNITED STATES NAVAL SERVICE.

Chief Fitch, McGee, Garfield, and two squadron sailors earned similar medals, posthumously. There were many heroes that day. Guys whose names I never knew. So many that died, and some that would never walk again.

The moment I stepped out of my car at the airport for my flight to Norfolk, I smelled the aircraft fuel. Most probably don't notice it. But flight deck guys do. The smell reminds us of an F-14 Tomcat in afterburner, or an F/A-18 Hornet trapping an arresting gear wire.

One by one, guys gathered in the hotel meeting room. Many had graying or non-existent hair, a few wrinkles, and plenty had paunches. I expected ten or twelve, but thirty-seven veterans from V-1 Division came.

We exchanged the perfunctory questions of where do you live and what do you do? How many kids? We swapped sea stories and a few guys brought up the fire. Where they were on deck when the ramp strike happened. What injuries they sustained.

I was surprised to see Czarnecki there. He had transferred to the hangar bay after the fire, but visited our coop often. Everyone liked him but understood him leaving V-1 Division. He wasn't scared and even worked on the roof for two days after we left Naples, but the thought of his friend Odie distracted him too much. We thought it a risk, and he did as well.

We'd invited Lieutenant Tunball but he'd declined. He'd left the Navy after eight years and worked for a defense contractor.

Eppers showed up looking nearly the same. His features were slightly older and his hair had grayed, but he was still smoking, stuttering, and exaggerating every story. He lifted up his shirt to show the scar from the piece of metal that had struck his back. He'd left the Navy four years short of the twenty needed for retirement. Eppers claimed a construction crew had offered him a job that was too good to pass up, but we figured he'd committed some offense on liberty. He was always one beer away from a dishonorable discharge.

"Spalding?" I squinted my eyes at the man that walked in with two stars over his chief's anchors.

"That's Master Chief Worthington to you, Petty Officer Donley." Spalding extended his hand and smiled.

"I heard you'd stayed in, but a master chief?"

Spalding adjusted his waistline. "Yep. Been in twenty-five years now. I even had another tour on the Bull before they decommissioned her. Kinda sad to see her go."

"Hey, whatever happened to Beckley? When we got back from the Med cruise, he just disappeared."

Spalding shook his head. "That old son of a bitch. His true colors came out in the fire. He abandoned us. You remember those rumors of him wandering around the ship during the fire?"

I nodded.

"All true. A few years after the fire, I ran into Senior Chief Perez at a bar. He'd had a few too many and told me the whole story. He said there was an investigation, and they found guys that had seen and talked to Beckley during the fire. Said he was acting all crazy. Of course, he claimed he was injured. Anyway, they sent him to shore duty and let him finish out his twenty. I saw him about six years ago. Works as a security guard at the mall. Called me shipmate. Can you believe it?"

"Unbelievable." I shook my head. "What about Climer? Ever see him?"

"Yeah, once or twice. He did his twenty and got out. I heard he's a fire chief up north somewhere."

Spalding excused himself as Parks walked up and shook my hand.

"You know, Parks, I always wanted to ask you something. Did you ever find out about that chief that was with you in the water? What was his name?"

"Michaels. Chief Michaels." Parks slightly grinned. "No, I don't know what really happened to me out there. But, you know, I travel a lot for business. Whenever I leave, my wife says, 'Be safe.' I tell her, 'Don't worry. The Chief will be with me.' I guess you could say I consider him my guardian angel."

An officer in a white uniform entered the room. I didn't recognize him and wondered if he was lost.

He walked straight toward me. "Hello, Brian."

I looked at his shoulders and noticed he wore three solid gold stripes, the rank of a commander. His nametag read McGee.

He held out his hand. "Ronald McGee. Willie's little brother."

I grabbed his hand. "Wow. What were you, thirteen, the last time I saw you?"

"Yep. The day I heard he'd been killed, I wanted to join the

Navy and take his place. I idolized Willie. It was kind of silly back then. But, I earned an appointment to the Naval Academy and got my wings. I fly Hornets. Almost too tall, but I made it."

"I feel bad. I haven't talked to your parents in years. I sent them an invite."

"Dad wanted to come, but his health is not great. He told me about it and asked if I'd represent Willie."

I put my hand on his shoulder. "Hey, guys!"

The chatter died slightly.

"Guys! This is Willie McGee's brother. Or Commander McGee, that is."

He smiled. "No, Ron is fine."

Several guys approached and shook his hand.

"Hey, Brian. You look like you gained a little weight." The voice came from behind me.

I turned. "Li'l V!"

He attempted a handshake, but I gave him a bear hug.

"You made it."

"Well, I figured you'd keep bugging me if I didn't."

"I heard you were teaching."

Li'l V folded his arms. "Yeah, I took some classes while I was still in the Navy. Finished my degree when I got out, and I've been teaching ever since and coaching a little. What about you?"

"I've got a little insurance business. Pays the bills, you know."

We found a table and sat down.

"Hey, Li'l V. Do you think about it much?"

"Think about what?"

"The fire. Chief Fitch. Garfield and McGee."

Li'l V looked off to the side. A tear rolled down his cheek.

He wiped it away and looked back. "I wish I could say no. But I think about it a lot. Not every day. About once a month or so, it'll pop in my head. I know I acted all tough and brave. But I was so scared. I thought we were all gonna die. I've woken up in the middle of the night screaming. You know. Nightmares. Scares my wife."

I leaned in. "But we didn't die. We survived. It made us stronger. And hopefully we've done some good with it."

He nodded. "The day of the fire was the day I realized something. We may think we're so important. That we're a great leader. Nothing will get done without us. But that day I realized, every day might be our last on earth. So, yeah. We'd better do some good with it while we're here. That's what I try to do. Live out my faith with my family, my students, and anyone else I come across. Try to do some good every day."

I reflected on Li'l V's words during the trip home. I had always thought of myself as a bystander to Li'l V's fearless heroics. Someone who couldn't relate to that level of valor. I guess he was as scared as I was that day. And it had stayed with him. We all carried some internal scars from the tragedy.

I have a recurring dream that I've rejoined the Navy. I'm back on the Bull. I'm my current age, but there's Li'l V, Spalding, and Beckley, and also McGee, Fitch, and Garfield. They're all just as they were back then before the fire. Doing the same jobs. I don't know why I have the dream. Maybe I'm going back to fix something. To prevent something. The older, wiser me could warn them. Maybe I'm wishing that terrible day on the flight deck never happened. Then I wake up and know it did happen.

The fire will always be with me. So will the memory of those heroes. The men with military bearing. The men willing to give their lives for their country. The kind of men that will run to the fire, not run from it.

ACKNOWLEDGEMENTS

Thanks to my wife Holly and our five children: Kevin, Brandon, Jordan, Jadyn, and Megan for your support on this project.

Thanks to my family who served this country and inspired me to join the Navy: My uncles Roger Sapp, Loren Groce, Ronald Johnson, and Allen "Buzz" Sapp; my Aunt Linda Hudson; my father, Darrell Sapp; and my brother, ITC Frank Sapp, who is serving in Afghanistan as I write this.

Thanks to Mary Demuth, Leslie Wilson, Anne Mateer, and the rest of Rockwall Christian Writers Group, as well as the members of Scribophile.com for your critiques.

Thanks to my beta readers: Robert Trisch, Mike Asbell, Bob Hamilton, and Roger Wilburn.

Thanks to my shipmates who entertained all my questions: CWO5 (Ret.) Eric Brown, Rodger Wilder, Gerald Leahy, and John Weidman. And to so many on the US Navy Flight Deck Veterans Facebook Group and the CVN-71 V-1 Division Facebook Group.

Thanks to Jeremy Gilstrap for the carrier drawing in the appendix.

Thanks to my editor, Lauren Ruiz, of Pure-Text.net, and proofreaders Mary Norsworthy and Debbie Vines.

A special thanks to William S. Phillips for allowing me to use his piece of art, Sunset Recovery, for the cover.

Sign up for Darren's monthly email on his website for writing news and release dates of future books. He will not spam you!

www.darrensapp.com

APPENDIX I:

Anatomy of a Flight Deck

1. Bow / Fore / Forward
2. Stern /Aft / Fantail / Ramp
3. Port
4. Starboard
5. Foul Line
6. Landing Area
7. CAT 1
8. CAT 2
9. CAT 3
10. CAT 4
11. JBD 1
12. EL 1
13. EL 2
14. EL 3
15. EL 4
16. Flight Deck Control inside the island
17. Yellow Shirt Shack inside the island
18. Crash Shack inside the island
19. Arresting Gear Wires
20. Four row
21. Six-Pack
22. Corral
23. Junkyard
24. Finger
25. LSO Platform
26. Point
27. Crotch
28. Patio

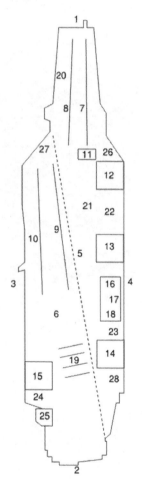

APPENDIX I:

Glossary

1MC - Public address system for entire ship.

5MC - Public address system for flight deck.

ABH - The rating for an aviation boatswains' mate. An ABH1 is a first class, ABH2 a second class, and ABH3 the lowest of the three. Other variations are ABHC, which denotes chief, or ABCM, a master chief, the highest enlisted rank.

AFFF - Stands for aqueous film forming foam. A water-based firefighting agent used on the flight deck and hangar bay.

Aft - Rear

Air Boss - The person over all flight operations working from primary flight control.

AN - Airman rate or rank equal to a private.

Arresting Gear Cable - One of four wire cables spanning the width of the landing area. An aircraft's tailhook catches the cable, ideally the third one.

At Ease - A command to relax from attention or parade rest.

Attention on Deck - A command to stop whatever one is doing and stand at attention because a senior person, such as an officer, has entered. Other versions might be ten-hut, atten-hut, or atten-huah.

Balls to Four - The watch from 0000 to 0400. Balls represent 0000, or midnight, although it's actually 2400, and the 4 comes from 0400.

Barricade - A large net spanning the landing area used to catch airplanes when their tailhooks fail.

Base - A military installation.

Bent - Damaged or broken.

Berth - Bed and/or lodging on a ship or shore station. A berthing compartment is a large room or space where several sailors live.

Bird - A slang term for aircraft.

Blue Shirt - Personnel that chock and chain aircraft and serve as safety checkers while moving aircraft. They also drive tractors, operate elevators, spot aircraft movement, and control the Ouija board in flight deck control.

Blue Water Operations - Flight operations so far out to sea, no alternate airfield exists for aircraft in flight.

Boat, the - A slang term for the ship.

Boondockers - Standard issue boots.

Bow - The front of the ship.

Brown Shirt - Squadron personnel called plane captains that care for a particular aircraft.

Bubble - The small room that raises and lowers on the flight deck for control of catapults.

Bug Juice - Kool-Aid.

Bulkhead - A wall in a room, space, or compartment.

Canopy - A glass enclosure covering an aircraft's cockpit.

Catapult (CAT) - The steam system used to propel an aircraft for launch.

Catwalk - A protected walkway next to, and lower than the flight deck, nearly the length of the entire deck.

Chevron - Petty officer stripes.

Chief - E-7 rank. They are typically upper management. It is commonly said that chiefs run the Navy.

Chocking and Chaining - Work done by a blue shirt to secure an aircraft's wheels with chocks and tiedown chains.

Chow - A meal.

Coke and Smoke - Taking a break that usually involves a cigarette and soft drink.

Combing - A curb shaped barrier along the flight deck edge.

Company Commander (CC) - Personnel in charge of boot camp recruits similar to drill instructors in other branches.

Compartment - A room or space on a ship.

Coolie - A blue shirt that chocks and chains. The lowest level in V-1 Division.

Coop - Sleeping compartment and living space.

Corfam - A type of leather used for shiny, dress shoes.

Corpsmen - Hospital personnel ranging from first responders to sickbay workers.

Corral - The area between elevators one and two.

Cover - Hat, helmet, garrison cap, etc.

CPO - Chief petty officer.

CQ - Carrier qualification flight operations where pilots perform numerous landings and takeoffs.

Crash & Salvage Crew - Typically called the crash crew, or simply crash, they are the flight deck fire and rescue workers.

Crunch - An accident on the flight deck where an aircraft strikes another object or another aircraft during routine movements.

DCC - Stands for damage control central. The place and group that coordinates all efforts to minimize damage and report the ship's situational effectiveness to the captain.

Dixie Cup - White sailor hat.

Don - To put on or wear.

Double-Time - To jog.

Dungarees - Standard working uniform for E-6 and below.

Duty Station - A location such as a base or ship where a sailor will spend a long period of time, usually more than a year.

EL - Short for aircraft elevator. El 2 means elevator number two. There are four elevators that run from the flight deck to the hangar bay.

Fantail - Rear portion/platform of the ship.

Finger - A small area between elevator four and the LSO platform where one small airplane, such as an F/A-18, is typically parked.

Fleet - A formation or group of ships, but also used to mean the Navy, in general, at sea.

Flight Deck Control - An area inside the island structure where all aircraft movement is monitored. The flight deck control officer or handler oversees this operation.

Float Coat - Nickname for a flight deck life vest that is worn deflated while working.

Fly One - Forward area of the flight deck including catapults one and two, and elevator one.

Fly Two - Middle area of the flight deck including catapult three and elevator two.

Fly Three - Rear area of the flight deck including catapult four and elevators three and four.

Fo'c'sle - Open area in the front of the ship, also called the forecastle, where the anchor chains are stored. Also used for ceremonies.

Fore - Forward.

Foreign Object Damage (FOD) Walkdown - The process of lining up personnel and searching the flight deck for any debris.

Foul Line - A red-and-white safety line running the length of the deck. During recovery/landing operations, personnel must stay to the starboard side of the line.

Galley - Kitchen.

Gear Puller - A yellow shirt responsible for directing a pilot clear of the landing area.

Gig Line - An imaginary line from the zipper to the belt buckle to the trim of the uniform shirt.

Green Shirt - Squadron maintenance personnel, or catapult and arresting gear personnel.

Hangar Bay - The largest enclosed section of an aircraft carrier used for aircraft parking and maintenance.

Hatch - Door.

Head - Bathroom.

Head Call - Going to the bathroom.

Helo - Helicopter.

Hit the Beach - Slang for going on liberty (time off from work).

Hummer - Nickname for the E-2C Hawkeye due to the sound the propeller makes.

Jet Blast Deflector (JBD) - A wall that is raised and lowered behind each catapult to spare personnel and aircraft from a jet's exhaust while taking off.

Knee Knocker - The lower portion of a passageway opening, sitting about a foot high.

Ladder - Stairs on a ship, typically at a steep angle.

Leave - Vacation from military service.

Leggings - A canvas sleeve that covers the ankle and lower leg.

Lifer - Career sailor planning on a minimum of twenty years in the Navy.

Litter - Rescue basket stretcher.

LPO - Leading petty officer over a unit. Typically a first class petty officer.

Mash - Physical exercise meant as punishment: **M**ake **A** **S**ailor **H**urt.

Med - Short for Mediterranean.

Mess Hall - Cafeteria, usually segregated between enlisted, chief, and officer.

Military Bearing - The ability to comprehend and follow orders.

Missile - Any loose item on a ship that can cause damage.

Muster - A gathering, in ranks, of sailors for roll call, work assignments, announcements, etc. A typical daily muster is held at 0700.

Non-skid - The asphalt material that covers the flight deck and hangar bay.

Old Man, the - Nickname for the captain of a ship.

Ouija Board - A table in flight deck control with a map of the flight deck. All aircraft and ground equipment have symbols, which are moved according to their relation to the flight deck.

Ordnance - Weapons and ammunition or the department responsible for those.

Oxygen Breathing Apparatus - A rebreathing oxygen system used for shipboard firefighting.

Paddles - The group/platform where pilots in white shirts guide a pilot on final approach for landing.

Padeye - Small metal divots with four to five bars to attach a tiedown chain.

Parade Rest - A command to stand with feet/legs spread shoulder length apart and hands locked behind the small of the back.

Passageway - Hallway.

Piece - Term for rifle.

Pissers - Urinals.

Port - The left side of the ship.

Pri Fly - Primary flight control. Located in the island structure, the air boss and mini boss oversee all flight operations from there.

Prop - Short for propeller.

Purple Shirts - Aircraft fueling personnel.

Rackmate - The person who shares the top or bottom of the bunkbed.

Red Shirt - Crash and salvage crew (pilot rescue) or ordnance personnel.

RCPO - Recruit chief petty officer. The recruit in charge while the CCs are away.

Reveille - Morning call to wake up.

RIO - Stands for radar intercept officer, the officer in the back seat of an F-14 Tomcat.

Roof - The flight deck.

Scuttlebutt - Can mean water fountain or gossip.

Seabag - Green duffle bag.

Ship's Company - Sailors assigned to a specific command (ship), as opposed to squadron personnel that live on the ship only while at sea.

Shitters - Commodes.

Sick Bay - Hospital and treatment area. Also called medical.

Sixteen-Count Manual Arms - A drill using a rifle to teach order.

Six-Pack - An area along the foul line in fly two where six airplanes are typically parked.

Skivvies - Underwear.

Smoking Lamp - A figurative term meaning that smoking is allowed when "the smoking lamp is lit."

SOP - Standard operating procedures.

SR - Seaman recruit. The rank at which everyone starts in boot camp. The lowest rank in the Navy.

Starboard - The right side of the ship.

Swab - A mop. Also a verb meaning to mop.

Tailhook Runner - The green shirt that ensures the tailhook is clear of the arresting gear after landing.

Tanker - An A-6 Intruder retrofitted with fuel tanks to refuel aircraft in mid-air.

Taps - Lights out for the night.

Touch-and-Go - The practice of an aircraft touching down and immediately taking off, simulating an at-sea carrier landing.

V-1 Division - A group of approximately 150 personnel that control the movement of aircraft on the flight deck. Other Air Department divisions are V-0 for administrative, V-2 for catapults and arresting gear, V-3 for hangar bay aircraft movement, and V-4 for aircraft fueling.

Walkman - A handheld cassette player.

Watchcap - Wool head covering worn by recruits the first five weeks of boot camp.

White Shirts - Final checkers for aircraft on catapult for launch. They also represent safety personnel, and those with a red cross on their white shirts are medical personnel.

Yellow Shirts - Aircraft directors or catapult officers. The yellow shirt indicates a leader on the flight deck.

Yeoman - A sailor performing administrative duties.

APPENDIX II:

Typical Aircraft on Carriers in the Late 1980s

A-6 Intruder

*C-2A Greyhound - (COD for Carrier Onboard Delivery)

*CH-53 Sea Stallion (Helo)

*CH-46/UH-46 Sea Knight (Helo)

E-2C Hawkeye (Hummer)

EA-6B Prowler (Sky pig/ Stretch)

F-14 Tomcat (Turkey)

F/A-18 Hornet (Cockroach)

S-3 Viking (Hoover)

SH-3 Sea King (Helo)

*Denotes aircraft not permanently assigned to the ship and used for delivery of items and personnel.

APPENDIX IV:

Military to Standard Time Conversion Chart

Military	Standard	Military	Standard
0000 or 2400	12 AM	1200	12 PM
0100	1 AM	1300	1 PM
0200	2 AM	1400	2 PM
0300	3 AM	1500	3 PM
0400	4 AM	1600	4 PM
0500	5 AM	1700	5 PM
0600	6 AM	1800	6 PM
0700	7 AM	1900	7 PM
0800	8 AM	2000	8 PM
0900	9 AM	2100	9 PM
1000	10 AM	2200	10 PM
1100	11 AM	2300	11 PM

A few examples:
- 0820 is 8:20 AM (Pronounced "zero eight twenty")
- 1951 is 7:51 PM (Pronounced "nineteen fifty one")
- 0001 is 12:01 AM or one minute after midnight.